Trotting Into Trouble

Also available by Amber Camp

The Horse Rescue Mysteries

Canter With a Killer

Trotting Into Trouble

A HORSE RESCUE MYSTERY

Amber Camp

NEW YORK

Published in the United States by Crooked Lane Books, an imprint of The Quick Brown Fox & Company LLC.

Crooked Lane Books and its logo are trademarks of The Quick Brown Fox & Company LLC.

Library of Congress Catalog-in-Publication data available upon request.

ISBN (hardcover): 978-1-63910-518-2
ISBN (ebook): 978-1-63910-519-9

Cover illustration by Brandon Dorman

Printed in the United States.

www.crookedlanebooks.com

Crooked Lane Books
34 West 27th St., 10th Floor
New York, NY 10001

First Edition: November 2023

10 9 8 7 6 5 4 3 2 1

For Warren and Maddy, your endless support means everything to me.

Chapter One

The near-skeletal mare stumbled as she backed out of the trailer, and before I could stop myself, I braced against her bony hip. Admittedly, it wasn't the smartest move to position myself on the downhill side of a falling horse, even if that horse was hundreds of pounds underweight. Thankfully, she regained her balance, and her muscles shook from the exertion. My heart broke as I looked her over again in the afternoon sunlight. Grady Sullivan, Connor County Sheriff and one of my oldest friends, had found her while he and his deputies were investigating a possible meth lab. They found the lab and several emaciated animals which were seized by various rescues, including mine. There had been no water, grass, or hay in the dry pen where she was held, and judging from her appearance, that wasn't a recent development.

As we loaded her at the scene, her owner screamed at us from the back seat of the sheriff's SUV that we were stealing his horse. Tanner, my volunteer-turned-employee, fought to keep his composure as the painfully thin mare struggled to get into the trailer. Tanner was a full head taller than me and built like a linebacker, incidentally the position he had played in high school a few years ago. It was probably a good thing the guy was safely under arrest; Tanner looked like he wanted to pulverize him. And given the difference in their sizes, my money was on Tanner. I definitely understood that impulse. There was just no reason for the neglect the poor mare had endured.

The resident horses at my rescue whinnied as we led the mare toward the barn. I glanced over my shoulder at the quarantine pen and shed that was under construction in the newly cleared paddock on the hill above my house. I'd been lucky so far that none of the rescues had brought any communicable diseases into the herd, but I didn't want to bank on luck forever. I kept them separated the best I could, but having a quarantine paddock was a much safer option. I wished the construction had been far enough along to house the mare away from the rest, but it wasn't, so wishing would get me nowhere. My little red barn was in desperate need of repainting, but the oak structure was as solid as the Ozark Mountain it sat on.

The first thing the mare did when we put her in one of the four the stalls I'd prepared for her was take a long drink of the cool, clean water. While she drank, a small gray nose poked through the outside window; its owner barely tall enough to make his presence known. It belonged to our resident donkey, Biscuit, who was convinced that he should always be in the middle of everything that goes on within the confines of Hillspring Horse Rescue.

"Want me to put him in the upper paddock?" Tanner nodded toward the probing gray snoot.

"Nah," I said, as I watched the mare pick up a mouthful of hay. "He can't help himself, but I don't think he's bothering her."

"I'll grab the camera then," he said. We kept a digital camera at the barn to document the condition of the horses on intake. It was hard to argue with photo evidence in court. Most of our cases ended in surrender to the rescue before they ever went to court, but I liked to prepare each file as thoroughly as possible, just in case. I also started mentally calculating everything the mare was going to need. That list started with an evaluation by our vet, sooner rather than later. I suspected that she had never had any dental care, and if she was an older horse, that would be an important part of her recovery. Horses are grazing animals, and the grinding motion of their teeth can sometimes cause them to wear unevenly, leaving sharp points that make it hard to eat or properly process their food. Her hooves were overgrown and cracked too, so she would need to be seen by our farrier as soon as possible.

She buried her nose in the tub of alfalfa hay and chewed another big bite. I wished I could feed her huge buckets of grain and treats to make up for her having been starved for so long, but knew that we had to be careful not to cause refeeding syndrome in an animal so emaciated. If starved animals, or even people for that matter, are fed too much too soon, it overwhelms the digestive and metabolic systems and can result in fatal complications. My medical background as a nurse was often applicable to caring for the horses, and though I no longer practiced as a nurse, I was thankful for my many years of education.

Tanner started taking photos of the mare and Biscuit let loose a mournful bray.

"It's okay, Bud," Tanner leaned out the window and scratched Biscuit's little chin. "We'll pay attention to you in a minute."

"I think we should blanket her tonight," I said as Tanner continued to take photos from various angles. "She doesn't have any fat at all to keep her warm and it's supposed to get chilly."

"Good idea. I think River's blanket will fit her."

I nodded, mentally sizing her up. Even though River, one of our residents, was about five hundred pounds heavier than the mare, he was about the size she *should* be, so his bright red blanket would be a good choice.

Suddenly, Biscuit's insistent braying changed to an alert, which is difficult to explain to anyone who isn't used to hearing him. But there's a definite difference in his normal "talking" and the bray he uses to let me know someone or something is here that doesn't belong. Since my dog never meets a stranger, Biscuit picks up the slack. It's easy to see why ranchers keep donkeys to protect their herds of cattle and sheep. I heard gravel crunching in between Biscuit's insistent honking.

Tanner and I looked at each other. Sheriff Grady Sullivan had been present at the meth lab, but he hadn't said he was going to come by for a statement or anything. At this point they had more than enough to charge the owner without anything related to the mare.

"I'll go see who that is," I said, leaving Tanner in the stall.

I heard the rumble of a diesel engine as soon as I opened the barn doors. The driver shut it off and climbed out of the big white truck. The truck was slick and pretty, a newer model probably worth as much as my house. So it was out of place that plastic had been taped across what I presumed was a broken passenger window.

"Hello!" He waved as he approached the gate. He looked familiar, and I squinted as I tried to place him.

"Good afternoon," I said. "How can I help you?"

"I was hoping you have a nice saddle horse for adoption."

"I'm so sorry, we don't have any up for adoption right now."

"You mean to tell me none of those horses are available?" He gestured to my little herd lazily grazing on the hill. Biscuit, who had taken his place between me and the stranger, eyed him warily. "Is this a rescue or a hoard?"

I clenched my jaw so I would keep my mouth shut long enough to calm my annoyance.

"The horses we have now are either unsuitable for adoption or used in our lesson program," I explained, my customer service smile plastered on my face. *Keep your cool, Mallory,* I told myself. I wouldn't do my rescue any good if I popped off at a potential adopter, no matter how rude he was.

He took his baseball cap off and rubbed his forehead with his sleeve. His more-salt-than-pepper hair was cut short, nearly shaved on the sides. And that's when I finally placed him. He was Coach Douglas Griggs, my favorite high school teacher. He'd put on a little weight, especially around his middle, but it was unmistakably him. I hadn't remembered him being this abrasive.

Coach Griggs taught math and coached basketball throughout my high school years and well beyond. He'd been new to teaching my freshman year, and back then he saw the best in everyone. It was only with his help that I was able to not only pass my math courses but score high enough to get a good scholarship. He'd taken the basketball team to the state championships more times than I could remember, and even after he retired from teaching he continued to coach the team. I'd seen him and the team featured in the newspaper many times over the years since I'd returned.

"Coach Griggs?" It came out like a question, even though I was sure of his identity.

"Do I know you?"

"I was your student."

5

"You don't say." He didn't seem impressed.

"You'd just started at Hillspring. You were the reason I passed math." I smiled for real this time.

He looked at me for a minute, still unimpressed. "Well, do you know anyone who might have decent horse for sale then? One that won't cost me an arm and a leg?"

"If you want to leave your contact information, I could ask around."

"I've been looking for months," he scoffed. "I don't need a scout. I need a horse."

I scratched Biscuit's little chest while I considered how to respond. If he was this friendly to all prospective sellers, I could understand why he was still looking. I couldn't think of any other reason he would have that much trouble finding a horse in an area where horses were anything but scarce.

"Surely you can find what you're looking for at any one of the area breeders, or even at one of the sales," I offered.

"You'd think so, wouldn't you?"

"I take it you haven't had any luck?"

"I wouldn't be *here* if I'd had any luck." He threw a hand in the air and turned back toward his truck.

"Well, I'll be sure to give you a call when a horse becomes available," I said, and made a mental note to put him on our "do not adopt" list. So far, his would be the only name there, but still.

He didn't say anything, just got into his truck and left.

"Was that Coach Griggs?" Tanner yelled from the barn doors.

I patted Biscuit and went back down the gentle hill to the barn. "Yeah. He wanted to adopt a horse. But he was kind of a jerk," I said, which made me really sad if I was being honest with myself. I'd always held him up on a pedestal. I credited him with helping me earn the scholarship that paid for college because he'd spent so much time helping me understand concepts that seemed so far out of reach at the time. He was definitely not the same man who stayed after school to tutor me. I wondered what had happened to change him so much.

"He's the reason I never played basketball. He was a drill sergeant, and I don't like being yelled at all the time." Tanner shrugged.

It made me wonder how hard Coach Griggs actually was on the kids, because I'd never thought of the football coach as being warm and cuddly.

"I'll get everyone fed if you want to start writing up the intake form," I patted Tanner's shoulder on my way by. Our intake form evolved as we added and took away based on things we learned along the way. It was important to document as close to arrival as possible though, not try to rely on memory.

Losing myself in the routine of caring for the horses is one of my favorite parts of running the rescue. There is such peace for me in the soft thunder of their hooves on the earth, the murmurs and neighs as they beg for food and attention, and that unmistakable earthy scent that is entirely unique to horses. And then there's Biscuit. He was my first rescue. He'd been used for roping practice and was found with a broken jaw and severe rope burns on his neck and back legs. Luckily, he'd also been a baby at the time, so youth and good vet care helped him recover with only faint scars to remind me of his ordeal. Instead of becoming wary and fearful of humans, Biscuit decided that we were the best things ever, especially if we happened to have treats in our pockets. He was *always* in the middle of whatever was going on at the rescue, and if it was beyond the reach of his soft little nose, he paced the fence as close as he could get.

"Hey Boss, I need help," Tanner said as he flung open the barn door. He was so rarely excitable that the tension in his voice snapped me to attention. "The new mare is down."

Chapter Two

Colic. One of the most dreaded words in the equestrian world. It was also the current condition of the emaciated chestnut mare. It had started yesterday, although after staying up with her all night, it just seemed like one long day. Colic is really just a symptom that means belly pain and can have a multitude of causes. It can be as complicated as lack of water intake that causes impaction in the intestines to as simple as increased gas that causes painful contractions. Whatever the cause though, complicated or simple, colic is a medical emergency in horses, which don't deal well with it, often hurting themselves or rolling to try to get away from the pain. And sometimes when they roll, their intestines twist, causing a lack of blood flow that can be fatal if untreated. The goal of colic treatment is to alleviate the pain and remove the underlying cause.

Biscuit's little nose reappeared in the outside window. We'd had a little reprieve from his curiosity when Tanner threw him a few flakes of hay, but he'd eaten his fill and was determined to find out what all the fuss was about. I reached through and stroked his soft snoot and gently moved it out of the way to close the shutters.

The poor mare didn't need the aggravation of inquisitive residents. Plus, the early morning sunlight was drilling into my tired skull like a jackhammer.

I pulled a towel off the stall door, marred by the last few years'-worth of wear from chewing horses, and tried to soak some of the sweat from her neck. She shivered. The crisp November morning air chilled us both. Tanner had gone to dry the horse blanket in my dryer at the house. I tried not to think about how difficult it was going to be to clean the drum and make it suitable for human clothes again, and bargained in my head that I wouldn't complain at all if the mare could just recover. She'd already seen more suffering that any animal should have to endure. I traced a long, jagged scar that ran from her milky white blind right eye, across her nose, and down to her split left nostril. Doc Brantley, our equally exhausted veterinarian, estimated her age to be in the neighborhood of seven. She was in the prime of her life, and she was almost too weak to stand up.

"How's our patient?" Doc Brantley asked as he took off his glasses and rubbed his eyes on his sleeve.

"It still seems like she's in a lot of pain," I said, fighting both tears and fatigue.

"We're getting to the point where we need to make some decisions." His mouth was drawn into a thin line.

"Can we try another shot of Banamine?" I asked, hoping that the equine analgesic might finally give her some relief. Though I had had years of experience with human patients in my former life as a nurse and then as a legal nurse consultant, I wasn't as versed in equine medicine.

"It hasn't been long enough yet," he said, glancing at his watch. "I want to tube her again."

He was referring to a nasogastric tube, inserted through her nostril and into her stomach that he used to administer fluids and mineral oil. He cautioned me that his diagnosis of impaction colic wasn't confirmed by anything other than years of experience, but I had never seen him miss a diagnosis. And because neither of us thought the mare would survive the five-hour trailer ride to the nearest veterinary college for colic surgery in her debilitated state, this was the best chance at saving her. Mineral oil isn't absorbed in the intestinal tract and can help horses pass a blockage. He'd already tubed her once, when he first arrived, and I hated to put her through it again, but it would be worth it if it worked.

Doc went back to his truck and gathered his supplies while I used the towel to rub down her neck and chest. She nuzzled my shoulder and the tears that had been threatening to escape rolled down my cheeks. I try not to attribute human emotion to the horses, but it was hard in that moment to dismiss the way she seemed to think I could make her feel better.

She stood like a trooper while Doc passed the hose through her nostril and into her stomach, only mildly protesting what *had* to be an uncomfortable procedure. I hoped that meant she was just a good girl and not that she was too weak to fight us. The first time he tubed her, I didn't know how many hours ago, she'd been sedated. She had been in so much pain she was trying to throw herself down on the ground. Thankfully, the old practice of walking a colicky horse fell out of favor, as current best veterinary practice recommends just keeping them from violently rolling or hurting themselves as they try to escape the pain in their belly. We had already tried a variety of veterinary medicine and old wives' tales, including taking her for a ride in the trailer. Doc said early on that the motion might help move things along, and for whatever reason, any horse owner knows that they always use trailer rides as a bathroom break.

It didn't take him long to give her another bolus of fluids and mineral oil. She snorted and shook her head as he removed the tube. I rubbed her shoulder to comfort her. Biscuit brayed as he stuck his little nose over the gate at the back of the barn. He wasn't used to being shut out of our activities, and he protested his exclusion loudly.

"Now, we wait," Doc said while he cleaned his equipment.

I nodded.

"Hey Boss," Tanner said and opened the barn door. "The blanket's warm and dry, but I think your dryer's gonna need an exorcism now."

I couldn't help but smile as he spread the blanket over the mare's bony back and jutting hips. I repeated my earlier bargain in my head, *I will not complain about my dryer if this sweet girl will just get better.* She seemed to relax as the warmth settled over her, even cocked one hind leg as horses do so often when they rest.

"Have you named her yet?" he asked as he leaned against the stall door. He took off his baseball cap and ran a hand through his unruly mop of curly brown hair. He was several inches taller than both me and Doc Brantley, but his wide shoulders slumped with exhaustion, making him seem smaller than usual.

"No, not yet. I'm already far more attached than I should be," I admitted.

"Mama always says you should name something if you want to anchor it here," he said, a bit sheepishly.

I smiled at the thought of Rachel saying that to Tanner. She was an old soul and she had raised one of the best young men I ever had the pleasure of meeting. I tried to send him home multiple times, tried to insist that one of us should get some rest, but he wouldn't hear of it.

"She looks like a Ruby, Boss."

"Ruby," I said, trying out the sound of the name as I looked at her. "I like it."

"It's settled then."

"We really shouldn't name her until the case is closed," I said.

He had recently made the same near-mistake I was about to make, getting attached to one of the horses before the court awarded him to the rescue. Luckily, for both Tanner and his new adoptee, the judge decided to remove the horse from his previous owner. We hadn't been sure that was going to be the outcome though, and Tanner would have been devastated to return Zeus to the man who had abused him.

"There's no way she'll get returned. Just look at her," he said, grimacing at her emaciated frame, tangled mane, and numerous scars.

"There's no guarantee about anything," I said, choosing not to give voice to my concerns about her even being able to survive.

She raised her tail, and we both held our breath, hoping that whatever was blocking her guts might be passing through. But instead of worms or fecal matter, she just passed a huge amount of air. My hope deflated with her lowered tail. Rescue work is rarely glamorous, the point illustrated by our intense desire to see the mare have a giant poop.

"That's great!" Doc Brantley leaned over the stall door, wearing the first hopeful smile I had seen in over twenty-four hours.

I snapped back to attention. Of course, passing gas was a good sign! I had been so focused on the ultimate goal, for her to pass the impaction, that I had forgotten everything I knew as a nurse.

Passing gas meant that her bowels were working, that *something* was passing through.

"Why don't you go get something to eat," Tanner gently took the lead rope from my hands. "I took the liberty of making some coffee while the blanket dried, and I owe you some bananas."

"You don't owe me anything. I told you to help yourself."

"I'll stay with her," he stroked her neck. "You guys go eat."

I opened my mouth to argue, but my stomach grumbled like an aggravated bear before I had the chance to speak. "Okay, thank you," I conceded.

Doc and I walked toward the house in comfortable silence. I stopped at the paddock gate and took in the rescue, washed in the warm morning sunlight. The faded red, four-stall barn sat on the gentle slope in the front. Paddocks extended down the hill almost to the county road in the front and up into the trees at the top of the hill beside my house. We had cross-fenced the original property that had belonged to my parents so that we could rotate grazing and get the most out of the available grass. I still had to supplement with hay and grain depending on rainfall and the individual needs of the horses.

A chill ran over my exhausted body, and I looked through the highline clearing to the huge show barn on the hill overlooking the rescue. I had almost lost everything, including my freedom, just a few short months ago. The owner of that show barn had been our longtime neighbor, Albert Cunningham, founder of Cunningham Performance Horses and descendent of the oldest banking family in our county. He hated my rescue and never missed an opportunity to tell me that my "mongrels" had no place next to his champions. When he was found murdered in that very barn, it didn't take long for the police to focus on me due to his long-standing and rather public animosity toward me. Well, that and the fact that the real murderer, his greedy son Braydon, tried to frame me for the killing.

After Braydon was arrested and my part in the investigation was made public, adoptions and donations boomed, and we were able to place three horses in loving new homes. Since Zeus, a big bay gelding, went home with Tanner, the rescue currently had six residents, the new mare making seven. With the exception of Biscuit, who was still trying to figure out a way to get into the barn, the remaining horses were grazing lazily on the hill above the paddock.

That media attention was a double-edged sword, good for donations, adoptions, and my brand-new lesson program, but really hard for me considering the situation. Braydon had tried to kill me when I discovered his deception. The requests for interviews and random questions lobbed at me anytime I left the house had just now started to die down. Hillspring is a quiet little town, so the murder and subsequent scandal were on everyone's radar.

I hugged myself against the chill and followed Doc Brantley into my house. He was a regular at the rescue, which also meant that he was a regular in my kitchen for coffee and refreshments. He made himself at home, grabbing a mug from the cabinet and helping himself to the coffee, which he drank black. I, on the other hand, preferred more cream and sugar than coffee in my cup. I picked up a bag of granola and absently picked through it, chewing on autopilot without really tasting it.

I glanced at the calendar, and on realizing that it was Saturday let out a sigh of relief. When school started, I moved my weekend riding lessons to Sunday afternoons to accommodate the kids who played soccer. Their games were all scheduled on Saturdays, and after a couple of them had tearfully told me they had to choose between soccer and riding lessons, I had rearranged my schedule. It also meant that I might be able to get some much needed rest before I had a paddock full of enthusiastic children to keep focused. Those lessons were part of the steady income that made the rescue possible, so being able to oblige them benefited me as much as it did them, probably more.

Dr. Vance Brantley, or "Van" as he preferred among his friends, seemed to be as much on autopilot as I was. It had been Tanner who started calling him "Doc Brantley," and it just stuck. Now half his clientele referred to him that way. He stared at my kitchen cabinet with tired, vacant eyes.

"Please extend my apologies to Amy," I said, referring to his very pregnant wife.

"She loves your rescue as much as I do." He waved me off. The support warmed me more than the coffee.

I had been warned by nearly everyone when I started the rescue that although it was a needed service it was doomed to failure, that there had been countless rescues that had already failed before mine, that I was stupid to leave a lucrative job as a legal nurse consultant to do something so risky. There have been some very close calls along the way, but as I entered into my third year, it looked like we just might make a go of it after all. My involvement in helping to solve the murder of my neighbor had brought in much-needed revenue, but that was not the way I wanted to succeed. Still, I'm glad there was a silver lining to that whole mess.

"I'm going back to the barn and see if I can get Tanner to go home and rest," I said, and downed the rest of my coffee. "Make yourself at home."

Trotting Into Trouble

I pushed a bag of bagels toward Doc and pointed toward the toaster. "There's cream cheese in the fridge."

He made a noise in the affirmative and toasted me with his cup of coffee. Banjo, my goofy blue heeler, looked at me expectantly as I passed his bed on the way to the door. He was completely unbothered by the extra person in the house, both because he was familiar with Doc Brantley and because he assumes everyone is a friend.

"Stay put," I said gently as I bent down to scratch his ears. He watched me go, but he didn't offer to bolt for the door.

I was descending the porch steps when my phone rang in my back pocket. I smiled when I saw Andy's name displayed on the screen. Andrew Hannigan had graciously agreed to represent me back when I thought I might actually go to jail, and more than a client-attorney relationship had blossomed.

"How's it going?" he asked as soon as I'd said my "hello."

"She's really sick," I said. I'd begged off dinner with him the previous evening in order to make the drive to the south end of the county to pick up the mare. "She colicked a few hours after we unloaded her. Doc Brantley has been here all night."

"You must be exhausted."

"To my bones," I admitted.

"I can come give you a break."

"I appreciate the offer, but I need to see this through."

"I'll bring dinner this evening," he said.

"That's sweet, but if I get the chance to rest, I intend to crash until tomorrow."

He chuckled. "I understand. Call me if you need anything or change your mind."

I agreed and we ended the call. I smiled at his offer. I had no doubt that he would be here in a heartbeat if I asked. I bit my lip as I thought about the fact that I hadn't told my daughter Ginny about him yet. For weeks now my best friend Lanie had been not so gently reminding me that I needed to tell her. The Christmas holidays were barreling toward me like a runaway freight train, and I needed to figure out a way to tell her before she came home and discovered for herself. I wasn't sure why it was such a big deal to just tell her I'd started dating someone. It wasn't like my ex-husband hadn't had girlfriends since our divorce, and Ginny didn't seem to resent him for it. I sighed. I was too exhausted to think about it, and even though Ginny would call from college that afternoon for her usual Saturday FaceTime chat, I could wait a few more days and still have time to tell her before her holiday break.

Biscuit had finally abandoned his efforts to get into the barn and joined the others to graze at the remaining grass on the frosty hillside. I found Tanner brushing through the mare's mane and speaking softly to her.

"Great news, Boss." He looked up, smiling, and pointed to a pile of the very thing we had all been waiting for.

I'd never been so happy to have a reason to clean out a stall before. The mare had stopped sweating and appeared relaxed and almost as exhausted as I felt.

"Wonderful!" Doc Brantley said from beside me. I wasn't sure when he had arrived back at the barn, but he was just as pleased as we were.

He completed his exam, deemed her to be on the mend, and then went over aftercare instructions with me before leaving. We were to keep her off grain for a few days, feed her small, easily digestible meals, and make sure she drank enough water. Tanner and I briefly discussed the best way to ensure that we did all of that and also make sure she got plenty of exercise. We decided we would turn her out in the small paddock just below the barn, the one we had come to call the "lower paddock," then stall her at night.

Relief seemed to invigorate Tanner, while I felt like I could finally let my guard down and relax. He buzzed around, feeding, putting out hay, and checking on the mare, while I felt like I was moving in slow motion.

I was barely conscious when I sat on the steps to the loft and leaned over on the two bales of hay stacked in the barn breezeway. I didn't remember dozing off, so when my phone rang in my pocket, I nearly jumped off the steps. It took several moments for me to figure out where I was and why my neck was so stiff. I managed to answer the phone before it kicked over to voicemail.

"Hello?" My voice was thick, and I still felt a bit disoriented. I picked up the jacket that I had dislodged when I jumped awake. It was Tanner's. He must've covered me up and let me sleep.

"Are you okay?" I recognized Sheriff Grady Sullivan's voice right away.

"Yeah. I was asleep." I leaned over and picked hay out of my ponytail. My blond curls seemed to grab debris like Velcro.

"Sorry," he paused. "It's almost noon."

"It was a long night. The mare colicked when we got home last night," I said through a yawn. He had been part of the seizure, so he knew she'd been in bad shape.

"I'm sorry to hear that, but I need your help."

Chapter Three

I rubbed my eyes and tried to stretch the kinks out of my neck and back.

"What do you need help with?"

"There's a loose horse at the Deadwood Lake Wildlife Management Area, at the South entrance. We've tried all morning to catch it and it keeps getting away."

"Any ideas who it belongs to?" I thought about trying to find the owner to help in the efforts. But I realized through my brain fog that Grady would have thought of that too.

"It's saddled, so we're afraid someone is injured. We've called in the volunteer fire department to help in the search, but we need to get the horse contained. I'm afraid he's going to get out into traffic."

"I'll be right there." I said, getting to my feet. I was glad that we hadn't had time to unhook the trailer from my truck the previous night.

"Hey, Boss," Tanner said as he descended the loft stairs. "Where are we going?"

"You should've woken me." I handed his jacket back to him. "And you should've gone home and gone to bed." I patted his shoulder. It was hard for me not to Mom at him, since he was just a few years older than Ginny.

"I slept some in the loft. I wasn't about to leave you in the barn, and if I woke you up, you would've found a million excuses not to sleep." He grinned. He knew me far too well.

"Well, thank you. I guess I needed it."

I looked in on the red mare. She was laying peacefully in the stall, her bony hips jutting out like driftwood. There were no signs of further colic, no sweat, no attempts to roll against the pain, just a sleepy, resting horse. I breathed a sigh of relief. She looked up at me, her eyes a stark contrast to her dark-red coat. The blind eye was a milky white, but the other one was bright sky-blue, hinting at Paint horse blood in her lineage. She wasn't out of the woods yet, but every hour she didn't colic again was another step in the right direction.

"Who was that on the phone?" Tanner gently reminded me that I hadn't answered his original question.

"Grady. There's a saddled horse loose at the Wildlife Management Area South entrance and they can't catch it."

"Okay," he said and grabbed a feed bucket off the hook. "I'll get some bait and meet you at the truck."

"You don't have to go. You've already gone above and beyond, and I can't pay you overtime just yet."

He waved me off. "You don't have to pay me overtime. I'm salary, Boss," he grinned.

I smiled back and thanked my lucky stars that I had such great volunteers-turned-employees. Tanner took the full-time position, which usually meant he nearly lived at the rescue; and Ashley took the part-time position because she was in college studying for a degree in social work. She had been with me longer, but she needed more time to devote to her classes. I let them both come and go as they needed, and that arrangement worked for all of us.

I grabbed a lead rope and a bag of horse treats and headed for my truck.

*   *   *

The drive to the south entrance of the Wildlife Management Area took about forty-five minutes from the rescue. Luckily, my best friend Lanie called, and we talked nearly the whole time. Tanner reclined the seat, pulled his baseball cap over his face, and slept through Lanie's account of the ongoing feud that flared up every time her sister-in-law came for a visit. Lanie's rant was also, thankfully, rather one-sided, so I didn't have to think much, just offer reassuring grunts and "um-hms" every once in a while. She wound down as we approached the rutted dirt road leading to the entrance and ended the call with a promise to catch lunch later in the week.

The parking area was nearly full, and it took some maneuvering to get my F150 and horse trailer parked in a place that would also allow me to get out again. Deer hunting is probably as popular as football in the South, and our county was no exception. The Deadwood Lake Wildlife Management Area was the bigger of two public hunting grounds in Northwest Arkansas, spanning five counties and covering nearly eight thousand acres. I doubted that I would have been able to find a spot at all if this had been opening weekend.

The parking area was little more than a large clearing at the end of a long, rutted gravel road. The south entrance was the least scenic of the access routes. The north entrance looked like something out of Middle Earth, with stately limestone bluffs overlooking the confluence where Mill River empties into Deadwood Lake. The south entrance was surrounded by small, anemic cedars, patches of briars, and stands of thistles that looked like they were from some alien landscape. I was thankful we'd had a couple of frosts so at least there wouldn't be ticks and chiggers.

Grady met us as soon as we got out of the truck. He was wearing his signature Stetson cowboy hat atop his salt-and-pepper hair. He was sporting some serious stubble that looked like he might be trying to grow a beard. I couldn't imagine Grady with a beard. He'd always been clean-shaven and somewhat Old Hollywood cowboy in his demeanor and aesthetic.

"The last time we saw the horse, he went back in there." He pointed across the parking area to what looked like a trailhead sign. "Some idiots chased him, but I sent them packing. He keeps coming back to the parking lot and then runs off into the trees anytime someone gets close."

"We'll start there then," I said, slinging the lead rope over my shoulder.

I dug around in my toolbox and pulled out two hunter orange vests and passed one to Tanner. The woods around us sounded like World War III had broken out, and the last thing we needed was to get mistaken for a deer in a forest full of heavily armed hunters. Granted, the horse trails were supposed to be off limits to the deer hunters on the other side of the wildlife management area, but I wasn't sure how well the area was marked. Grady led the way to the trailhead sign. Tanner followed with the bucket of feed while I trailed along behind, wishing I'd slept longer.

The whole area was covered in hoofprints, but it was impossible to tell if they were from the horse we came for or from any one of the other riders in the area. There were four other horse trailers in the parking area besides mine. I personally knew several hunters that liked to go in on their horses or mules and pack out their deer. Plus, this was a popular trail-riding area, and even though I wouldn't ride in public woods during deer season, it didn't mean everyone made the same choice.

We'd walked only a few yards down the trail when we heard the telltale snort of a spooky horse. I spotted him just to the left of the trail ahead of us, watching us warily.

"Hey there, Buddy," I said and whistled at him. He raised his head and snorted again.

Tanner rattled the feed bucket, and the horse took a wary step toward us. He was beautiful. His black coat gleamed in the little patches of sunlight that filtered through the cedars and scrubby blackjack oaks. He had a wide, white blaze on his face and three white socks, leaving only his left front leg entirely black, the same leg he used to paw the ground in front of him. He tossed his head, bouncing the circle reins up his neck but, luckily, not over his head. He was fully tacked out with a Western saddle and fringed breast collar. The rifle scabbard strapped to the right side of the saddle was empty. I hoped that he had escaped from someone's deer camp and that there wasn't an injured rider dumped somewhere in the woods. I hoped Grady had called in the volunteer searchers for nothing.

I hung back while Tanner passed me and approached with the feed. It looked like the horse was going to dip his head in and take a big bite when a man wearing a hunter orange vest over camo coveralls crashed through the underbrush and fell, face-first, into the trail. The horse reared up, pivoted and rolled back like a champion reiner, and galloped off into the forest.

I cursed under my breath while the man on the trail rolled over and spat out some dirt and debris. He moaned and reached for his rifle, which had landed just out of his reach. I could smell the alcohol wafting off him from several feet away.

"O God," he moaned.

His receding hairline was now sporting pieces of leaves and what I hoped was just mud. He continued to fumble for the gun. I rushed over and nudged it out of his reach with the toe of my boot.

"Did you fall off your horse?" I turned back to him.

"Huh?" He looked like he was struggling to focus on me. "What you talkin'bout?"

"There's a horse loose here. Is he yours?"

"No." He pulled himself up to a sitting position and swayed unsteadily.

I yelled for Grady, who had apparently been just behind us because he materialized almost immediately. He helped the man to his feet and ushered him back toward the parking area. Grady radioed for a deputy to collect the rifle and then caught the man just before he face-planted again.

"I think he's dead," the guy mumbled.

"Who's dead?" Grady asked, bracing the man as he stumbled again.

"He don't look good," the man slurred and clutched onto Grady's arm. "I never seen nothing like that. I think he's dead."

I could hear Grady radioing in that little bit of information and the new orders to be on the lookout for a possibly injured individual. I left him to deal with that and took off down the trail after the horse. I was afraid the intoxicated man had been talking about the horse's rider, which renewed my sense of urgency. Tanner followed, considerate enough not to outrun me and leave me in the dust. We'd only jogged a few yards down the trail, which was also down a gentle slope, when we caught sight of the horse again. He seemed to be sticking close to the trail, which was a blessing since the briars and bushes were getting thicker the farther in we went.

As we approached, the horse turned and faced us warily, head high, his dark eyes ringed with white as he widened them to watch us. He snorted and pawed the ground.

"Want me to hang back, Boss?" Tanner offered me the feed bucket.

"He seemed to respond pretty well to you earlier before that guy scared him off. Might as well try again."

Tanner approached the horse, head down, slowly and calmly on a diagonal path to him, careful not to come at him directly. He rattled the feed bucket and paused every few steps to allow the horse to look him over. When he was a few feet away, the horse turned and trotted a few steps down the trail, snorting again. Tanner stopped and stood relaxed instead of pursuing what was clearly a scared animal.

They continued like this for several minutes, back and forth, until something spooked the horse again and he took off through the underbrush. This time there was no drunk hunter stumbling onto the path, so I had no idea what had set him off. We had no hope of keeping up with a bolting horse on foot, and I started to regret my decision to not bring horses of our own. We followed the hoofprints and trampled vegetation the best we could, since neither one of us was a seasoned tracker.

"We may have to go back and get River and Zeus," I said, trying not to gasp for air.

"I think that's him, just over there." Tanner pointed to a small clearing on the other side of a rocky creek bed.

Trotting Into Trouble

We fought our way through the cedars and, sure enough, the horse was grazing on the hill above the bank, just outside the treeline. He noticed us as soon as we emerged into the dry creek. The air was thick with the smell of the evergreens we had disturbed, reminding me again of the impending holidays.

"I'm oh for two, Boss. Why don't you give it a shot this time?"

I nodded and took the feed bucket. Exhaustion and my natural grace, which is to say that I have no natural grace, caused me to spook the frightened horse yet again as I scrambled through the weeds and loose rocks. I fought back annoyance and frustration and reminded myself that horses are rarely contrary without a good reason. And to be fair, my lurching and tripping wasn't exactly the picture of a confident horsewoman.

At least he didn't bolt again. He trotted a few feet into the trees onto what looked like a 4 x 4 trail. Deep ruts had been cut into the earth, dried now and cracking with the lack of rain. He bent down and sniffed what looked like a camo coat that had been thrown into the underbrush. I circled around so I could approach him from the front, but not *directly* in front of him. I watched him closely, looking for any sign that he would run, but he just shook his head and shifted nervously. I eased forward, slowly and steadily, until I had a hand on his shoulder. He dipped his head in the bucket and took a huge bite of feed.

"Good boy," I said softly, and stroked his neck. I slowly worked my hand up his neck until I could get a hold of the reins and slip them over his head. As soon as he felt tension on the reins, he set back against me and slung his head from side to side to try to dislodge my grip.

"Whoa!" I took a few jerking steps forward, but I held onto the reins. "Whoa there!"

Thankfully, he stopped fighting and stood, defiantly, at the end of the reins. I took a step forward and tripped over something. The horse snorted but didn't set back again. I glanced down and found that I had tripped over the coat. The problem, though, was that someone was still in it.

Chapter Four

I'd been so focused on the frightened horse that I failed to notice the body. The way he was lying, half in the dense shrubs that the old-timers call buck brush, made it look like it was just a coat tossed off the trail. But looking down, after tripping over a leg nearly buried in leaves, I could see that it was a man. I leaned over and pulled back the branches covering him, looking for any signs of life. There weren't any. His face was ashen, and his eyes were open and fixed. I tried to lean over a little further to look for the rise and fall of his chest even though I knew he wasn't breathing. Trying not to contaminate what I hoped wasn't a crime scene, I used a stick to poke him in the shoulder. He was stiff.

I heard a branch snap behind me and spooked worse than the horse did. I was relieved to find that it was Tanner.

"Don't come any closer," I said, holding up my hand to stop him. The horse danced nervously beside me at the sudden movement.

Tanner stopped, but looked confused. "What's wrong?"

"Call Grady," I said, and swallowed, hard. "I think I found the horse's rider."

He looked down at the body beside me, but like me it didn't seem to register right away that it was anything besides a coat. He took a tentative step forward and craned his head to look into the brush. When the reality dawned on him, he went gray and cupped a hand to his mouth.

"Oh, no," he gasped.

"Tanner," I said to get his attention again. He nodded, letting his hand drop to his side. "Take the horse back to the trailer and call Grady."

The horse was reluctant to leave, and I suspected that he had kept coming back here every time someone tried to catch him—back to his fallen owner. A lump rose in my throat at the thought. I stroked his neck and told him what a good boy he was to bring us here. He allowed me to pass the reins off to Tanner, but he looked back one more time before following him down the creek bank.

I went back to the body. I was careful not to disturb anything as I circled the patch of brush to view the man's face. This had to be what the intoxicated man was talking about. He'd said, "He doesn't look good, I think he's dead." I hoped there wasn't more than one dead body in the woods. As I kneeled down I had a sinking feeling of recognition.

Oh, God. I know him.

I gasped so hard I choked. After recovering, I gently pulled back the brush and confirmed that I was looking at Coach Douglas Griggs. I scanned over his head and face, looking for evidence that he had fallen off the flighty horse and cracked his skull. There was some debris in his hair, and he looked like he had rolled, or *been* rolled, into the underbrush, but there was no telltale blood or wounds on his face or head. The only blood visible was a small patch on the front of his denim overalls.

It was then that I noticed the reason I hadn't immediately recognized that there was a person in the camo coat. His right arm, which was beneath him but still partially visible, was inside the sleeve of the coat. The left sleeve, however, was empty and slung haphazardly across his body. And the lower half of his body had been half covered in leaves and sticks. I could see where the forest litter had been disturbed to bury his legs. The coat pocket that was visible had been turned inside out.

This wasn't an accident.

At least it wasn't a riding accident. Coach Griggs hadn't partially redressed himself, and he sure hadn't tried to bury himself in leaves and litter.

My chest tightened and I felt my eyes sting as tears threatened to fall. I circled the brush again, looking for anything I'd missed the first time around. He wasn't wearing an orange vest. In addition to coaching and teaching math, Coach Griggs also taught hunter's safety, driver's ed, and chaired many of the committees at the school. He always preached safety. He would never have been in these woods without a vest. I didn't see a rifle anywhere near him. Since the scabbard on the saddle had been empty, I wondered where his weapon had ended up. I guessed there was a possibility that he hadn't come to the woods to hunt, but none of this was adding up for me. He should have been wearing a safety vest even if he'd just been out for a ride.

I was poking through the underbrush searching for anything out of place across the rutted trail when Grady and Corporal Bailey pulled up in a Polaris side-by-side. Grady frowned at me but didn't say anything right away as he got out of the passenger side. Darrin stayed in the 4x4, his long limbs folded in what looked like an uncomfortably narrow seat.

"He's over there." I pointed at the camo coat. "It's Coach Griggs." My throat felt tight at saying it aloud.

"Darrin will take you back to your truck and I'll come by later to get an official statement," Grady said, positioning himself between me and the body.

"He's been rolled into the bushes," I said, ignoring his stern expression, which was getting more so by the minute. "Someone covered his legs with leaves, but they didn't finish covering the rest of the body, so they were either lazy or they got interrupted. And his coat is only half on."

"Mal," Grady held up a finger.

"He isn't wearing a hunting vest," I plowed on. "I have a really hard time believing he would be out here without one."

"Mallory, this will be investigated. And I can always call in the state police if we need help."

"Of course," I said. "I'm just sharing my observations."

I couldn't tell if Grady smirked or grimaced before he turned toward Coach's body. I hadn't considered that he might have to call in the state police again. It made sense though, because the murder had occurred on state wildlife management land. If he did, I hoped it wouldn't be the same two detectives who had responded to Albert Cunningham's death. I hadn't had a great relationship with the lead investigator since she'd been convinced I was guilty.

"He came to the rescue yesterday," I said to Grady's back. He jerked upright and turned to face me again.

"What? Why?"

"He was looking for a gentle riding horse," I said, trying to remember the exact conversation through my fog of exhaustion.

Grady rubbed the stubble on his chin. "Okay," he said, and he still seemed to be considering something, "I'll talk to you later."

I left Grady to begin taping off the area and joined Corporal Bailey in the side-by-side. He hadn't been my biggest fan either, but he'd warmed up a bit since then.

"Sheriff said the mare from last night colicked. Is she alright?" he asked as soon as I took my seat next to him.

"She's doing much better this morning." I smiled at his concern. "She's not out of the woods yet, though. She's in really rough shape."

He clenched his jaw. "That worthless piece of . . ." he stopped himself and glanced at me, ". . . garbage is probably going to make bail. His mama has already been calling and asking where she can pay to get her baby boy out of jail."

"Thanks for the heads up." I watched the trees whizz by as he barreled down the trail. I couldn't stop thinking about Coach Griggs. I knew he wasn't everyone's favorite teacher, and his reputation as a tough coach was even stronger. I shook my head against my own thoughts. There was no reason to think he'd been the victim of anything but a terrible shooting accident. There was no telling how many hunters were in the woods, and a stray bullet can travel a very long distance. The person responsible had probably panicked and tried to hide their fatal mistake. I told myself there was no reason to think he'd been murdered on purpose. I needed to focus on the immediate issues and let the police do their job, as Grady kept reminding me.

We pulled into the parking area, and it was mostly abandoned. I noticed a few trucks with the Connor County Volunteer Fire Department logo in the back windows, but they were likely in standby mode, since I'd already found the missing rider. I saw a group of CCVFD T-shirt-clad men and women gathered by the front of one of the trucks. I followed their collective gazes to a sheriff's SUV on our left. Lieutenant Calvin Burns dodged a blow from the drunk hunter Grady had escorted away from us on the trail. The hunter clumsily swung and missed. His wrists were handcuffed together, making his movements even more awkward. Even though Cal was squat and square, he was surprisingly agile, and had no trouble staying out of danger.

Much to his credit, Cal didn't appear to lose his temper with the man. He just dodged the swing, grabbed the man's arms, recuffed him behind his back, and put him in the backseat of the SUV, all without being overly rough or forceful. I'm not sure I would have been able to keep my cool like that, but I certainly admired Cal for being patient. Once the man was secure, Cal rubbed his bald head and motioned for Darrin to come over to the SUV.

"One of us will be out later," Darrin waved as he exited the side-by-side.

I nodded and headed for my own truck. Tanner was stretched out in the back seat, his boots sticking out the driver's side window and his cap covering his face. I hated to disturb him since I knew he'd only been out a few minutes. I pulled myself up on the side of the trailer and looked in on the big black horse. Tanner had switched the leather bridle and bit for the halter we'd brought with us. The horse eyed me suspiciously but was otherwise calm and collected.

"He loaded right up," Tanner said, and yawned.

"I didn't mean to wake you."

"It's okay. I didn't know how long you'd be, so I thought I'd catch a nap."

"You can go home and get some rest as soon as we get this guy back to the barn," I said as I climbed into the driver's seat.

"I'm fine," he said, and yawned again. "I want to make sure Ruby is still doing alright."

I smiled. I knew it wouldn't do any good to argue with him about naming her. Besides, I really liked the name. It suited her.

I was glad that Grady, or one of the deputies, had cleared out the parking area. It was much easier to make a big circle than it was to turn the truck and trailer around. I was a much better driver than I had been when I first opened the rescue, but it still took me longer than I would like to back up the trailer, a fact that Tanner found immensely amusing.

The drive back to the rescue was uneventful, and I kept myself alert by checking the trailer frequently in the mirrors. I really wanted to upgrade with a camera so I could keep tabs inside the trailer, but that would have to wait until other expenses were covered. I avoided the winding streets of downtown Hillspring, taking the straighter and less hilly county roads even if they did add a few miles to the trip. I took extra care in navigating the rough, steep driveway and made a mental note to get some quotes on the dirt work to repair it.

Biscuit started braying, or "honking" as Tanner calls it, the minute we came to a stop. The horses joined in the chorus, and soon even the horses at the Cunningham Farm on the hill next door were neighing at the new arrival, who returned the greeting with excited whinnying of his own. He stomped a little in the trailer, but nothing that made me concerned.

"I'll get the front stall ready," Tanner called back over his shoulder on his way to the barn. He stopped for a moment to scratch Biscuit's little chest, then led him to the back paddock, where he closed the gate to allow me a clear path to the barn.

I didn't waste any time unloading the horse. I didn't know how long he'd been tacked up, but I figured he would appreciate being unsaddled, fed, and watered. I planned to wait until Grady had time to notify Mrs. Griggs and then I would offer to deliver Coach's horse back home. He danced around a bit, trying to see all the other horses at once, whinnying again, his sides shaking with the effort. He wasn't pushy on the lead rope though, just followed me, head held high, to the breezeway of the barn. I cross-tied him using the ties that Tanner had rigged up for saddling the lesson horses.

"Almost ready." Tanner popped his head up over the stall door.

"No problem. I'm going to get him unsaddled and brushed before I put him up."

I walked to the back of the barn where we kept the brushes and tack. I grabbed a brush from the crate on the shelf, and when I turned back to the horse, something caught my eye. Something metallic was glinting in the fringe of the horse's breast collar. I squinted, trying to get a better view, but the horse shifted nervously and blocked me. Afraid he had snagged a piece of wire or metal in the fringe, I tucked the brush under my arm and spoke softly to him while I approached from behind.

My attention was still focused on that stupid fringe, so I missed the subtle changes in his body language. It was a complete surprise when his left hind hoof connected with my right calf with a pop that sounded like a gunshot. I gasped and stumbled backward into the wall.

"Did he just kick you?" Tanner was out of the stall and at my side with impossible speed.

"Yep," I said, still a little breathless from the sudden shock of pain.

"Anything broken?" Tanner asked as he reached out to touch my leg and then yanked his hand back, unsure how to help.

I put some weight on it and though it hurt, *really hurt*, it definitely wasn't broken.

"No. It just hurts." I looked at the horse, who was watching us as closely as he could over his shoulder.

"You should go put some ice on that. I'll get him settled."

"I'll ice it as soon as we're finished," I patted Tanner's shoulder. "I'm not going to let him think he's won. But I *will* watch him a little closer from now on. That was a dumb, rookie mistake."

Tanner drew his mouth into a thin line, but he didn't argue with me. I limped to the front of the breezeway and continued to watch the horse closely, but I was careful not to act afraid or nervous. Bad habits are easily reinforced because horses are natural observers. I felt stupid for making a mistake like that. I knew better than to trust a horse I didn't know. I grumbled at myself as I kept an eye on the horse while I pulled the fringe back on the breast collar. It wasn't wire or stray metal caught there. It was a thumb drive. And it had been zip-tied to the hardware.

Chapter Five

After untacking the big black horse, I him settled into the stall with some fresh hay and water, then limped to the house to get my laptop. I didn't want to cut the drive off the breast collar, since I didn't know if it was important to the investigation, but my curiosity got the better of me. I decided I could bring the laptop to the barn and see what was on it before I turned it over to Grady.

I let Banjo follow me back to the barn, and he bounced along happily sniffing everything along the path. I fired up the laptop as I hobbled down the gentle slope. I don't know why I felt such a sudden urgency, but I wanted to get a look at the thumb drive's contents as soon as possible.

"Let me do that so you can go put some ice on that leg," Tanner said as he met me at the barn door, hands on his hips.

"I don't want your fingerprints on anything," I said, avoiding eye contact. "Mine are already on everything."

"You're not going to be a suspect this time and neither am I. We were both here with a reliable witness."

"Still," I said, and failed to come up with a better rebuttal.

I went to the back of the barn where I put the saddle and tack. I quickly inserted the thumb drive in the USB port and waited at an awkward angle, holding the laptop on the saddle rack with one hand. It was a short wait. The thumb drive was encrypted. I didn't have a clue what his password might be, or even how to start guessing. How did people in books and movies always conveniently know a hacker? I didn't know anyone who could type furiously on a laptop and produce tech magic. I ejected the drive and closed my laptop. I would have to hope that Grady had access to people who could get past the security.

"Nothing?" Tanner asked from behind me.

"It's password protected."

"Well, I guess that would make sense. Anyone hiding a flash drive on their horse is bound to be pretty paranoid." Tanner shrugged. "Unless it's just vet records and registration stuff."

"In that case, why would it be password protected?"

"True." He took off his cap and scratched his head. "That would kind of defeat the purpose."

"I just can't figure out why anyone would put a thumb drive on their horse's breast collar," I said, looking back at the offending drive.

"People are weird," Tanner said with great conviction.

Before I could agree, Biscuit started braying his announcement that someone he didn't recognize was coming up the driveway. I hadn't expected Grady this soon. I shoved the laptop under my arm and limped out to the paddock. Except it wasn't Grady.

Andy pulled his silver Lincoln Town Car in beside my truck, which was still hooked to the horse trailer. Biscuit continued to bray. Even though Andy had become a frequent visitor over the last few months, he was still new enough to set off Biscuit's discerning alarm about half the time. He rounded the back of the trailer and headed toward the house. Banjo raced past me to greet him.

"We're out here," I called to him, since my leg was getting stiffer by the minute and I was moving at a snail's pace.

He turned around with a smile that quickly faded. His dark-brown hair was tousled, unlike the deliberate style he wore during his workweek, and he had traded his suit for a flannel shirt and jeans. He was handsome in an entirely disarming way no matter what he wore, but I definitely preferred the lumberjack look.

"What happened? Are you okay?" He put the bags he was carrying on the trailer fender and hurried to open the gate for me.

"Glad you're here," Tanner said from behind me. "Maybe you can talk her into putting some ice on that leg, because she won't listen to me."

"I'm *fine*." I glared playfully at Tanner, who glared right back.

"You don't look fine," Andy said as he took my laptop and then held onto my arm to steady me.

"Gee, thanks," I said.

"That's not what I meant," Andy pulled me in close to him, a fact that I did not mind in the slightest. I inhaled his woodsy cologne and enjoyed how strong and solid he felt against me.

"That new horse kicked the thunder out of her," Tanner continued. "Sounded like a gun going off."

"The sick one?" Andy shoved the laptop into one of the bags and then scooped them up with his free hand.

"No, the dead guy's horse."

"Okay, I'm going to need you to start at the beginning."

* * *

After Andy and Tanner had settled me in my own living room with my swollen leg on pillows and my ancient ice pack perched precariously on my calf, I filled Andy in on everything that had happened since our call that morning. Tanner interjected occasionally, mostly to gang up on me and force me to take it easy or allow them to wait on me. Admittedly, I wasn't used to being pampered by anyone, let alone my friend and employee and the man I was dating. And as they coordinated their efforts to prepare the takeout Andy had brought for me, I dozed off pondering whether or not I could call Andy my boyfriend yet.

When I jerked awake from the weird, disjointed nightmare I was having, I heard voices on the porch. Banjo was curled up on his fluffy dog bed and I didn't hear Biscuit, so I assumed those voices belonged to Andy and Tanner. I winced as I moved my leg off the pillows. Someone had moved the ice pack, and I wasn't sure it had done any good. My leg throbbed. I pulled my bootcut jeans up over my calf and gasped at the carnage. There was a perfect hoofprint marring my skin in varying shades of purple and black, so perfect that I could make out the nails in the horseshoe. In fact, I could even see that one of those nails had been loose and bent over at about a forty-five-degree angle from the shoe itself. I would need to take a look at the shoe and see if the nail needed to be removed or if the whole shoe needed to be reset.

I ran my hand over my skin, and it felt hot to the touch. Remembering my extensive nursing training, I knew I needed to watch out for signs of blood clots after an injury like this. I winced again as I pulled my jeans back down and tried to stand. This wasn't the first time I'd been kicked and likely wouldn't be the last, but it was certainly the *worst* I'd ever been kicked. My eyes watered as I took the first tentative steps. I opened the front door and was surprised to find that it was dark. I hadn't realized how long they'd let me sleep.

"Oh hey," Andy said as he stood up from my rocking chair. "I hope we didn't wake you."

The owner of the other voice turned out to be Grady. I didn't see Tanner or his truck in my driveway.

"When did Tanner leave?"

"About an hour ago. He fed the horses before he left."

"Why didn't you wake me up? I didn't want Tanner to deal with everything alone," I ignored Grady for the moment.

"He asked me to let you sleep," Andy said.

"Do you feel like giving me a statement?" Grady interrupted without getting up from the rough-cut cedar chair that occupied the other corner of my porch.

"Sure." I leaned on my open door. "I need to tell you something first."

"Tanner already told me about the thumb drive. I've taken it into evidence."

My initial reaction to this information was anger, and it must've shown on my face, because both men looked at me like I was about to explode. I took a deep breath and dialed it back. Why should I be angry with Tanner? He hadn't done anything that I wouldn't have done myself. And from knowing Tanner as well I did, I knew that he was trying to be considerate by taking the lead. I told myself I would take a harder look at what made me angry later. At that moment, I needed to focus my foggy thoughts on getting my statement recorded.

"You guys come on in," I said as I turned back into the house.

I grabbed a soda from the fridge and flopped down at the kitchen table. Grady followed and sat across from me. He hung his

Stetson on the back of another chair. It didn't take long for me to write out what had happened, and Grady had already asked Tanner everything extra he wanted to know.

"Have you notified Mrs. Griggs yet?" I asked as I handed over my written account.

"Yes," Grady said, his mouth drawn into a thin line that told me the notification had been difficult for him.

"I'll reach out to her and see when she wants me to bring his horse home."

"It's actually *her* horse." Grady stood and picked up his hat. "She said Coach was trying to break some bad habits before he turned the horse over to her."

"Bad habits like kicking?" Andy said from the living room.

"Speaking of which," Grady leaned over and looked at my legs. "How are you?"

"Sore, but I'm okay."

Grady grinned. "Would you admit it if you weren't?"

"Maybe."

He put on his Stetson and tipped it, still grinning like the Cheshire cat.

"I'll call if I have any questions. Have a good evenin', Andy."

"You too, Sheriff," Andy said and joined me in the kitchen.

"Thank you for staying."

"No problem." He smiled and took my hand. "Go put that leg up and I'll heat up the leftovers."

I opened my mouth to argue, but he gave a me stern look, so I held up my hands in surrender and hobbled out to the living room. My jeans pulled uncomfortably at my calf, and I couldn't find a position that gave me any relief. I wasn't sure if Andy and I were at the stage in our relationship where it was acceptable for me to change into my PJs at this hour, but necessity overrode my concerns.

Instead of PJs, I opted for comfy knit capris and my favorite soft T-shirt. I was just settling my leg on the pillows again when Andy brought me a plate of take-out Chinese from the new place in town, the one we'd planned to visit the night before. That felt like weeks ago.

"I'm not sure chow mein reheats very well, but hopefully this will be edible." He was smiling until he saw the modern art mosaic on my leg. "I think you need to see a doctor about that."

"There's not really anything they'll do about it." I shrugged. "They'll just tell me to ice it and keep it elevated."

"I guess you would know," he said, no hint that he was being sarcastic.

"Thank you for this." Even reheated, the food smelled amazing, and my stomach growled in anticipation.

"I figured if I was going to see you this week, I was going to have to see you here."

"I'm sorry." I dropped the forkful that I was about to cram in my mouth.

"No, that's not what I meant. I just wanted to see you," he said, and scooted closer to me on the sofa.

"I wanted to see you too. I hate that I slept through your visit."

"There's no law that says I have to go home. I'm an attorney. I should know."

* * *

The heavenly smell of fresh coffee pulled me out of my slumber the next morning. I yawned and stretched, finding that my leg was still plenty sore and stiff. I followed the delightful aroma to my kitchen, where Andy stood in front of my stove. He was shirtless, and I shamelessly stood for a moment and admired the view.

"Good morning," he said with a broad smile. "I'm ashamed to admit I don't know how you like your eggs, so I hope scrambled is okay."

"Scrambled is perfect." I suddenly realized I hadn't even looked in the mirror before coming to the kitchen, and I hoped I didn't look like I usually did in the mornings.

I excused myself and limped as fast as I could to the bathroom. My curly blond hair was a matted mess, as usual, and my face was puffy and pale. I groaned as I thought about Andy seeing me this way. It wasn't like he hadn't seen me at my worst already; he'd stayed with me at the hospital after Braydon Cunningham tried to strangle me. But somehow, after spending the night *together* for the first time, I wanted to look better than I usually did.

I raked a brush through my hair and splashed some cold water on my face. Then sighed at my reflection and went back to the kitchen. I hadn't scared him off yet, and the sooner he got used to Morning Mallory, the better. I sidled in next to him and reached for a coffee mug. He plated the eggs and then leaned over to kiss the back of my neck. A girl could get used to mornings like this, tangled hair and all.

"How's the leg?" He murmured into my hair.

"Sore," I swiveled to face him. "But you're good at making me forget about it."

Breakfast took a while because I kept getting distracted, so I was later than usual getting out to feed the horses. I checked on Ruby first, and thankfully, she was up and munching on hay in the corner of her stall, her thin frame almost skeletal, but relaxed and comfortable. She made a soft "whuffling" sound when she noticed me watching her. I was running out of time to get the lesson horses ready before the kids started showing up, but I couldn't resist getting in the stall with her and brushing her down.

After spending extra time with Ruby, I hurried through the rest, which was still almost a glacial pace because sharp pain stabbed through my leg with every step. I separated Goldie, Stormy, and River from Biscuit, Buck, and Tunie so they would be easy to catch and tack up when my first two students arrived. I didn't have enough horses to have very big group lessons, so I staggered them throughout the afternoon. Goldie, a senior palomino mare and one of my first residents, nuzzled my pockets to see if I was hiding any treats. She was the most patient of my lesson horses, although they were all wonderful. She would tolerate the beginners' mistakes and often just anticipated what they actually wanted, regardless of the mixed signals they gave her.

River, though a bomb-proof gelding, was more literal in his interpretation of cues. So, I often started the independent beginners on Goldie and worked up to him. Stormy was our oldest resident, somewhere in the neighborhood of thirty, but he was sound and gentle, so I used him as my lead-line horse. I was always careful not to overdo it, just because of his advanced age, but he seemed to enjoy packing the littlest students around the paddock, and I think it taxed me more physically than it did him.

I didn't have a student advanced enough for Tunie yet. An off-the-track thoroughbred, her registered name was Fortune in Iced Tea, and she'd been seized when law enforcement raided a puppy mill. Because they hadn't expected to find a horse, they called us to take her in, and when the court awarded her to the rescue, she became one of our residents. She was standoffish and temperamental and had yet to bond with anyone, so finding an adopter had proved difficult, which was unfortunate since she was in the prime of her life at nine years old.

I looked in on Coach's big black horse. It took a minute to catch him even in the stall, which wasn't helped by my hitching gait that seemed to spook him, and the fact that I had to be extra wary about his back end. I did finally get him settled enough to halter and tie so I could check the shoe that had left an imprint on my leg. The nail would need to be pulled, but everything still seemed to be secure. The nail was bent flush with the shoe, so it wasn't likely to hang on anything. I texted Tanner and asked if he would pull the nail the next time he came out. Though he wasn't a certified farrier, he was great at simple trims and easy maintenance. He responded like he usually did: *"K,"* which as a nurse, always translated in my head to "potassium" rather than an abbreviated "okay."

As I removed the halter, I wondered what Coach had named him and felt a stab of pain somewhere in my belly on realizing that Douglas Griggs would never take our team to state again. It was such a source of pride for our tiny town and a great opportunity for local athletes to earn scholarships. I hobbled up the steps to the loft where I kept a makeshift office area that was usually more dust than anything else and pulled a padlock and key out of the desk drawer. I wanted to secure the stall door while students were in the barn because I now *knew* the black horse was a kicker.

After locking the stall door, I threw a few flakes of hay into the dry paddock to keep the horses occupied until the kids got there. As I checked my phone screen to see how long that would be, I suddenly panicked at seeing "Sunday" displayed below the time. Ginny had never called yesterday, and I'd been so busy with the sick mare, finding poor Coach Griggs, and then being exhausted that it had never registered. I quickly pulled up the FaceTime app and dialed my daughter as I made my way back to the house. She picked up right away, so I sat in the rocking chair on the porch.

"Hey Mom," she said as she walked through her dorm room. "I'm sorry I didn't call yesterday. I lost track of time and I wasn't sure you'd still be up when I got out of the library."

"Yesterday must've been hectic for everyone." I gave her a brief rundown of everything that had happened, omitting that I'd found the body of my favorite high school teacher.

"Are you sure you're okay?" she stopped working on her hair and looked directly into the phone.

"Yeah, I'm good. Just waiting for the kiddos to get here for lessons."

"What's going on?" She crossed her arms and stared into the camera, lips drawn into a thin line.

I sighed and told her about Coach Griggs.

"I'm coming home. I only have one more mid-term, and I'll see if I can either take it early or take it remotely."

"No," I said firmly. "I'm doing fine. Really."

She stared at me for a moment. "Are you sure?"

"I'm sure. As much as I want to see you, I would rather you finish your semester and come relaxed and ready for a vacation."

She opened her mouth to say something, but the door opened behind me.

"Ready for another cup of coffee?" Andy held out the cup with a grin.

I froze. I briefly considered hanging up, but I knew Ginny had already seen him. My mind was racing. Why hadn't I just told her I was seeing someone? My thoughts snapped into place like cherries in a slot machine. Just because a man was handing me a cup of coffee didn't have to mean anything. He could be the dad of one of my students. He could be a volunteer. But I would have to admit I was seeing him soon enough anyway, so why the hesitation?

"I didn't realize you were on the phone." Andy sat the cup on the windowsill beside me since I hadn't taken it from him.

"Hi, there," Ginny said from the phone in my hand. My head snapped back around in time to see her waving at him.

"Oh, hey." Andy leaned over beside me and came into frame in the little window. "You must be Ginny.'

"I am. But I'm afraid I don't know who you are."

"I'm Andy, I'm your mom's . . ." he paused, and I kept staring at Ginny. I tried to keep my expression neutral and also tried to figure out why this was such a big deal.

". . . attorney," he finished.

"Does the sheriff think you have something to do with that guy's death again?"

"No, nothing like that." I shook my head. I glanced at Andy. His eyes were downcast and he looked like he wanted to be anywhere but here.

"Then why do you need an attorney?"

I paused for a beat while my thoughts continued to race. I wanted to do my soul-searching alone some evening, relaxed on the sofa with a glass of wine, not at hyperspeed with my daughter on the phone waiting for me to answer her. Regardless of *why* I'd put off telling her that I was dating Andy, the fact remained that I *was* dating him, and I hoped to continue to do so. I opened my mouth to tell her the truth and then snapped it shut again as I realized I didn't know what the truth was. Andy and I hadn't

really talked about labels, and calling him my "boyfriend" felt like
we were back in junior high.

"I don't *need* an attorney. Andy is my . . ." I hung up on that
word again, but I couldn't figure out a better one.

"Oh my God, Mom! He's your boyfriend!"

*   *   *

I was saved from Ginny's barrage of questions when my first student
of the afternoon pulled up. The little redheaded girl, Piper, almost
jumped out of her mom's SUV before it came to a complete stop,
and she was chattering at me before she got the door shut. I caught
most of it. She'd brought carrots for Biscuit and Goldie, and she'd
drawn a beautiful picture of Goldie to hang in the tack room.

I gushed over her artistic talent as we crossed the paddock.
My first lesson of the day was a group lesson—well, if you can
consider two a group—for Piper and a little boy about her age
named Henry. They were both in second grade, but she was
homeschooled, and he went to Hillspring Elementary. They had
both worked up to about forty-five minutes of actual riding time,
which meant their lessons usually ran to almost two hours when
I factored in tacking and untacking, and of course, the obligatory
horse cuddles.

After the first group lesson, I scheduled a lead-line class with
an adorable six-year-old to allow the horses to rest before I finished
the day with another group. It was exhausting when I did them
myself, but I loved every minute of it. Ashley, my volunteer turned
part-time employee, scheduled herself for the lead-line class and
the second group lesson this time. After the exhausting events of
the previous day and a half and the throbbing pain in my leg, I
was more than happy to let her take over.

I was watching Ashley expertly guide the twins, Riley and Julia, around some ground poles on River and Goldie when Andy joined me at the paddock fence. I was thankful for another distraction, because my thoughts had started to wander to Coach Griggs.

"Pick up your outside rein, Julia," Ashley called from her spot in the center of the paddock.

"I didn't realize you were on the phone with Ginny earlier," he said quietly, picking at the top board of the paddock fence.

"It's okay, really."

"And I didn't realize you hadn't told her."

I was thankful that Ashley and the kids were far enough away that they couldn't hear us.

"We haven't really discussed things," I said, a little more defensively than I meant to. "Have you told your mom about us?"

"Yeah," he said. He rested his elbows on the fence and clasped his hands. "She wants to meet you."

For the second time that day, I was speechless.

"Are we moving too fast?" He turned to face me as he reached for my hand.

"No, not at all," I said. "It's just that I haven't been this serious about anyone since my divorce, and I wasn't sure how to tell my daughter." The words tumbled out so fast that they surprised me too. But that was it. That was why I'd been so hesitant to tell Ginny. I was getting *serious*.

Chapter Six

Our conversation was interrupted by Ashley signaling the end of the lesson and the twins begging for "just five more minutes." Their dads, Marcus and Leo, who had dropped them off for the lesson promptly an hour ago, pulled up behind my truck. Leo got out of the driver's side of the Subaru Outback and waved at me. He and Marcus had opened a bed and breakfast last year across the street from my dad's house in Hillspring. They were wonderful neighbors and helped me keep an eye on my stubbornly independent father, Jasper Hall.

I helped the twins get the horses unsaddled and brushed and trailed behind them during their mad dash to the car.

"Another great lesson?" Leo asked as he opened the door for the twin tornados to climb inside. He was met with enthusiastic agreement from both.

"Did you thank Miss Ashley and Miss Mallory?"

"Thank you!" They leaned out the window on the passenger side and called to us in unison.

"Is there any way we can come an hour later next week?" Leo turned to me after shutting the car door. "The girls have a birthday party invite and we RSVP'd before we thought to ask about the lesson." He rolled his eyes.

"Shouldn't be a problem at all." I smiled and felt a pang of nostalgia. I remembered those days, the birthday parties, the field-trip chaperoning, the science-fair projects. Part of me desperately missed those days.

"Perfect. See you then."

He climbed back into the driver's seat. Marcus looked up from his phone, smiled warmly, and waved as they drove away.

"The new mare looks terrible," Ashley said as she opened the paddock gate and let the lesson horses out with the rest of the little herd.

"I know. She breaks my heart." I looked down the hill where the mare stood sleepily in the afternoon sun. Her hip bones and ribs looked even more prominent in the sun, since the light cast deep shadows on her emaciated frame. I hoped she would pull through and we would get to see her dull coat shine in the sun someday.

"I have something I need to talk to you about." She bit her lip.

I glanced up at Andy, who had retreated to the house and was waiting patiently on my porch steps.

"Sure, Ashley. Anytime."

"I'm going to have to drop down to one or two days a week," she said quickly, the words rushing out. "My course load is awful next semester, and I can't run the risk of falling behind. I can take all the classes on Sundays, though. That way, maybe you can add a few on another day, if you want."

I paused for a minute as I considered giving up the classes. She was right though; if I wasn't committed on Sundays, I could add some odd lessons here and there throughout the week. And that would mean more income for the rescue as well. I had a wait list for classes. It wasn't a long list, but each one represented untapped income and the opportunity to foster a love for horses in the community.

"Mallory?" Ashley said, snapping me out of my thoughts.

"Sorry, I was just thinking about what you said. Of course it's okay."

"Thank you so much. I don't want to leave you in a bind though."

"It'll be fine. Tanner just about lives here anyway." I chuckled.

Biscuit took full advantage of the gate Ashley had just opened and checked her pockets for any goodies she might be hiding there. She talked softly to him and scratched his small chest, something he seemed to enjoy immensely.

"I'm going to visit with my little buddy here before I head out," Ashley said as I paused at the gate.

"Take as long as you want. I don't think Biscuit will complain."

She laughed and patted his shoulder. "Nope. Little love sponge would just stay here all day if I kept scratching the itchy spots."

I made my way back to the house. My leg throbbed. Andy was still sitting on the steps, his laptop perched on his thighs. He pushed his glasses up as I approached.

"You look so happy when you're working with the kids." He smiled and closed the laptop.

"I love it. But right now, I just want to sit down and put this leg on a pillow."

He jumped up and rushed to my side. Normally, I would have bristled at being treated like a damsel in distress, but something about his cologne and two-day-old stubble short-circuited my brain, so I just leaned into him and let him guide me to the sofa. Banjo, having been unfairly banished to the backyard during lessons, burst through the doggy door in the back and launched himself right into my middle. I coughed and threw my arms around my squirming dog, who seemed to be determined to wash my entire face before finally settling down next to me.

Andy sat in the overstuffed chair beside the sofa. Somehow, my realization that my attraction to him was deepening made me feel self-conscious and even more awkward than usual.

"I just . . ."

"About earlier . . ." Andy said at the time.

"You first," I said.

"If we need to put the brakes on, it's fine." He took off his glasses and rubbed his eyes.

"I don't know how to do this anymore," I said, and tried to sit up a little straighter while keeping my leg up on the pillows. "I'm not sure I ever did. But I do know that I don't want to put the brakes on anything."

"I'm glad to hear that." He leaned forward and took my hand. "Because I don't want to either."

I didn't want to ruin the moment, but my leg was throbbing in time with my heartbeat, and elevating it hadn't alleviated as much of the pain as I'd hoped.

"Would you mind getting me some ibuprofen from the medicine cabinet?"

"You should really have that looked at," he said as he stood.

"If it gets worse, I'll make an appointment."

He didn't look convinced.

"I promise."

I grabbed my phone off the end table when he left to get the ibuprofen. There were several texts from Lanie.

I have so much to tell you!

And then, *WHERE are you???*

And finally, about thirty minutes after that one, *Oh crap! It's lesson day. I forgot. Just call me when you get done.*

I decided to find out what she wanted to tell me her after I made the call I'd been dreading all morning. Still procrastinating, I texted Grady first to see if he had Patricia Griggs's phone number and could save me the time of trying to find it online. He replied, quickly and in standard Grady brevity, with a simple "yes" and then the number. I sighed as Andy handed me a couple of ibuprofen tablets and a glass of water.

"I guess that wasn't good news?" He pointed to my phone.

"I have to call Coach Griggs's wife. I want to give her my condolences, and I need to take his horse home."

"Want me to stay, or give you some privacy?" He sat on the edge of the sofa next to me.

"Please stay." I leaned into him, letting him prop me up.

I punched the number in Grady's text and waited either for Patricia to pick up or for the call to switch over to voicemail.

"Hello?" a shaky female voice finally answered.

"Hello, is this Patricia?"

"Yes. Who's calling?" She sniffled loudly, and my heart broke for her as images of Coach Griggs flashed through my mind.

"Mallory Martin. I'm so sorry for your loss. I was one of Coach Griggs's first students at Hillspring and he was a wonderful teacher. I was also involved in the search. I have the horse rescue just north of town," I said, and paused for a beat.

"Sheriff Sullivan told me that you have the horse." Her voice hardened.

"Yes, I do. I can bring him home any time that's convenient for you."

"Keep him."

"What?" My voice squeaked. "I'm sorry, I don't understand."

"I don't want that horse. He's the reason Doug is dead." Her voice cracked and she sobbed quietly.

"I'm so sorry. I didn't mean to upset you." It still wasn't making any sense. Surely Grady had told her how Coach died, that it wasn't a riding accident.

"You can come by in the morning and I'll sign over the registration papers to the rescue. I'll give you his vet records and anything else related to that black devil, but I don't ever want him back on this place."

"Yes, ma'am," I said, and unconsciously nodded my head. "I can be there at nine, if that works for you?"

"Yes, that'll be fine," she said, and we ended the call.

"What happened?" Andy asked. I'm sure my face displayed the confusion I was feeling.

"She doesn't want the horse back. She said he's the reason Coach was killed. But I don't understand why she thinks that. He was shot."

"Maybe she blames him for just being out riding. Grief is a funny thing. People look for things to blame to help make sense of the senseless."

"I guess you're right," I said, and snuggled against his chest. I could definitely get used to having him around.

I wanted to curl up beside that wonderful man and go to sleep again. I wanted to forget the awful images of Coach Griggs and the strange conversation with his grieving wife. Fatigue still pulled at my eyelids even after getting a good night's sleep. How had I stayed up all night in college and then gone to class the next morning like it was nothing? Was I really *that* old? The throbbing in my leg that just wouldn't stop and the realization that I needed to call Lanie pulled me back to reality.

"I need to call Lanie real quick," I said as I struggled to sit up again.

"Go ahead. I need to work on some research and return some e-mails. Can I use your office?"

"'Office' may be a stretch but you're welcome to use my desk."

"I like your desk," he said, pausing to rub my shoulders. "It overlooks the barn and paddock. It's peaceful."

I mumbled in the affirmative and closed my eyes while he massaged my aching shoulders. It hurt so good. After a few minutes of bliss, he patted my back, grabbed his laptop, and headed down the short hallway.

Lanie picked up on the second ring.

"Hey! Sorry I forgot today was lesson day, but I have so much to tell you!"

"I've got quite a bit to tell you too," I said when she paused.

"Oh yeah? Well, you go first then."

I told her about finding Coach Griggs's body, the new mare, Ginny "meeting" Andy, and then circled back around to how weird Mrs. Griggs had been when I called.

"She's just grieving," Lanie said.

"That's what Andy said."

"Listen to him. He's a smart cookie."

Banjo jumped to attention and my head snapped around in the direction he was looking. Andy came running into the living room and Banjo jumped down to greet him, wagging his whole butt.

"Mal, I think maybe the new horse is in trouble," he said, pointing toward the barn.

"Lanie . . ."

"Go," she said, having overheard Andy. "Call me later."

"I do want to hear your news," I said as I hauled myself to my feet.

"I know. It's okay. Go on now and we'll talk later."

I thanked her and ended the call as I shoved my feet into the sneakers I'd shed by the front door. Banjo ran in excited circles, happy to be going outside with us. Every move I made sent shooting pain through my calf, and the ibuprofen didn't seem to be taking the edge off at all. I limped down the steps, and sure enough, the mare was wedged under the paddock fence on the downhill side.

I picked up speed as I crossed the driveway, limping faster as Andy easily caught up with me at the paddock gate.

"What do we need to do?" Andy jogged alongside me down the hill.

"I don't know yet," I said, trying to assess the situation as we got closer.

My best guess was that she had rolled, gotten her legs caught under the fence, and just kept wedging herself farther underneath it as she tried to get free. She lifted her head and "whuffled" quietly at me when I came into view. Her breathy neigh combined with the look on her face clearly said, "Help me."

"It's okay, sweetheart," I fell to my knees and stroked her face through the fence. "We'll get you out of this mess."

I hoped she hadn't started rolling again because the pain in her belly had returned. Although there were no other signs of colic. She wasn't sweating. She wasn't looking back at her belly. I hoped she had just been trying to scratch an itch, like horses love to do, and had misjudged her surroundings, which horses also seemed

59

to love to do. There's a running joke in the horse community that even if you bubble-wrapped horses, they would eat it and colic.

I quickly looked over what I could see of her. She'd scraped her left front knee, but other than that, what I could see didn't look much the worse for wear. But she was stuck under that fence like she'd been planted there. I pulled myself up and winced at the sharp stab in my calf at the change in position.

"We're going to have to take out this section of fence," I said, looking at Andy and wondering if he was wishing he'd gone home this morning.

"Do you want to saw the boards loose, or take it apart?"

"I don't think we can risk the chainsaw. I have no idea how she would react to that."

"Do you have a handsaw?" He bent to look at the rusted nails holding the boards to the posts.

I wasn't sure how old the fence actually was. Dad had built it long before I moved home, and I wasn't sure if we even *could* take it apart.

"There's a handsaw in the shed," I gestured toward the house. The little garden shed housed all manner of random tools.

"I think that will be the quickest, safest way to get her loose," he said, already jogging toward the house.

I nodded.

The sweet mare made the quiet "whuffling" sound again. I jogged around to the gate and made my way quickly to her side. She relaxed as I patted her neck and spoke softly to her.

"You're such a good girl, Ruby." My heart ached as I thought about everything she'd been through and how long she'd suffered at the hands of her previous owner. I am always dedicated to making sure abused animals don't go back to their abusers, but I would move heaven and earth to make sure this sweet mare never returned to hers. She was laying on her right side, which meant that her blind eye was on the ground side. That was good. Being able to see likely helped her stay calm.

It was only a few minutes before Andy returned with the handsaw. I stood and reached for it, but he was already working on cutting the top plank.

"I got this." He smiled. "You just make sure she's alright."

He made short work of the first two boards and was well into the third before Ruby started getting restless again. I knew her bony frame had to be uncomfortable. The Ozarks are known for their rocky hillsides, and mine was no exception. I continued to talk softly to her and scratched her neck and chest. By that time, Biscuit had figured out something was going on and trotted down the hill. He immediately went to Andy and scooched himself in between Andy and the fence.

"I'll get him," I said. I heaved myself upright again and decided to just ignore the pain in my leg since it wasn't going away anyway. I was thankful that I hadn't been able to break Tanner's habit of hanging halters and lead ropes beside the gates. I grabbed the halter, which was about two sizes too big for Biscuit's little head, and dragged him into the upper paddock behind the barn. He started braying when I closed the gate behind me. He always took personal offense at being excluded from whatever was going on.

In the short time it took me to banish our over-eager helper, Andy had removed all but the bottom board from the fence. Ruby was getting restless again, but Andy was talking softly to her and pausing every few moments to pat her gently on the shoulder. I stopped and watched him, and my breath caught in my chest. His tenderness was his most endearing quality. It didn't hurt that his stubble, tousled dark hair, and arms straining in his flannel shirt made him look like an Instagram-worthy lumberjack. I grinned to myself as I remembered that my first impression of him on that day I'd come to his office needing counsel had been that he looked like a young Mr. Rogers. Maybe he had the same quiet, gentle manner, but there was also passion and strength. All of that bundled up in a man I was finding more irresistible by the minute. I snapped myself out of the reverie and stepped forward to hold the bottom plank as he sawed through it so it wouldn't fall on the mare.

"Almost done." Andy smiled at me, only slightly out of breath.

He finished quickly, and as soon as we pulled the last board away, Ruby snorted and struggled to her feet. She was still weak from starvation and her bout of colic, but after one unsuccessful try, she was up and shaking off the dirt. I hurried to check the side that had been on the ground and found only one additional superficial scrape.

"Is she alright?"

"She seems to be," I rested my hand on her shoulder and smiled triumphantly.

"Now we fix it?" Andy wiped his brow on his shirt sleeve and held up one of the boards he'd just sawed in two.

"Now we patch it and save the actual repairs for another day."

"How do we patch it?"

"There are some livestock panels leaning against the back of the barn." He looked clueless, so I added, "Big metal panels, almost like the stock gate, only in squares and not as heavy."

He nodded and started up the hill.

By the time we finished wiring the stock panel across the new hole in the fence, my leg was hurting so bad I couldn't ignore it anymore. I tried to pull my jeans up and look at my calf, but it was too swollen. Red flag number one. I took a few steps toward the house, and the stabbing pain took my breath away. Red flag number two. As a nurse, I knew both of these symptoms weren't reassuring signs, and I also knew that I needed to give up and go to the ER.

"Mal?" Andy took my arm just before my failing leg dumped the rest of me in the dirt.

He scooped me up like it was nothing.

"You're going to ruin your back," I said, wincing and trying to will myself to weigh less.

"I'm taking you to the ER."

"I have to put Banjo in the house. And I'm filthy. I need to change clothes."

"I'll put Banjo in the house, and they don't care about a little dust." He rocked me back and balanced me on his thigh while he opened the gate.

"Put me down. I can walk."

"I'll put you down in the car."

He left the gate open, deposited me gently in the passenger seat of his car, closed the gate, put Banjo in the house, and nearly set a land speed record to the county hospital ER.

Chapter Seven

Andy and I spent our second night together in Hillspring Memorial Hospital. He'd stayed with me the night I spent there after Braydon Cunningham tried to choke me to death. There were blood tests, an ultrasound, more blood tests, and finally a diagnosis of hematoma. Hematomas occur when large blood vessels are damaged, causing blood to pool in the tissues, like when you've been kicked by a large, shod horse. Thankfully nothing was broken, and hematomas usually go away without much treatment. The ER physician told me that if it didn't improve in the next few days, I might need to have it drained. And he told me to take it easy.

The sun peaked over the hills on our drive home, sending long bands of light and shadow across the winding road. Andy insisted on my riding in the backseat where I could elevate my leg, so I had a great view of the limestone bluffs that lined the short drive between Hillspring and my rescue. They weren't bluffs by Rocky Mountain or Blue Ridge standards, but they were beautiful nonetheless. The yellows, reds, deep browns, and every shade in between had already peaked, but the little bit of color that hung on looked like jewels in the golden morning light.

White Oak Creek, winding alongside the road on the other side, was especially full after the fall rains. If it had been warmer, I would have rolled the windows down so I could hear it roll and tumble over the rocks on its way to Deadwood Lake. Even though the drive was just a few minutes long, I fell asleep before we got home. My rough driveway jolted me awake. Andy pulled his car in next to Tanner's big black truck.

I smiled at the splash of yellow road-striping paint behind the wheel well on the passenger side of Tanner's truck. That little detail had been what had helped me figure out that Braydon Cunningham killed his dad. Tanner's truck got the blemish driving to the rescue after the roadwork signs had been knocked over. Braydon had come home the night he killed his father and got the same paint on his white BMW. After I'd told Tanner about it, he decided to leave it there. He said he liked the fact that it had helped bring a killer to justice.

I opened the door to get out, but Andy ran around and met me before I could stand up.

"I don't need crutches."

"Hey, Boss. I thought you were still in the house. Are you okay?" Tanner came jogging up from the barn. "Guess that was a stupid question." He looked at my compression-wrapped leg and jeans that had been cut off at the knee. I'm sure I was a terrible patient, but I refused to wear a hospital gown and there was no other way to get to my injury.

"You're here early," I said, taking the crutches from Andy when he ignored my protests.

"It's not *that* early. What happened to the fence?" He hooked a thumb toward the paddock we'd disassembled and patched.

I filled him in as Andy ushered me into the house. I also told him about my appointment with Mrs. Griggs and that she didn't want the horse back.

"I'll drive you over," Tanner said when I'd finished and settled myself on the sofa to try to get a nap before going to the Griggs residence.

"That would be great. I really need to go into the office today," Andy said.

"Guys," I said, and they both turned to face me. "I can drive myself."

"We know that Boss," Tanner said and shoved his hands in his pockets. "We just want to help."

Andy nodded. "The doctor *did* tell you to take it easy. And it *is* your right leg that's injured. That'll make it hard to drive."

I have always hated it when I need help. Being fiercely, sometimes irrationally, independent has always been one of my toxic traits. But something about these two melted my defenses. Tanner was as close to a son as I would ever have and Andy . . . well, Andy was melting *all* of my defenses.

"Thank you both," I said. "I would appreciate that very much."

"Great! It's decided then," Andy clapped Tanner on the shoulder. "I should be able to get away from the office early today."

"You don't need to . . ." I started, but Andy raised his eyebrows in a look that said, *Didn't we just talk about this?* I held my hands up in surrender.

Andy leaned over and kissed me on the forehead while Tanner tried to look anywhere but at us.

*   *   *

I felt like I had only slept a few minutes when the alarm on my phone went off. I stretched and used those blasted crutches to pull myself tentatively to my feet. I hobbled to the bathroom, took a lightning-fast shower, ran a brush through my hair, gave up on it looking anything close to decent, and pulled it up in a messy bun. I took more time reapplying the compression wrap to my leg than anything else. The perfect imprint of the hoof and horseshoe were outlined in an ugly purple-black. My entire calf was varying shades of red and purple. It was still ridiculously sore, but the wrap and rest were definitely helping. Tanner knocked on the door just as I was pouring coffee into a travel mug.

"Come on in," I yelled from the kitchen. I heard the door open and close. "Want some coffee?"

"That would be great," he said while he scratched Banjo's round rump. "I pulled that nail. Liked to never caught him."

"Oh good, thanks," I said over my shoulder. "He certainly isn't very friendly."

"Needs some lessons from Biscuit," he said as he coaxed Banjo into a game of tug of war with the rope toy.

I grinned as I filled a travel mug for Tanner too. He added almost as much cream and sugar to his as I liked in mine.

It took two tries to climb into Tanner's big black truck, but I was finally able to heave myself into the passenger seat. The Griggs lived on the other side of Hillspring, the south side where the mountains gave way to rolling hills and pastures. We passed cattle farms, commercial chicken farms, and one goat dairy where goat kids bounced happily in a manicured field that looked like it could be featured in *Hobby Farm* magazine.

My phone's GPS took us right to Coach Griggs's driveway. His house sat next to the paved county road. It was a log-cabin-style house with a gigantic wraparound porch featuring not one but two oversized porch swings, both covered in bright pillows. The front yard was a maze of flowerbeds and raised flower boxes. I'd bet the whole place smelled like floral perfume in the spring.

We pulled in next to a small silver sedan and I took a deep breath. I got out, leaving the crutches in the truck, and was halfway up the walkway before I realized that Tanner wasn't with me. I turned around and went to the driver's window.

"You coming?" I asked as he rolled down the window.

"I didn't know if you'd want me to," he said sheepishly.

"Of course I do."

He followed me onto the porch, where our arrival was announced by the sharp yapping of a tiny dog. I could barely hear Mrs. Griggs shushing the ferocious beast over its steady staccato barking. When she opened the door, a Yorkie that weighed maybe four pounds came bursting out with the bravado befitting a tiny dog. It continued to bark until Tanner snatched it up and started telling it how vicious and scary it was and how terrified he was of such a guard dog.

Mrs. Griggs smiled at Tanner, and it almost reached her swollen, puffy eyes. She clutched a handkerchief in one hand and the front of her sweater in the other. I got the impression that she was physically trying to hold herself together.

"Please, come in," she said, opening the door wider for us. "I'm sorry about Timmy. He thinks he's a rottweiler." Her long, graying hair fell over her shoulder in a loose braid.

"He's a guard dog, aren't you?" Tanner scratched Timmy's ears and the little dog did his best to wash every inch of Tanner's face while he wagged his entire back half. I wondered if there were any animals that didn't love Tanner, or vice versa.

Mrs. Griggs led us into a large living room. The back of the room was dominated by a huge fireplace, and glowing coals winked at us from behind the screen. I envied her having a fireplace. Nothing felt better on cold winter nights than settling in next to a roaring fire.

"Would either of you like a coffee? Tea?" She shoved the handkerchief into her pocket and used both hands to pull her sweater even tighter around her thin frame. "Maybe an iced tea?"

"No thank you," I said, and angled myself to perch on the edge of the sofa. "We're okay."

Tanner hovered at the other end of the sofa, still holding Timmy, who showed no sign that he was anything but enraptured by the attention.

"Is he allowed on the sofa?" Tanner asked.

"Oh yes, he has run of the house." She gestured in a wide circle. "Go ahead and have a seat."

She sat in the chair closest to me and pushed a folder toward me on the coffee table.

"Everything for that horse is in there. I don't want him, and I don't want to profit from selling him. I just don't ever want to see him again."

"I'm so sorry for your loss, Mrs. Griggs." I took the folder but didn't open it.

"Patricia." She swallowed hard. "Thank you."

69

"Grady, um, Sheriff Sullivan told you it wasn't a riding accident, right?" I blurted out and then instantly worried that I was being insensitive.

"He did." She nodded. "It was a hunting accident. But he wouldn't have been there at all if it wasn't for that awful horse."

She took a deep breath and pulled out the handkerchief to dab at her eyes.

"We rode together, you know?" Her breath hitched as she stifled a sob. "My mare died last summer. She was so old. He bought that black devil for me. But he'd been drugged or something, because he was horrible after we got him home. Doug was trying to put some miles on him and work through his issues *for me*." She sobbed in earnest. "He died because he was trying to fix that horse for me."

"Oh, Patricia, I'm so sorry."

I wanted to reach out and hold her hand, but she folded in on herself again, clutching the front of her sweater.

"You know what doesn't make sense?" she asked. She was looking at me, but seemed far away, lost in her thoughts and grief. "Sheriff Sullivan said he wasn't wearing an orange vest. Where was his vest? He had it with him when he left. He liked to keep peppermints for the horses in his pockets when he rides, and I saw him put a handful in the hunting vest before he left. He wouldn't have gone hunting without it. He just wouldn't. His rifle is missing too. Where did it go?"

"Those are great questions," I said, but I wasn't sure she was even hearing me. She seemed to have turned inward on herself.

"I'm supposed to go collect his things at the school tomorrow. I didn't know he even still had things at the school after he retired, but I guess he had a desk in the athletic department. I don't think I can face it."

She suddenly leaned forward and took my hand. The abrupt gesture startled me, but I recovered quickly and tried to squeeze hers reassuringly.

"Can you go get his things? I wouldn't ask, but my son can't make it until later this week."

"Of course." I agreed before my brain fully engaged.

"Thank you. The appointment is at one PM."

"Okay," I said and wondered what I was getting myself into. "Who should I ask for?"

"The secretary is Leslie Danvers. I made the appointment with her." She held on to my hands with a ferocity that made my heart ache. Her grief was palpable.

Somewhere outside, a horse whinnied.

"That's Doug's horse," Patricia said, and pulled her hands back to clutch at her sweater again. "He doesn't understand why Doug hasn't come home." She collapsed back into the chair, her shoulders shaking with quiet sobs.

"Ma'am, I'd be happy to go tend to him if you'd like," Tanner said as he put Timmy gently on the floor and the little dog immediately pawed at Tanner's leg in a desperate attempt to get him to pick him back up.

"If you don't mind, I would really appreciate that," Patricia said, still sobbing.

"Yes ma'am. Does he get grain?"

"Yes, Doug feeds, I mean Doug *fed* him in the evenings, but I don't know how much. He has some grass in the pasture, but Doug always gave him some hay too."

"I'll take care of it." Tanner tipped his ever-present baseball cap as he passed her on his way to the door. Timmy followed him like a tiny shadow.

"Your son is a good man," Patricia said when the door had closed and Timmy returned to sit at her feet.

"I can't claim him, but you're right. He's a treasure." I beamed with secondhand pride. I made a mental note to set up a lunch date with Rachel so I could tell her all the ways in which her son was an exceptional human being.

"Have you eaten?" I asked, noting how pale she looked.

"I can't bring myself to fix anything." She rubbed her eyes again.

"It's important to keep your strength up," I said, and got to my feet. I remembered how hard it had been for me to eat anything after Mom died, how hard it was to do the small, everyday things under the weight of all that grief.

I made my way to the kitchen, found eggs and sausage in the fridge, and pulled a skillet down from the hook above the sink. As the eggs and sausage sizzled, I admired the modern farm-house feel of Patricia's kitchen. The white cabinets had been stenciled with pale blue flowers. The white tile countertops gave way to a deep-apron double sink with drainboard, the kind that I had always wanted but never turned loose enough money to buy.

I popped some bread in the toaster, and by the time it was finished, the eggs were done too. I plated everything and carried it to Patricia, who was still sitting in the living room. She stared out the window but didn't appear to be looking at anything in particular. I handed her the plate and she snapped back to attention.

"I wanted to tell you not to bother, but the truth is, I'm hungry." She blushed deeply and her swollen eyes glistened again.

"That's a good thing." I sat back down on the sofa. "I'm glad to help. I'm going to leave my phone number, and if you need anything else, you call. I'll be checking in on you too, starting tomorrow when I bring Coach's things home."

She patted my hand and it looked like the effort took all her remaining strength.

"I'll bring his saddle and tack when I come back."

She nodded. I put out food for Timmy before I let myself out. Tanner was coming around the house from the barn as I came down the porch steps.

"The horse is fed, watered, and I went ahead and picked out his hooves."

"That was really nice of you." I smiled at him as I limped toward the truck.

"Did she know what that weird flash drive was?"

"I didn't have the heart to ask." I climbed into the truck, careful not to overexert my injured leg. "I have to come back tomorrow anyway. Maybe she'll be in a better frame of mind then."

As we pulled out of the drive, I texted Grady.

Have just been to see Mrs. Griggs. Did you ever find an orange vest? She mentioned that he had one when he left.

He replied before we got to the main road.

Can't discuss open investigation. Stick to horse rescue.

I sent an emoji to convey my feelings about his suggestion.

Tanner glanced at my phone but was too polite to ask.

"Grady won't tell me whether they found a vest or not." I tapped my phone screen while I considered texting Corporal Bailey. I figured I had nothing to lose.

Hey, it's Mallory. Full disclosure, already asked Grady and he won't say. Did you find an orange vest anywhere at the scene? Wife said he had one when he left.

I watched the three little dots start and stop three times before he finally responded

Did not find one. Don't ask me anything else. Sorry.

I texted back quickly: *Thanks! Sorry to put you on the spot.*

"Well?" Tanner said after waiting a few moments after the last text.

"Darrin said they didn't find a vest."

"That's weird."

"Let's go back to the scene," I said. "It won't hurt to just take a look around."

"Are you sure you can hike back in?"

"I'll use the crutches and take it slow."

He took advantage of the clear roadway and made a U-turn.

"While we have a few minutes, there's something I've been meaning to ask you," Tanner said, glancing over at me.

My heart sank. I just *knew* he was going to tell me that he needed to scale back his time at the rescue too. Unlike Ashley, Tanner wasn't in college, but he had confided in me that his dad was pushing him to take over more responsibility at their farm. I knew the day would come when those two amazing kids would move on, but I definitely wasn't ready. Not that I ever would be.

He swallowed hard and took a deep breath. Not a good sign.

"What is it?" I asked, trying to sound neutral and supportive.

"Have you ever thought about taking on a partner at the rescue?"

"What?" This wasn't anywhere close to what I'd expected. It wasn't even in the same zip code as what I'd expected.

Tanner took another deep breath and launched into what seemed like a well-rehearsed pitch. He outlined all the ways a partnership would be beneficial to the rescue, and to me personally.

"I put together a proposal," he said, then paused to glance over at me again. "It's in the glove box."

I pulled out a file folder and leafed through the typed document.

"Dad has wanted me to take over the farm my whole life, but that isn't where I see my future. I love the horses. I love working at the rescue. As a minority partner, I could take over a lot of the responsibilities you hate."

"This is very thorough," I said as I lingered on a section at the back.

"I've got so many ideas for fund-raising and expansion. And even if you don't want me to come in as a minority partner, I would like to take on a more managerial role. I've researched some grants I think we have a good shot at getting, and I'm taking an online course on grant writing."

I wasn't sure what to say. I had no idea that Tanner wanted to make the rescue his life's work. He'd always been dedicated and reliable, but this offer completely blindsided me. I wondered what on earth I thought I was going to find where Coach Griggs had died when I couldn't even effectively observe those closest to me.

Tanner turned the truck onto the road leading to the Deadwood Lake Wildlife Management Area south entrance while I continued to look through his proposal.

"Oh God," he said, slowing the truck. "I've offended you."

"No, not at all," I said. "I'm surprised, but not offended."

"I know I ambushed you with this, so I certainly don't expect an answer on the spot."

"We can definitely talk more. This proposal is impressive, and I like your fund-raising ideas." I paused and tried to choose my words carefully. "Honestly, though, I haven't considered taking on a partner. I started the rescue because it was a lifelong dream."

"Like I said, I can understand not wanting to jump right into a partnership. I know I'm young and I've only worked at the rescue for a couple of years now." He pulled into the parking area and turned to face me. "I would welcome the opportunity to prove myself as a manager."

"Alright," I said, seriously considering his proposal. "Let's sit down and talk about it. I haven't taken a hard look at the finances recently and we would need to draw up a job description."

He smiled so broadly it almost looked painful. He was still grinning when he got out of the truck and opened his toolbox. I followed, debating about whether to take the crutches or not. I decided against it. I figured they would be more of hindrance than a help, even though I'd promised to use them to get Tanner to agree to come back.

"What do you think we're going to find?" Tanner asked as he pulled on his orange vest.

"Probably nothing," I said as I took the other one.

"Want me to grab the crutches?" Tanner asked, and I swear he smirked before he turned toward the truck.

"I think I'll be okay."

We'd been walking for what felt like miles when we finally came to the dry creek bed. Tanner took the same rough path I'd taken to get to the horse. Today, however, I wasn't sure I could scramble up the other bank.

"I'm going a little farther down and see if I can find a better place to climb."

"I could pack you up there," Tanner said, and shrugged.

"I am *not* going to let you carry me up a creek bank." I recoiled in horror at the thought of him picking me up, much less trying to heave me up a rocky, steep incline. "It looks like it gets lower just around that bend down there."

I pointed, hoping the briars weren't as thick as they appeared. He nodded and headed toward the underbrush where I'd found Coach Griggs. I slowly and carefully made my way down the rocky bed. Thankfully, the bramble that I had seen from the trail gave way to a clear, gentle slope and I was able to climb out of the creek easily. I could just make out Tanner's giant outline through the brush, and I started to head back in his direction when something caught my eye.

Chapter Eight

Orange. A tiny patch of hunter orange was visible in the tangled underbrush between me and Tanner. I told myself that it could belong to any one of the hunters in the woods, and there could be hundreds of them. It could even be from last year, although it didn't look faded as I limped closer.

The little patch of hunter orange was in the middle of a pile of rocks. Most of it was still *under* the pile of rocks, but a small part had been dug out and something had chewed through the pocket, leaving behind peppermint wrappers. It was definitely Coach Griggs's vest. I bent down and took photos at every angle I could think of, then yelled for Tanner.

"Looks like coons or possums dug it out to get to the candy," he said as he bent over and studied it. "But why would he bury it?"

"Maybe he didn't," I said as I pulled up Grady's contact on my phone. "Maybe whoever shot him was trying to hide it. It would look less like a hunting accident if he was wearing a vest."

Tanner nodded and straightened up.

Grady picked up on the first ring. I told him what we'd found and that we'd be waiting for him. He cursed—I wasn't sure if it was at me or the situation—told me he would be there as soon as possible, warned me not to touch anything, and hung up.

Tanner cleared off a log nearby for me to sit down on while we waited. He continued to look through the underbrush. He'd used his pocketknife to trim a fallen branch, which he then used to poke through the leaves.

It took Grady longer than I expected to come crashing through the woods like a bull elk. I yelled and waved them over from my perch on the log. He'd brought a team with him, flanked on both sides by deputies. They went to work right away photographing the scene as I had done, but with better equipment.

"What are you doing back here?" Grady didn't bother with greetings.

"It was bothering me that Coach wasn't wearing a vest. And then, when his wife confirmed that he'd been wearing one when he left home, I couldn't help but wonder what happened," I confessed.

"Then you *call me,*" he hissed.

"I texted you. Would you have come back out here and looked if I'd called instead?"

He glared at me but ignored the question. "I'm waiting for the ballistic report, but the preliminary looks like we have a solid suspect."

"Who?" I pulled myself to my feet.

"I'll let you know when there are formal charges."

"The drunk hunter we met on the trail," I said, more to myself than to Grady.

"Don't start speculating," he leaned in and spoke deliberately. "You remember how awful it was when people thought *you* were guilty."

I opened my mouth to respond, but snapped it shut as I realized he was right.

"Will it do any good at all to tell you again to leave the investigating to me?"

"I'm not investigating," I protested. "I just wanted to come out here and . . ."

"And what?" he interrupted me. "If you're not investigating, what do you think you're doing?"

"I wanted to satisfy my curiosity so I could let it go!" I clenched my fists at my sides.

Grady sighed and cocked his head to the side as he looked at me. He seemed to be trying to decide if he was going to say something else or not.

"Patricia Griggs asked me to get Coach's things from the school tomorrow," I said as I turned back down the trail. "Just so you know I'm not poking around on my own."

Tanner followed me as I went back the way I'd come.

"Grady yell at you?" he asked as we descended the gentle slope into the creek bed.

"Of course." I laughed, but the truth was, it had hurt my feelings a little. I wasn't going to do anything that would jeopardize his investigation, and I thought he ought to know that.

*   *   *

I nodded off on the way home, which was a huge testament to my trust in Tanner and his ability to drive us safely back to the rescue. I didn't wake up until he switched off the ignition. And just for a minute when I woke up I didn't know what day it was, where I was, or what was going on. My ibuprofen had worn off and the throbbing in my leg helped reorient me quickly.

"Go get some rest, Boss. I'll take care of the horses."

I didn't even argue. All I wanted was to crawl into bed and sleep until sometime the next day.

"I'll take this and look it over and we can talk more later." I held up the folder as I collected my crutches from the back seat.

He gave me a thumbs-up.

I just about crawled inside, took some more ibuprofen, and sent a text to Andy.

I'm going to crash. I don't intend to get up until tomorrow. I'll call you when I get up. If you still want to come by, there's a key under the pot of mums on the porch.

I didn't wait for him to reply, and I'm pretty sure I was asleep before my head even hit the pillow.

*   *   *

By the time I woke the next morning I had finally gotten enough rest to feel human again. The throbbing in my leg had receded to a dull ache. I peeled off the compression wrap to let my skin have a reprieve. The hoof-shaped wound had taken on an angry black-purple color, but the swelling had improved, and I could move my foot without sending sharp, stabbing pains up my leg.

After I finished in the shower, I pulled my wet hair into a messy ponytail and made my way to the kitchen to brew some much-needed coffee. Much to my delight, it was waiting for me along with Andy, who was typing away on his laptop at my kitchen table.

"Good morning, Sleeping Beauty," he said with a grin.

I blushed like a teenager. I'm sure I was the picture of "beauty" in my oversized fluffy robe, messy hair, and absolutely no makeup whatsoever.

"How long have you been here?" I asked as I poured my coffee. I vaguely remembered stumbling to the bathroom sometime in the night, but I hadn't noticed an extra person in the house.

"I didn't want to risk waking you last night, so I came early this morning. There's a plate for you in the oven. How's the leg?"

"Ugly, but better."

He'd fixed an entire breakfast—eggs, bacon, toast—and kept it warm for me. A girl could definitely get used to this kind of pampering. I told him about finding the vest as I ate my breakfast.

"Are you sure you want to get in the middle of a murder investigation again?" he asked when I'd finished.

"I didn't really choose to get in the middle of either one," I said, feeling a little defensive. "And Mrs. Griggs asked me to pick up Coach's things from the school today. Besides, it isn't really a murder investigation. Grady thinks it was a hunting accident."

"It's suspicious that someone tried to hide the vest." He rubbed his chin. "It means whoever shot him knew they did it and tried to conceal damning evidence."

I nodded enthusiastically. "And then there's that USB drive I found on the breast collar, of all places."

"It's all just very odd," he said, and reached across the table to take my hand and give it a squeeze.

"You don't think it was an accident?"

"It could've been. The shooter could've tried to hide the vest to lessen their culpability. A jury, if it came to that, would be less sympathetic to someone who shot a man wearing hunter's orange." He shut his laptop and stood up. "But it could be something else too. Did you ask his wife if he had a habit of keeping USB drives on his horse?"

"No." I stood up too. It was getting close to time to feed. "She was so upset I couldn't bring myself to ask."

"Maybe you could ask her today." He leaned over and kissed me on the forehead. "I've got to get to the office."

I smiled from ear to ear, both at the tender kiss and the fact that he wasn't telling me to stay out of the investigation.

He paused in the doorway, laptop under his arm. "I'm having dinner with Mom tonight. Would you like to come?"

We'd talked briefly about this, my meeting his mom and his meeting my dad, but had never made any concrete plans.

"No pressure," he said, and bent to scratch behind Banjo's ears. I must've looked as ambushed as I felt. "Dinner's at six. I can swing by and pick you up. You can think about it and let me know."

"Okay," I said as noncommittally as possible.

I dressed quickly and grabbed my phone. I had several texts from Lanie, the last of which asking me if I was still alive. Crap. I'd told her I would call her back and then completely forgot. I didn't bother with texting. I called her on my way out the door.

"I've been trying to get a hold of you!" she said as soon as she picked up. "Are you okay?"

I told her about the new mare getting stuck under the fence so hopefully she would understand my initial distraction. And after that, I told her about my night in the ER. I ended with telling her about visiting Mrs. Griggs and finding the vest. Other than a few gasps and murmurs as I talked, I didn't really give her a chance to respond.

"Holy moly," she said when I finally slowed down enough to allow her to speak. "That's a *lot*. I guess I'll forgive you then."

"It's been a weird few days," I said. "I have to go to the school and get Coach's things this afternoon."

83

"Want me to go with you?"

"Surely he couldn't have had that much stuff still there. He was retired, after all."

"Okay," she said, but she sounded funny. "Come over for supper tonight, I have a lot I need to tell you and I'd rather do it in person."

"That sounds ominous."

"No, nothing bad. I just need to bounce some . . . ideas off you and it's more than I want to dive into on the phone."

"Well, Andy invited me to dinner tonight . . . with his mom."

"Are you finally going to meet his mom?" She still sounded off somehow, not like herself. I figured she was still a little peeved at me for forgetting to call her back. And that was fair. She was always so supportive and available, and I often felt that I took it for granted.

"I don't know. I can't decide. I don't know if I'm ready for that or not."

"You like him, don't you?"

"Of course! He's wonderful." I held back details of our night together, but it definitely added a check mark in his favor.

"Then go meet his mom," she sighed.

"I can meet her another time," I said, secretly grateful at being able to use Lanie as an excuse to postpone the meeting.

"No, you're not going to use me as an excuse to put it off."

Dang it. She knew me too well.

"A raincheck then? I really want to hear your ideas."

"Yeah," she said. "Call me when you're free."

We ended the call, and I was left feeling guilty and unsettled. I felt bad both for leaving Lanie hanging and for wanting to weasel out of meeting Andy's mother. What was wrong with me?

Why was I balking at every turn with him? When I really pressed myself, I knew I wanted a relationship with Andy. He was kind, gentle, and considerate, and there was no denying the chemistry. I continued to ponder my shortcomings as a friend and girlfriend as I fed the horses and cleaned out the stalls.

I had learned my lesson the first time with Coach's horse, so I tied him up safely in the breezeway while I worked on his stall. He pawed the ground and pulled at the lead rope. Being cooped up in a stall wasn't doing him any favors, and I needed to figure out what to do with him ASAP. He wasn't safe for adoption yet, even though he was beautiful and in great physical condition. That was in contrast to the sweet red mare in the lower paddock, who was in abysmal shape but was as sweet and well-mannered as any horse I'd ever seen.

I finally decided to put Coach's horse in the field between the rescue and the Cunningham Farm. After Braydon Cunningham was charged with murdering his dad, he received another shock when Albert's will named his younger sister Mae as the primary beneficiary. She inherited the farm, the horses, and most of the money. Braydon was left with mere pennies in comparison to what Aunt Mae received.

I had met her briefly at Albert's remembrance and then again when she came a few weeks later to assess the property. She was distraught over the dual tragedies in her family, but she was warm and welcoming, the complete opposite of her brother. She told me she was planning to settle her affairs in Illinois, and then she was moving to the Cunningham farm permanently in the spring. She'd called me over during her tour of the farm and asked about the untouched, unfenced land that sat unused between my rescue and Albert's manicured pastures. After I tried diplomatically to

85

tell her that it was just easier than fighting her brother over a few inches of boundary, she waved me off and declared that she would have it fenced, and I should start using it straightaway.

After that, she'd insisted I come to the house, where she had fixed tea for us and insisted the staff join us in the formal dining room. They all seemed as shell-shocked as I was, but Mae didn't seem to notice. She talked loudly and gestured wildly, and I thought she was the perfect person to bring life back into that stuffy house. I was looking forward to having Mae Bennett as a neighbor.

The big black horse turned as soon as I unbuckled his halter and bucked all the way up the highline clearing to the back fence. He was going to be a major project. I watched him for a while to make sure he was going to settle down. He whinnied frantically, and horses from all over the rescue and the Cunningham farm answered him. He ran, bucked, and reared some more, followed by another round of whinnying, then finally started grazing. Luckily, he was respectful of the fences.

I stopped in the lower paddock and checked on Ruby. Her bony hips and shoulders were dirty where she had rolled after being turned out from her overnight stall. She quietly munched the alfalfa hay and continued to show no further signs of colic, and every day that it didn't recur made me more hopeful for her recovery. I braided her mane while she ate. I didn't have any rubber bands with me, so they would shake out in no time, but I loved just being with her. It reminded me of being a horse-crazy little girl on this very farm. I buried my face in her shoulder and hugged her neck, feeling thankful to my very bones for being able to live out my childhood dream of operating a horse rescue. As long as I had this little piece of Heaven, I could fix the mistakes I'd made in my relationships.

Trotting Into Trouble

And speaking of relationships, it had been too long since I'd visited my dad. I gave Ruby a good scratching on her withers and chest, then headed to the barn to grab Coach's saddle and tack. After I stashed them in my backseat, I went to the house to get cleaned up. I could swing by Dad's place on my way to the school.

Chapter Nine

When I pulled up in Dad's tiny driveway, he was weeding one of the many flowerbeds that surrounded the modern log cabin. Almost four years ago, he'd been hospitalized with pneumonia, then developed sepsis and required extensive rehab after being in the ICU for so long. I'd taken a leave of absence to care for him, and it was in those days of physical therapy appointments and pulmonology follow-ups that I'd gotten serious about starting a rescue. When I started looking for land, Dad talked me into taking over the family farm. He'd said that, without Mom, he didn't want to keep it up and had been thinking about moving into town anyway. He'd initially moved into an apartment but found that didn't suit him, so he bought the little cabin. I'd been worried that he was just trying to help me get started until I saw how much he loved his new house and how he'd worked so hard to make it a peaceful haven.

The red-tin-roofed cabin perched on a gentle slope, just back from Mason Street. Although his cabin was relatively new, it sat on a lot in one of the oldest parts of Hillspring, flanked on either side by homes that had been built in the 1800s. And even though it was modern, it somehow still fit in without looking like a sore thumb, probably due to Dad's extensive landscaping and the big, homey wraparound porch.

"Hey Punkin'," he called as soon as I got out of the truck. Jasper Hall was never going to stop calling me by my childhood nickname, so there was no use in even trying.

"Hi Dad."

He met me at the yard gate, and I pulled him in for a hug.

"Where's my granddog?" he asked, looking around me for Banjo.

"I have to go to the high school later and I didn't want to leave him in the truck."

"The high school?"

"Yeah," I said, following him into the yard. "You'd better have a seat."

We took seats at his patio table, which was situated on a terrace, the only flat spot in his entire yard. I told him what had happened over the last few days, including Coach's visit the day before he was killed.

"You say the drive thingy was zip-tied on the breast collar?"

"That's the weirdest part," I said. "It was encrypted, and I can't figure out why anyone would put something like that on a breast collar."

"I can't say that's the place I would keep *my* valuables," Dad scratched his head, ruffling his snow-white hair.

"I'm going to try to find a way to ask Mrs. Griggs if he had a habit of doing things like that when I take his stuff out to her this afternoon. It's bugging me."

"What else is bugging you?"

"What do you mean?"

"It's odd, sure enough, to keep something like that zip-tied to a breast collar. But it seems like there's more bothering you."

"The whole thing is bothering me," I said, holding back a lot of what actually was bothering me since Dad wasn't exactly discreet. I didn't want him gossiping about details that Grady might not want discussed in public, like the body being hastily half-buried and the vest we found in the rock pile.

"Talk to Grady about it then," he said, and shrugged like it was the most obvious answer in the world.

"Grady doesn't want me involved at all. He's made that perfectly clear."

"I'll talk to him," he said like he was going to intervene with a difficult teacher or speak to my principal.

"Dad, no," I said. I appreciated his loyalty and unwavering support, but the last thing I needed was my dad talking to the sheriff on my behalf. "Don't you need me to get some of your winter clothes out of the attic?" I hoped the change of subject would be enough to put the subject to rest.

"I'm not sure I want you up on that rickety old ladder either," he said, but got to his feet even as he protested.

"I'll be fine." I made a conscious effort not to limp as he led me into the laundry room where the pull-down ladder door occupied most of the ceiling in the little space. I'd told him about getting kicked, but left out the trip to the ER.

I pulled the chain for the light and stood up as well as I could in the cramped space. I wasn't normally claustrophobic, but the tiny attic felt oppressive and I felt confined in the clutter.

"What are your winter clothes packed in?" I asked as I looked down through the opening in the floor.

"Blue tote. Should be labeled 'winter stuff' or something like that."

I turned back to the stacks of boxes and searched for a blue tote, and of course it was against the back wall. On my way to retrieve it, I banged my leg against a stack of books and newspapers, sending them crashing to the floor, and the sharp pain brought tears to my eyes.

"All okay up there?"

"Yeah," I said through gritted teeth. "Fine."

I wasn't fine. I sat on the little patch of bare floor and resisted the urge to rub my throbbing calf. It was tempting to just sit there and have a good cry. The stress, worry, and exhaustion of the last few days caught up with me again. I took a deep breath and shook off the self-pity as I reached for the books and newspapers I'd just knocked over.

"Dad," I called over my shoulder, "we really need to clean out your attic. Why do you have a collection of old newspapers up here?"

"I saved them for this or that. I keep thinking I'll make a scrapbook or something."

I sighed and felt instantly sympathetic with Mom, who had frequently been forced to deal with the effects of Dad's collections. Luckily, he was selective about it and kept most of his house neat and clean, if a bit cluttered. The books stacked easily, but the newspapers kept sliding back out on the floor. I bent down to pick up the increasingly unruly pile when a front-page article caught my eye.

Local Parent Pleads Guilty to Murder for Hire

The article was accompanied by a photo of a smug-looking young man who could easily pass for a high school student. I pulled it out of the stack and leaned back against the wall to read it. It had happened right after I'd graduated from college and had already moved away, so I hadn't heard about it at the time. The article was relatively short for a front-page feature, but it detailed the charges against a man named Rex Mansfield, the parent of a football player in a nearby town. He'd hired another man, Damon Earnhardt, to kill the coach he believed to be standing in the way of his child's chances for a scholarship. Luckily, Damon appeared to have had a crisis of conscience and went to the police before he completed the job.

The article sparked a firestorm in my brain. I had idolized Coach Griggs so much that I hadn't even considered the fact that he might have been doing something that got him killed. The Coach Griggs Tanner described wasn't the Coach Griggs I remembered, so what had changed him so much? Granted, as a teenager who didn't follow sports, I didn't know if his coaching style had changed as much as his general attitude. But why would anyone zip-tie a thumb drive to their horse tack if they didn't have something to hide?

I pulled out my phone and sent a quick text to Tanner.

Did you ever hear any rumors about Coach Griggs when you were in school?

I watched the three little dots on the screen that indicated he was responding.

No. Did you find out something?

"You still looking?" Dad asked from the bottom of the ladder. "If you can't find it, don't worry about it."

"I knocked some stuff over. I found it. I'll be down in just a minute."

I responded to Tanner before I grabbed the tote. *No, nothing like that. Just curious. The whole thing is bugging me.*

He sent a thumbs-up emoji in response.

I grabbed the blue tote labeled with my dad's deliberate script and slid it down the ladder to his waiting arms.

"Careful, Dad. It's heavy."

He grunted in response.

"Need anything else while I'm up here?"

"Not that I can think of," he said as he pulled the lid off. "Looks like everything is in here."

I climbed down out of the attic and carried the tote into Dad's bedroom.

"Need some help sorting it out?" I gave the top jacket a sniff. "They're kind of musty. I'll throw them in the wash."

He took the jacket from me. "I can do my own laundry. I'm not so old I can't take care of myself."

"I know that. I *like* helping you."

He surprised me by pulling me in for a fierce hug. I hugged him back. He was right. In spite of his age, he wasn't a frail old man. He still felt just like he did when I was a kid. If I closed my eyes, I could almost pretend that time hadn't touched either of us. He kissed me on the forehead, then held me at arm's length.

"I need to get out to the farm and visit the horses. It's been too long."

It had only been a few weeks, but I didn't argue.

"I'd better get going," I said as I glanced at the clock on the wall.

He walked me to my truck and waved as I pulled out of the drive.

*   *   *

Hillspring High School sat nestled in one of the many valleys that punctuated the topography of our little Ozark haven. The school I'd attended was buried somewhere inside the renovations and additions that sprouted from the old center structure like a patch of mushrooms. The result was an entirely unique and charming multilevel series of buildings. The administration office was on the downhill side, so I parked in the lower lot.

The other thing that had changed since I'd attended was the locked front doors that required me to press a buzzer for entry.

"Name of student?" came a tinny voice over the crackly speaker.

"I'm Mallory Martin. I'm supposed to meet Leslie Danvers to pick up Coach Griggs's things."

The door clicked loudly as the lock released, and I pulled it open. The front hall was emblazoned with the Hillspring Bobcat painted in various murals on the concrete block walls. A memorial to Coach Griggs was set up in front of the trophy display case that sat beside the doors to the principal's office. There were numerous letters and photos, and judging from the glowing praise, he had been well-liked despite Tanner's misgivings about his coaching style. I pulled back the top few pages and looked through the lower layers. There was nothing there to indicate that he had had any enemies. Of course there probably wouldn't be. Administration was likely monitoring the content pretty closely.

"Ms. Martin, you can follow me."

I turned to face a young woman about my height with thin, mousy brown hair. She wrung her hands so fiercely I was afraid she was going to cause abrasions. She paused long enough to push a loose tendril behind a prominent ear, then returned to rubbing her knuckles. Her tasteful dress and sweater hung loose on her tiny frame, giving the impression that she was somewhat disheveled despite the neatness of her clothes.

"Mallory, please." I smiled warmly, trying to put her at ease. "Leslie Danvers?"

She nodded, and I followed her down the hall. We made a left turn and climbed two flights of stairs before she led me onto a covered concrete path that linked the main cluster of buildings with the gym. The gym was a large red-metal building that had also been painted with murals of the mascot. "Bobcat Pride" crowned the double doors. We were greeted by the sounds of squeaking sneakers and bouncing basketballs the minute we opened the doors.

"This way."

"Thanks for allowing me to pick up Coach's things," I said quietly as I followed her down another set of stairs. "Patricia couldn't face it just yet."

"Of course." She glanced back over her shoulder. "This is such a terrible thing."

The offices were two doors down from the locker room, and in spite of being in an area of the gym that had no windows whatsoever, it was bright and well-lit. Leslie paused at the door, her hand hovered just above the doorknob, as we both listened to the crash inside.

Leslie turned to me and whispered, "No one is supposed to be in here."

"Maybe we should . . ." I started to say "go get the principal" or someone else, but she yanked the door open before I got the chance.

I followed. As soon as we'd come through the door, a man whirled around to face us.

"Mr. Green! What are you doing in here?" Leslie's voice cracked and she hugged herself nervously.

"I left a note on your desk." He smiled broadly, the kind of smile that told me he knew exactly the effect he had on the opposite sex, and ran a hand through his dark wavy hair. He could pass for a lesser-known Jonas brother. "I thought I would help and gather up Coach Griggs's belongings. I know how busy you are."

She blushed and looked away.

"Mrs. Griggs sent Ms. Martin here to get his things."

"Mallory," I corrected again, and extended my hand to him. The lower desk drawer was still open where he'd been rifling through it.

"Cameron Green. I teach English and English literature."

His handshake was weak and damp. I fought the urge to wipe my hand on my jeans.

"I'm afraid I didn't plan very well, and I didn't bring any boxes with me."

"I'll go get one," Leslie said, and hurried out of the office.

"Did you know Coach well then?" I asked, hoping he caught my insinuation that it was odd to catch him in the office.

"We're a pretty tight-knit group here, small school and all." He used his foot to close the drawer behind him, and I swear I saw him put a piece of paper in his pocket. It wasn't lost on me that he had answered my question without answering my question.

He made a show of cradling the framed photo of Coach and his wife on the desk before handing it over to me.

"Such a shame." He frowned and shook his head. "Of course, not everyone is heartbroken."

I watched him for a moment. He glanced at me a couple of times, clearly wanting me to ask him what he was talking about. I decided to take the bait.

"Are you saying that someone might be glad Coach is dead?" I did my best attempt at pearl-clutching, sans the pearls.

Cameron leaned in conspiratorially and motioned for me to come closer. I suspected he taught drama as well. If not, he'd missed his calling.

"It would seem that he had an enemy."

I briefly considered that Cameron was yanking my chain, but his revelation had the desired effect. My curiosity was piqued.

"How could someone dislike him enough to be considered an *enemy*?"

"Last Friday, he had a very loud confrontation with one of his player's parents. It happened right out front. I saw it myself. I thought they were going to come to blows."

"Did you tell the police?"

He looked surprised. "No. They haven't asked. I expected them to come by after I heard what happened, but I haven't seen anyone."

It was my turn to look surprised. What on earth was Grady doing?

"Would you be willing to speak to them?"

"Sure, if you think it's important." He shrugged.

"What did they argue about?"

"I imagine it was something about basketball."

"Do you know who the parent was?"

"I do." He smiled broadly. "Bruce Porter."

I opened my mouth to say something, but Leslie burst back into the office, dropping the boxes she was carrying as she fumbled with the door. Cameron bent to pick them up, and Leslie blushed deeply again. I felt bad for her. She seemed so shy and timid.

"Thank you," I said as I picked up the last box.

"That was Coach Griggs's desk," Leslie pointed at the desk Cameron had been rifling through. "I'll help you pack his things."

I smiled, but inwardly I was cursing. I'd hoped to be alone to do a little rifling of my own.

"I hope you'll excuse me," Cameron said as he made his way to the door. "I have a class starting soon."

I followed him into the hall.

"Please let Sheriff Sullivan know what you saw. It may be absolutely nothing, but he needs to know."

"I'll do that," he said and turned that thousand-watt smile on me. It didn't affect me the way it had Leslie. Maybe it was my recent encounter with another gorgeous playboy who had tried to kill me that caused me to be less than impressed. Or maybe it was because he just rubbed me the wrong way.

Leslie had started without me. She had nearly filled one of the boxes, and I wondered how much stuff Coach could possibly still have at the school. He was retired, for crying out loud.

Turns out the answer to that question was *a lot*. We filled the three boxes Leslie brought and stuffed some more into a trash bag. Thankfully, even though she was sparse on friendly chitchat, Leslie wasn't afraid to work and helped me load all of it into my truck.

"It feels so final to pack up his things," I said as I shut my truck door.

"Will that be all then?" Leslie asked after an awkward pause.

"Yes. Thank you for your help."

She looked somewhat surprised and then quickly looked away. "You're welcome." She started wringing her hands again. "We're having a memorial Friday in the gym. It's important for the kids to honor Coach Griggs's memory. Would you please extend our invitation to Mrs. Griggs?"

"Of course."

She nodded curtly once, as though that settled our business completely, then scurried back into the school building. I took a deep breath, gathered my strength, and turned my truck toward the Griggs's house.

Chapter Ten

Patricia Griggs met me in the driveway as soon as I got out of my truck. She looked less fragile than she had on my previous visit, but her eyes still bore the evidence of her grief.

"Oh dear," she said as she opened the back door. "I didn't realize there was still this much there."

She reached and took a box off the top of the stack.

"We can just stack them up in his office." She took the lead, and I followed her into the house and down the hall.

She opened the door to a small room that contained a tiny desk and a massive TV.

"It's not really an office," she shrugged. "He didn't have much paperwork after he retired. But it was somewhere he could hole up and watch sports."

"A man cave," I smiled, and she returned it.

"He hated that term," she said with a chuckle. "But that's what it is . . . was."

And just like that, the weight of grief settled back over her and the sparkle that lit her swollen eyes was gone again.

I glanced around the room as we stacked the boxes, but there wasn't anything out of the ordinary. There was no computer or laptop on the desk, and I couldn't find a delicate way of asking where his might be, if he even owned one. And it didn't matter anyway since I'd turned the USB drive over to Grady and didn't have a clue what the password might be. However, I took the opportunity to bring it up as I headed back to my truck for the saddle.

"Would you like me to take the saddle to the barn?"

Patricia hesitated for a moment.

"No, I think I would like that in here too." She hugged herself the way she'd done when Tanner and I were there. "I just don't want anything to happen to it."

"Did Grady, I mean Sheriff Sullivan, tell you what I found on the breast collar?"

She looked confused for a moment, then nodded as it dawned on her.

"Oh yeah, the flash drive."

"Was it normal for him to keep things like that on his tack?"

"He had weird habits like that. He was raised by his grandparents, who lived through the Depression. His grandmother didn't trust banks or safe-deposit boxes or anything like that. She would squirrel money away in the pockets of her coats, in jars hidden in the back of cabinets, and coffee cans she stashed in the chicken coop. When we cleaned out her house after she died, we found little wads of money and important records hidden in the weirdest places. That's a habit that Doug picked up too."

That made a *little* more sense. I could remember my own grandparents giving me quarters from a tin can they hid behind a loose piece of trim in the hall closet.

"But like I told the sheriff, I don't know the 'cryption' key or password, or whatever you call it."

I cursed inwardly. But it did make me feel better that Grady had asked. He was taking it seriously even if he refused to talk to me. At all.

"Doug's laptop was stolen out of his truck. They smashed the window and took it. So he was probably extra paranoid in hiding important records," Patricia said matter-of-factly, like it was a normal thing to have happen.

I remembered the plastic covering the passenger window on Coach's truck the day he came to the rescue. The laptop had been stolen recently.

Patricia waited for me at the door while I went to get her husband's saddle. My breath caught in my chest. She was waiting for me to bring her one of his treasured belongings, something she could cling to, something she couldn't bring herself to put in the barn. Regardless of how Coach had changed over the years, his wife loved him very much.

I pulled the saddle out by the horn and slid my arm underneath it. I yelped and jerked my hand back as something in the gullet cut me. Something on the underside of the saddle had torn a jagged line across my thumb and wrist. It wasn't deep, but it smarted plenty. I pulled the saddle out in the sunlight. If it had a nail or fitting coming loose, Patricia would need to know before it was put on another horse.

But it wasn't a nail or fitting. It was a key. Coach Griggs had used a small screw to secure a key onto the wooden tree of his saddle.

*   *   *

Grady pushed his Stetson back and scratched his forehead as we both stood over the upturned saddle.

"Have you looked over the rest of it?"

"Yes," I said. "I never thought to look in the gullet of a saddle for a freaking key. But I've been over it now with fine-tooth comb."

"Have you asked Mrs. Griggs if she knows what it goes to?"

"No. You told me to stay out of it."

"Are you this difficult with everybody or do you just save it for me?"

"I save it for you." I feigned annoyance and put my hands on my hips.

He grinned as he bent down and tried to loosen the screw, but it wouldn't budge. I fished my multi-tool out of my pocket and handed it to him. He looked amused all over again as he took it and opened the screwdriver. It only took him a few minutes to remove the screw and drop it in an evidence bag. I stayed with the saddle while he went to talk to Patricia. I could hear him asking her what the key might unlock and why her husband would hide things like that. She told him a version of the story she'd told me earlier about the odd habits he'd picked up from his grandparents, but she also had no idea what the key opened.

I put the saddle over a stack of boxes so the fenders wouldn't get bent out of shape from resting on the floor. I could no longer convince myself that Coach's death was a terrible accident. I'd suspected as much all along, but it was easier to convince myself before it was obvious that he was hiding something. As I glanced over the "office" again, I finally admitted it to myself.

Coach Griggs had been murdered.

After Grady left, I offered to make Patricia something to eat again.

"I'm doing alright," she said and mustered a weak smile. "I ate breakfast."

I gave her a skeptical look.

"I promise," she said in response.

"I'll go tend to the horse." I started for the door.

"I did that too. It's helped to stay busy. And my son will be here in a day or two." She reached out and took my hand. "I didn't have any right to ask you to do all this. I don't even know you."

"I was here when you needed someone and I'm glad to help." I squeezed her hand back. "Coach helped me so much in high school. I would've never qualified for my scholarship without his tutoring."

"I'm glad he made a difference." She took on a faraway look, as though her thoughts had either taken her away from the present or ceased entirely. When I lost Mom, I sometimes found myself just *blank*.

"Sheriff Sullivan asked me about the key and that computer thingy." She suddenly snapped back to the present and clung to my hand like it was her only anchor to this world.

"What did he say?"

"He wouldn't tell me. Just said it was an open investigation."

I bit my lip and hesitated. She seemed to be a little better than she'd been on my previous visit, so I decided to blunder ahead.

"Can you think of anyone who would want to hurt Coach?" I asked tentatively.

"He'd been getting calls nearly every evening from the parent of one of his players. Doug was proposing a change to the way the kids qualify for athletic eligibility to the school board next week. I don't know all the ins and outs of it, but the guy was pretty upset." She paused and took a deep breath. "And then there was Ben Archer."

I waited for her to elaborate, but she released my hand and walked into the kitchen.

"Coffee?"

I'd had enough caffeine to fuel a jet engine, but I thought it might keep her talking if I had a cup.

"I'd love some."

She poured two large mugs and joined me at the table, passing the cream and sugar as she sat down. We both added an embarrassing amount of each to our coffees.

"Who's Ben Archer?" I asked when I'd finally given up on her continuing.

She seemed to be waiting for me to ask. "He was on Doug's team about three years ago. Doug caught him dealing drugs on campus and turned him in. Doug worried himself sick over that kid and went to all the hearings. Then, when Ben was sentenced he threatened Doug in open court. Said he would kill him for ruining his life."

I sipped my coffee while I digested this information. It seemed like Coach had at least two people who might have had sufficient motive to kill him. I wondered if the parent calling him at home was the same one Cameron had seen arguing with him at the school.

"Do you know who the parent was? The one who was calling him in the evening."

"Bruce Porter," she said, her face drawing up like his name tasted bad in her mouth. "Even before Doug drafted his proposal for the school board, Bruce would call him about every little thing. His son wasn't getting enough time on the court, or he was getting too much and the poor baby was *tired*. It was ridiculous."

My suspicion that they were one and the same was confirmed. I tried not to seem too eager.

"Did anyone know he was going riding that day?"

"Probably." She shrugged. "He'd been sharing short videos of his work with that awful horse to a group on Facebook. *Hillspring Hill Riders,* I believe it's called. He posted there all the time. He even met a few of them to ride off and on. We both did—well, before I lost my mare, that is."

We talked for a while longer about horses and our kids. Patricia was very proud of her son, who had ended up in the same profession as Coach, teaching math and coaching basketball out of state. I tried, unsuccessfully, to talk her into keeping the big black gelding. She was adamant that she never wanted to see the horse again, and wouldn't accept any payment for him either. It was clear that she blamed the animal for the part it played in her husband's death. And while I felt sorry for the horse, I didn't judge her misplaced blame. I had no idea how I might react had I been in her shoes.

She walked me to the door, clinging to herself again. I kept getting the impression that she was physically trying to hold herself together. As I turned to say goodbye, she grabbed my arm so quickly and so forcefully that I jumped like I'd been attacked.

"You have to make sure Sheriff Sullivan takes this seriously," she said, holding onto my arm with an iron grip. "You seem to know him pretty well, and he came when you called. I'm right, aren't I? You're friends?"

"Yes, but . . ."

"It wasn't an accident!" she cut me off. "Someone killed him. Please don't let Sheriff Sullivan sweep this under the rug."

"Grady would never . . ."

"He's already got his mind made up." Her mouth formed a thin line. "He dismisses everything I say. I need you to talk to him. *Please.*"

I opened my mouth to protest, but she didn't give me a chance.
"You don't think it was an accident either," she plowed on.
"You wouldn't have asked me about people who might want to
hurt him if you thought it was a simple accident. I know I don't
have any more right to ask this of you than I did to ask you to get
Doug's things, but I don't know anyone else that can help."

My head started nodding before my brain caught up. She took
that little bit of agreement as gospel and grabbed both my hands
in hers.

"Thank you," she said, tears welling in her eyes. "I don't know
how I'll ever thank you enough."

"I can't promise anything," I managed to say.

"You just being willing to try is enough. I know he'll listen to
you."

Oh boy. Little did she know.

* * *

I was lost in thought as I drove back through town, mulling over
everything Patricia had told me. What had I gotten myself into? I
was curious about what had actually happened to Coach Griggs,
and I wasn't prepared to stick my nose back into a murder investigation. But I *could* stick to some research and background, and
then if anything turned up, I would have a stronger case to present to Grady. By the time I reached Hillspring city limits, I had
formulated a loose plan of attack.

First, I wanted to find out what sort of changes Coach was
going to propose to the school board. If those changes kept Bruce
Porter's son from playing basketball, it might have been motive
enough for murder. Some parents take high school sports way too
seriously. I was reminded of the Texas mom who tried to eliminate

her daughter's cheerleading competition in the early nineties. Sports parents can be an intense lot, some of whom I witnessed firsthand when Ginny played soccer. And that intensity only gets worse when high-dollar scholarships are on the line.

Second, Ben Archer certainly had a motive for revenge. He'd openly threatened Coach in front of a court full of witnesses. I needed to find out if he was still in prison. Being incarcerated is a pretty good alibi. Grady would be able to find this out much more easily than I could. I considered stopping by his office to try and discuss it with him, but I thought better of it and found myself pulling into Lanie's parking lot instead. I needed solid leads to present to Grady. If my information was helpful, it might distract him from how mad he was likely going to be.

Eve, the floor manager at Junk & Disorderly, Lanie's eclectic flea market/antique store, looked up from her phone when the sleigh bells on the door jingled. Her black hair was pulled back in a high ponytail and she was wearing a pale-yellow dress that contrasted beautifully with her dark skin.

"Hey." She smiled as I approached the counter. "Lanie's not here this afternoon."

"Oh shoot." I frowned. "I guess I should've called first."

"You're welcome to stay and help me unbox the stuff she brought in yesterday." Eve hooked a thumb toward the back room. "I think she bought a whole storage unit."

"Sure," I said. "I'll be glad to help."

"I was only kidding." She looked surprised.

"I don't mind. I can spare and hour or so."

She wasn't kidding about the amount of stuff. There were six pallets of wrapped items and boxes. Eve had to break away every time someone came into the shop, so I worked alone a lot, which gave my mind plenty of time to wander and obsess. I leaned against a tall box and opened the notes app on my phone. I quickly typed out a list.

- *Find out if Ben Archer has been released*
- *Find out what Coach was proposing to school board*
- *Look into Facebook riding group*
- *Find out who the intoxicated hunter was and what was his blood alcohol level*

I paused at this last one. I didn't want to tip Grady off that I was looking into anything, so I decided I would try to corner Darrin. Corporal Bailey wasn't my biggest fan to begin with, but we had forged a relationship of mutual respect after the whole mess with Braydon Cunningham. I knew the hunter I'd met on the trail was Grady's prime suspect, but I had my doubts about his ability to function at the level necessary to try to hide his crime. He was staggering drunk, and Coach's body had been partially concealed. Granted, it was a lousy job and appeared to have been hastily done, but even so, it looked like it was beyond that man's capacity in the state he was in.

Deciding that was enough for now, I went back to work unboxing the pallet. I sorted things as best I could in ways that made sense to me: kitchen stuff together, art and knickknacks together, and so forth. Lanie would have to inventory and price it all, but at least it would be waiting for her. Eve made polite conversation in between customers, but I'm sure I wasn't very good company because I was so preoccupied.

"You're amazing," Eve said as she surveyed the stockroom, hands on her hips. "This would've taken me forever."

"It's been busy this afternoon," I said.

I pulled out my phone and sent a text to Tanner on my way back to my truck.

Finished at Lanie's, just checking in.

It only took a few seconds for him to respond. *All good Boss.*

I sent a "thumbs-up" emoji and pocketed my phone as I approached my truck. My brain registered that something was wrong, but it took a few seconds to realize what I was looking at.

Chapter Eleven

Grady couldn't respond in person, so he sent Corporal Darrin Bailey. Darrin circled my poor truck and scratched his head. When he got to the driver's side, he took an evidence bag out of his pocket and pulled the screwdriver out of my ruined tire. It also looked to be the tool that was probably used to gouge out the word "stop" into my driver's side door.

He sealed the bag and then looked around the employee parking lot.

"Do you know if Mrs. Harris has any cameras out here?"

"I don't think so." I shook my head. "I know she has two out front, but I don't think she put any in the employee lot."

The lot was small and surrounded on three sides with a tall privacy fence, so I didn't have much hope that the vandalism was captured on anyone else's cameras either.

"I called and texted Lanie, but she hasn't responded yet. Eve, the store manager, didn't see anything out of the ordinary."

"I'll still need to talk to her. Have you made anybody mad lately?" Darrin added with a smirk.

My first thought was that this had something to do with Coach Griggs and someone was following me or watching me, or both. That thought sent a cold chill down my spine and I suppressed a shiver. I wasn't sure I wanted to admit that I was looking into things for Patricia just yet, so I blurted out the next idea that ran through my brain like a squirrel darting through traffic.

"Just that guy from the drug bust the other day," I said. "He was pretty upset when Tanner and I took the horse. It was my truck at the scene."

"He's still in jail." Darrin looked at me like he was sizing me up. "Are you sure you're not sticking your nose where it doesn't belong?"

I opened my mouth to protest but couldn't bring myself to outright lie to him, so snapped it shut again.

"Patricia Griggs thinks her husband was murdered," I said, throwing caution to the wind.

"So do I."

"You're a smart man, Darrin. You can't think it was a simple accident. Wait, what?"

"I think he was murdered too. And we are investigating it. Thoroughly, I might add." He grinned at me again. Apparently, he found this very amusing.

"Well, okay, good. Although I'm not sure what's so funny." I gestured toward my truck and tried not to cry. I love my truck.

"It's not funny." He wiped all traces of amusement off his face. "In fact, I'm taking this very seriously. And you should too. You need to distance yourself from the investigation. If this *was* someone related to Coach Griggs's death, you could be in real danger."

"If it *is* related, then I must be on to something."

I didn't give him time to argue. I launched into everything I'd found out so far, which admittedly wasn't a lot. But by the time I'd started winding down, he'd taken out his notebook and jotted down some notes. He seemed particularly interested in the names that Patricia had shared with me.

"I'll look into this," he said when I'd finished. And then he made a point of emphasizing, "*so you don't need to.*"

"Understood."

Darrin went inside to talk to Eve, leaving me with the remains of my poor truck. I pulled out my phone and called a tow truck first and Andy second. He got there before the tow truck.

"Wow!" he said as he got out of his car.

"Yeah. Not exactly the detailing job my truck needed."

He put his arm around my shoulders and gave me a squeeze. It felt good to lean into him.

"I can chauffeur you around for a few days."

"Are you sure? I need to run to the feed store," I said as I eyed his town car. "But I can ask Tanner to do it."

"I've got a trunk and a back seat. We can pile in just about everything except maybe hay."

"Are you finished at the office?"

"I can be. It's a light day." He pulled me in for a hug. "Let me help you. Besides, I don't like the idea of you being alone right now. Someone is obviously following you."

The thought sent a chill down my spine and I hugged him back, fiercely.

While we waited for the tow truck, Andy called his assistant, Sherry, and updated her on the research he needed her to complete and the briefs he wanted her to draft. Sherry had taken an instant dislike to me when I'd first showed up at Andy's office without an appointment. I had needed an attorney when I thought I was going to be framed for my neighbor's murder. No matter how nice I'd been in the months since, I just couldn't seem to win her over. So I mostly just avoided her when possible.

Randy's Towing took my truck to the body shop while Andy drove me to the feed store. Andy and I managed to cram my feed and supplement order into his Lincoln Town Car like an old school game of Tetris. I dreaded unloading it when we got home. I usually pulled my truck through the paddock directly down to the barn, but I doubted that his car would make it.

"You know," Andy said as we pulled out onto the main road. "I should trade this old car in on a truck. Then I could help out more when you need it."

I froze. Not only did it seem like he'd read my mind, I also felt . . . cornered.

"You don't need to do that," I said, trying to collect myself and not allow my panic to show on my face, as nearly all of my emotions tend to do.

He must have seen the look of horror on my face, because he pulled into the Hillspring Storage and More parking lot and turned to face me.

"Wouldn't that make more sense?" He reached for my hand. "There's not much use for my car on a horse rescue and I could haul my kayak without messing with the little trailer."

"Andy, I don't want you to trade off your car for me." I was suddenly aware that I was breathing heavily, and I was gripping my seatbelt like it was some kind of lifeline.

"Okay," he said quietly. "I was just throwing out ideas."

He gave my hand a squeeze, then pulled back out onto the road. We didn't talk the rest of the way home and my mind was a tornado, swirling and chaotic. I was forced to reexamine my hesitancy when Andy tried to take our relationship to the next steps. That was the last thing I wanted to do. I was happy with how things were. Why did we need to mess with what was working so well? I was still trying to figure out why I was such a disaster when Andy turned up my rough driveway and jolted me back to the present.

We worked without speaking and unloaded the feed. I kept feeling like I should say something but didn't know what to say, so we had been suspended in awkward silence for nearly a half-hour between the ride home and unloading the feed when Andy carried the last bag into the barn.

"You need to call your insurance provider and see if they cover a rental," he said, leaning against the barn door. "I can come by tomorrow afternoon and take you, if you need me to. And I don't like the idea of you staying out here alone. Give Lanie a call."

"Do you want to talk?" I asked, half hoping that he did and half hoping that he didn't.

"I don't know that there's anything to talk about." He crossed his arms and regarded me, furrowed brows behind his glasses. "I think I'm pushing you to move faster than you're comfortable with."

When he said the words out loud it was like punch in the gut. He reached forward and rubbed my shoulder. I pulled him in for a hug and felt him kiss the top of my head. It felt like a goodbye. It felt even more like it when he turned and climbed the gentle hill back through the paddock and got in his car, all the while not looking back at me.

Chapter Twelve

I tried to soothe the hollow feeling that had settled in my chest by doing chores and grooming the horses. When that didn't work, I grabbed my orange vest, saddled River, and took to the old logging roads that crisscrossed the mountain behind my place. The land now belonged to my late neighbor's sister, Mae Bennett, and she had offered me an open invitation to ride whenever I wanted. Which was nice, since riding circles in the paddock gets old and riding on the shoulder of a road isn't the safest choice.

River's flaxen mane bobbed in time to his gentle gait. I had no idea what his pedigree might be, but I suspect he had at least *some* Missouri Foxtrotter in his heritage. While not fully gaited, he definitely had a faster, easier walk than a typical quarter horse. He was alert and curious as we explored the trails, and I suspected that the ride was good for him too. He had mostly been toting youngsters around the paddock lately, and while he was great for lessons, his heart was on the trail.

We topped the mountain, and I turned River around to take in the view between the tall oaks, pines, hickories, and cedars. To my right, Deadwood Lake wound through the crooked hollow, gleaming in the afternoon light. My place wasn't visible from the top, but I could see the manicured pastures of the Cunningham farm and the tiny dots of grazing horses. The last of the leaves that hung onto the oaks rattled in the gentle breeze, their color faded to a dull brown.

River drew in a deep breath and cocked a back leg, relaxing in the cool air that blew up from the lake. I tried to do the same, but when I took a deep breath, it caught in my chest. I found myself sobbing as I clutched the reins. Thankfully, River was unbothered by my sudden mental breakdown.

It felt like everything was reeling out of control. I'd managed to get myself in the middle of another murder investigation, though admittedly at least I wasn't a suspect in this one. I was still in the middle of it though, and apparently the possible focus of the killer if the damage to my truck was any indication.

I was also afraid I'd messed up everything with Andy. He'd been nothing but wonderful and supportive, and I'd responded by pushing him away every time he tried to get closer. I angrily wiped the tears off my cheeks, disgusted with myself. I *wanted* a relationship with Andy. He was kind and generous, and our chemistry was undeniable. For once in my life, I decided to tackle this problem like an adult. I dismounted and pulled my cell phone out of my shirt pocket and dialed Andy before I lost my nerve. He picked up on the second ring.

"Are you okay?" he asked as soon as the call connected. It was a legitimate question. I'd called him in the middle of one disaster or another for days now.

"Physically, yes. And before you say anything, just let me get this out. I don't know why I'm so freaked out about taking the next steps in our relationship. I really don't, but I promise you I'll try to figure it out if you'll be patient with me. I want to meet your mother, and if it's not too late, I'd love to have dinner with the two of you tonight."

The line was silent when I stopped talking. I wished I could see his face and regretted calling instead of doing this in person.

"Mal, you don't have to do this. You don't have to compromise how you feel to be in a relationship with me. I've told you before, we can take this as slow as you want."

I smiled and patted River on the shoulder as he lazily picked at the sprigs of grass growing sparsely on the hilltop.

"I think it's good to push me a little now and then. Otherwise, I might never move. I really do want to have dinner with you and your mother tonight." River snorted, and then whinnied loudly in answer to one of the Cunningham horses below.

"I'll pick you up at five thirty then," he said.

After we hung up, I found a big limestone rock shelf to use as a mounting block and climbed back on. I *can* mount from the ground, but it's not pretty, and I try not to if I can help it. I patted River on the neck and squeezed his sides gently with my calves to ask him to head back down the trail. The road we were on circled the back of the Cunningham farm and came out on the road about a quarter-mile from my driveway. Any other day, I would've made the whole circle, but I needed to get back in time to make myself presentable. I didn't want my first impression to include barn aroma and horse dirt.

It didn't take River long to bring me back to the barn. By the time we returned, my leg was aching in time with my heartbeat. Luckily, when I pulled up my jeans and took a look at my leg, the swelling wasn't any worse. To be fair, it wasn't any *better* either though. I took a little extra time to brush River down and give him the apple-flavored treats he loves so much.

Before I headed to the house, I checked on Ruby, who was lazily munching her soaked hay. I couldn't imagine that the watery mess was very appetizing, but we were on strict orders from Doc Brantley to soak it for a few days to help reduce her chances of colicking again. Luckily, she didn't seem to mind. Her skeletal frame was still heart-wrenching to look at, but it was nice to see her filling her belly. And it was comforting that her belly didn't seem to be bothering her anymore. I talked softly to her and coaxed some of the knots out of her mane with my fingers. She needed a bath, but I wanted her to rest a few more days before we tackled that.

After deciding everyone was okay, I showered quickly and pulled on my favorite sweater over a pair of knit leggings. I was trying to find that sweet spot between too dressy and too casual and hoped I'd found it as I checked myself in the mirror. I was just about to start taming my blond curls when I heard gravel crunching in the driveway. Since Biscuit hadn't sounded the alarm, it had to be someone he knew. I glanced at the clock, which told me it was early for Andy.

I got to the door just as Grady was about to knock. He tipped his Stetson as soon as I opened the door.

"Hey," I said. "I wasn't expecting you."

"Sorry to drop in unannounced."

"I didn't mean that. You're always welcome here. It's just that I gave my statement to Darrin earlier." I opened the door and gestured for him to come inside.

"I just wanted to come talk to you, off the record, so to speak."

"That's a first," I snorted.

"Do you have to be difficult *all* the time?"

"Yes," I said, grinning. "It's in my contract."

"Remind me at some point to renegotiate the terms. But right now, I want to warn you to be careful. We had to release Marvin Randall." When he noticed my lack of recognition of the name, he added, "the intoxicated hunter who nearly face-planted on you."

"Oh. Well, that would rule out his involvement then, wouldn't it? My truck was vandalized this afternoon and Darrin seems to think it might be connected to Coach Griggs."

"That's what I'm telling you, Mal. He was released *before* someone vandalized your truck."

"He wouldn't have any reason to do that." I shook my head.

"I'm not stupid. We both know you're poking around. You went back and found the vest, or did you think I would just ignore that little fact? Plus, you've been in contact with Mrs. Griggs on multiple occasions."

"How would *he* know any of that?"

"I think he's following you."

That sent a cold chill to my very bones. I'd suspected as much, not necessarily about Marvin Randall, but about the killer in general. Hearing Grady confirm it was terrifying.

"I think he remembers a lot more than he's admitting to." Grady's mouth drew into a thin line. "He drives an older black F150 with a dented driver's-side front fender. Keep an eye out. Stay vigilant. And put my number on speed dial. If you see *anything* out of the ordinary, call me immediately."

"I'll do that," I said, and hugged myself against the chill. "And for the record, I don't think you're stupid."

"I can't tell you everything, just know that we have compelling evidence against Marvin Randall. We don't have enough to keep him in custody, but I need you to know that I'm not focusing on him for no reason."

"I understand. And I won't get in the way."

He nodded. He looked like he wanted to say something else, but drew his mouth into a slight frown instead. Banjo, having just realized we had company, came trotting into the living room and wagged at Grady. While he generally liked all people, Grady was one of his favorites and he was always glad to see him. Grady bent down and scratched his ears.

"Sherlock is going to hate me, coming home smelling like a dog again."

I giggled. I hadn't realized that Grady's big gray cat was named after the famous detective.

"What?" he asked as he straightened up.

"Nothing. It's just adorable that the sheriff's cat is named Sherlock."

I would have bet money that he blushed ever so slightly before we both turned toward the window. It was the sound of gravel crunching again.

Andy got out of his car, his starkly professional attire replaced by a long-sleeved tee and jeans. I much preferred this look and the shadow of stubble that colored his angular chin.

When he realized who it was, Grady's attention turned back to me.

"I know you have your guard donkey out there," he said with a grin, "but you should think about putting in a security gate. Something you can lock down after hours."

"I doubt I can afford anything like that, but I'll look into it."

"Bill should be able to connect you with a wholesaler."

He was right. Lanie's husband would have those connections. He'd taken over the family construction business several years ago, keeping Harris Construction and Renovation one of the most successful in the area.

Andy knocked lightly as he opened the door.

"Sheriff," he nodded as he entered and stood between us.

"Evenin'," Grady nodded back as he opened the door to leave. "Take care, Mal."

"Everything okay?" Andy asked as Grady pulled out of my driveway.

I gave him a quick recap and asked him to wait just a minute while I slapped on a little makeup and tried to tame my curls a bit.

He opened the car door for me, and I was greeted by the amazing scent of takeout from Rossi's Italian Kitchen. My mouth watered at the thought of cheesy garlic bread from one of my favorite restaurants.

"Do you think the horses will be okay?" I asked as he climbed into the driver's seat.

"Whoever vandalized your truck waited until you were parked where there aren't any security cameras. Everyone in town knows that your security footage is what helped strengthen the case against Braydon Cunningham. But I can understand why you'd be worried. We can reschedule, if you want."

"I'm sure it'll be fine." I opened the security app on my phone and watched us pull out of the driveway.

I'd put up just one camera before Braydon Cunningham attacked me. The recording it provided was crucial in proving my innocence and a key piece of evidence used to deny his bail. Since the arrest and news coverage drew people to the rescue in unprecedented numbers for a while, I added several more security features, including more cameras and an actual security system. Knowing that I could turn on alerts did a lot to ease my mind.

The short drive to the assisted living facility was a relatively short one. Applewood Estates sits atop a craggy limestone bluff that overlooks Deadwood Lake. The location would be perfect for a gothic castle or haunted hotel, but Applewood Estates is an open, warm, and welcoming facility. The views are spectacular, especially in the evenings when Deadwood Lake catches the sunset and holds it like paint washed from an artist's brush. The main building is flanked by a mixed orchard on the right and a chicken coop and community garden on the left. The chicken coop and garden raised beds were all designed to be accessible to people with varying degrees of mobility, and all are situated to allow wheelchair access. The nurse in me understood the extra work all of that must create for the employees, but I could also appreciate the unmeasurable benefit to the residents' health and well-being.

I got out of the car before Andy had the chance to open the door for me. I often forget that he likes to do that. It took both of us to carry in all the takeout bags, and I wondered if it was just going to be the three of us. The front doors were secured with a numerical keypad and Andy shifted his load onto his knee while he punched in the code. I had never been inside this facility before, and the interior was just as homey as the grounds. It reminded me of Old Faithful Lodge in Yellowstone National Park. The ceiling featured large open-log beams that framed the central rock fireplace like a rustic cathedral. The hardwood floors echoed with our footfalls.

"Mom's apartment is down here," Andy gestured to a hall that extended off to the right, labeled with a gold "B."

I followed him past numbered apartments down a deceptively long hall. We stopped in front of B11 and Andy knocked on the door.

"Come on in," came a soft voice from inside.

Andy shifted the takeout bags and opened the door for me again. As I crossed the threshold into Annette Hannigan's apartment, I wished I'd asked Andy if he'd let her know I was coming.

"Just put the food on the table." She gestured toward an adorable bistro-style table in the center of the kitchen.

"Hey Mom, Mallory was able to get away after all," he said as we both put our bags on the table.

"Oh good." She smiled broadly, one side of her face lifting higher than the other. "I wondered why you smelled like perfume."

Andy told me that she'd had a series of strokes that had affected her mobility and sight, but it wasn't until that moment that I realized she was blind. Her delicate face retained the beauty of her youth, the changes brought on by age just enhanced her high cheekbones and full lips instead of diminishing them. Her long white hair was braided loosely in a cascade over her shoulder. Her long lavender sweater dress completed the impression of quiet serenity.

When she moved toward me, I could see her contracted left hand, another result of her strokes.

"So pleased to meet you," she said, extending her right hand in my general direction.

"Likewise," I said, taking her hand in mine. "Andy has told me so much about you."

"Oh no," she laughed.

"All good, I promise."

Trotting Into Trouble

Andy insisted that we sit down while he unboxed everything. Annette asked me about the rescue and about Ginny, which is always a favorite subject of mine. I told her that my daughter was majoring in veterinary sciences and hoped to practice in Hillspring, or at least nearby. She beamed as she talked about how proud she was of her only son, while Andy looked like he wanted to crawl into the cabinet.

Annette carried the conversation through dinner, and though she still had trouble with some words, she would just plow on, and her meaning was never lost on me. I often have trouble filling awkward silences and I'm terrible at small talk, so it was nice for her to be able to take up the slack. Plus, she had led a fascinating life. She'd lost her husband, Andy's father, to a heart attack when Andy was four and his sister was two. She had supported her children on her own, working jobs that allowed her flexibility and control over her schedule. I was fascinated by her stories. She had worked as a campground caretaker, school bus driver, medical courier, and many others.

"You've led such an interesting life," I said. Andy smiled at me. He'd told me a little about his childhood, but hearing it from his mother's perspective was enlightening. She was fiercely independent and dedicated to her children. No wonder Andy had grown up to be the strong, sensitive man he was.

"I never brought a killer to justice, as you have," she said as we dug into dessert.

"I can't take credit for that, really." I blushed.

Andy took this opportunity to tell his mom about Coach Griggs, how I'd found him, and the latest development with my truck. He started clearing the table and waved me off when I offered to help.

"It would seem that you've gotten *someone's* attention, that's for sure," she said.

She was right. The message couldn't have been clearer. But who knew that I was looking into anything? Obviously Patricia Griggs, since she as the one who'd asked me to do it. Leslie Danvers and Cameron Green could have figured out that I was involved because they'd been there when I collected Coach's things and I hadn't exactly been subtle with my questions. But whoever had vandalized my truck had obviously been following me, so it wasn't out of the realm of possibility that the killer had been doing so ever since I'd found Coach's body. It would've been easy to watch me load the horse and get a good look at my truck.

"Where'd you go?" Annette asked quietly.

"I'm sorry?"

"I don't have to be able to see to know you left us for a bit just now."

I laughed. It must have been very hard to be a teenager with Annette as your mom. It seemed that not much got past her.

"I was thinking about what you said, about getting someone's attention."

"I don't like to think about you being on some killer's radar," Andy said, not meeting my eyes. "I know you don't want to hear that, but I worry about you, Mal."

"I'm glad you care about me." I turned in my chair to look at him. "But I'm not going to be intimidated."

"I knew I would like you," Annette reached for my hand, and I moved it closer so she could take it. "From everything Andrew has told me, you're my kind of people."

We fell back into easy conversation about what it was like to live in the assisted living facility and how Annette had initially thought she would hate it. Instead, she felt like she was thriving in the supportive environment and had made many new friends. When Andy reminded us that it had gotten late and we should be going, I felt a pang of regret that I had dreaded this meeting and put it off for weeks. Annette was lovely, and I'd genuinely enjoyed her company. She gave me an open-ended invitation to return, with or without Andy, which made me grin at his mock indignation.

We drove back to my house in comfortable silence. Biscuit trotted to the gate as I got out of the car and squawked a quiet half-bray in greeting. I pulled out the baggie of treats I keep in my purse and gave him a couple while I scratched his neck. He nuzzled my cheek with his little impossibly soft snoot. If he'd been a mini, I would have undoubtedly house-trained him by now. I heard Andy chuckling behind me.

"What? I can't resist him."

"It shouldn't surprise me that you have horse treats in your purse."

I shrugged and did my best impersonation of innocence as I wrapped my arms around his waist.

"I really enjoyed tonight."

"I wasn't kidding, Mal. I'm worried. I don't like the idea of a killer following you."

"I guess you'll just have to stay here then."

Chapter Thirteen

For once, I beat Andy to making the coffee. I'd just started breakfast when he wandered in, hair tousled in the most endearing way.

"Good morning," I said, smiling at him.

He responded by pulling me to him for a hug and kissing the top of my head.

"I . . ." he started, and then trailed off.

"What?"

"Nothing really, I was just going to say that I could get used to this, waking up to you." He looked a bit wary after saying it. To be fair, I *had* pulled away nearly every time he'd tried to get closer. But the truth was, I could get used to this too. It felt good to wake up to him, to have someone to share morning coffee with, to have someone worry about me again.

"I hate to cut this short, but I have an early meeting and I didn't really prepare last night."

"No problem. Do you have time for eggs, or this a toast-only situation?"

"Toast only, I'm afraid."

"Coming right up," I put the eggs back in the fridge.

I put the bread in the toaster while Andy showered. Then I grabbed a notebook from the spare bedroom that serves as a home office of sorts and sat down at the kitchen table. Whether I wanted to be or not, I was in the middle of a murder investigation. The killer clearly thought I was involved, and if I wanted to get out of the crosshairs, I needed to start eliminating people from my list. I figured I could look into who had vandalized my truck without breaking my promise to Grady. Whoever had done that was also probably the person who killed Coach Griggs, and even if not, I still needed to know who was responsible. I opened the notebook and the notes app on my phone and started organizing my thoughts.

The list of things I *knew* was much shorter than my list of questions. I didn't even have a solid motive. I remembered the article I'd found in Dad's attic and wrote the question down. *Was Coach involved in something shady/illegal?* Motive seemed as good a place as any to get started. I did feel guilty though. Coach was the victim, but at the same time I knew that good people frequently make bad decisions. If I was going to look at the situation objectively, I needed to ask myself the hard questions. I tried to be open-minded, but found myself arriving at the same conclusion Grady seemed to be making: that the most logical suspect was Marvin Randall. He was the only intoxicated hunter they'd found that day, which didn't mean that someone else couldn't have killed Coach and escaped before we got there. But, more often than not, the simplest explanation is the answer.

I shook my head, frustrated that I had immediately started focusing on the murder instead of the vandalism. I started a new list; even though Darrin had probably already talked to

Lanie's neighbors, I needed to find out if they'd seen anything for myself.

A knock on the door jarred me out of my thoughts and I flinched at the noise. My reaction was more than my dog could muster. Banjo looked toward the door briefly before resuming his nap.

"Hey Boss?" came Tanner's voice from the front door. "Are you home?"

Normally, I would have told him to come on in, but the door was still locked because I hadn't been outside yet. I stepped over Banjo and answered the door.

"Where's your truck?"

I told him about the events of the previous evening as I ushered him inside.

"Wow, I'm sorry that happened." He shuffled from one foot to the other, uncharacteristically nervous.

"Everything okay?"

"Um, I was just wondering, um, if you'd had time to look over my proposal?"

"No, I haven't had a chance yet." I felt a pang of guilt when the expression on his face went from awkward and hopeful to genuinely hurt. "I have some time this morning though," I lied.

"Great!" His face lit back up like a marquee. "I'll just be outside if you have any questions."

"I haven't had a chance to look at financials yet either," I said as he turned to leave.

"I took the liberty of pulling that together too. I'll grab it out of my truck."

I weighed the idea of leaving all the things I hated doing—the feed orders, lesson scheduling, farrier scheduling, fund-raising, and worst of all paying the bills—to a manager, focusing on the things I loved instead. I would be free to add more lessons, ride more. Heck, I could even host some trail rides if I wanted to. I wasn't sure how we would swing paying Tanner any sort of fair wage though. I figured the only reason either of my employees agreed to the pay I was able to afford was because both of them still lived at home. Donations were winding down as life got back to normal after the media coverage surrounding Braydon Cunningham's arrest died down as well. The few lessons we scheduled every week weren't enough to sustain the rescue and were dependent on the weather. It was getting colder all the time, and I couldn't imagine any of the kids coming to lessons when the temperatures dipped to freezing or below.

I retrieved Tanner's proposal from my desk and sat back down at the table with my coffee. If I was brutally honest with myself, I had to admit that I was dismal at marketing. The positive attention after Braydon had tried to kill me was a happy accident. I'd been near bankruptcy when all that took place. And I would be right back there again if I didn't figure out better ways to draw in some steady income.

Tanner started talking the minute he walked back through the door. "I just pulled the last six months' worth of statements and receipts. I didn't think it would do any good to go back further."

He sat at the table across from me and turned the pages around to face me.

"If donations and lessons stay stagnant, we'll be in the red by April."

"And they won't. We'll lose lessons any time now as it gets colder," I said, giving voice to the very concerns I'd had a few moments ago.

"I've been brainstorming ways to bring in money that isn't dependent on weather or access to the rescue. It hit me when I was watching infomercials the other night."

"That we need gimmicky products?"

"Maybe," he grinned. "But what I was thinking about is sponsorships. Or virtual adoptions, whatever we want to call them."

I raised an eyebrow.

"People want to help, that's been evident from the uptick in donations. But a lot of people can't adopt an animal as big as a horse, and they can't always visit here. So, we can bring the horses to them, virtually. We can launch a website and offer video updates, a newsletter, personalized photo packages, just whatever in exchange for a subscription or monthly donation. We can sell calendars that feature the success stories of the ones who've found homes. The possibilities are endless." His eyes lit up as he spoke.

"Those are really good ideas," I said, and I meant it. He'd been thinking about the same things I was, but, unlike me, he'd come up with some great solutions.

"My biggest concern is that I can't guarantee income for you. I never know from one month to the next if we'll have enough to pay you and Ashley, and I can't expect you to live with your parents forever."

"I thought about that. Give me a year. Promote me to manager and let me see if I can expand enough to justify my position," he said firmly. His voice was confident, but his demeanor revealed his nervousness. He didn't look me in the eye, and was clasping his hands so tightly his knuckles had gone white.

I mulled it over. I hadn't considered the possibility of even having employees when I started the rescue, much less hiring a manager. But I'd never seen Tanner want anything as badly as he seemed to want this. And if he succeeded, then not only would we both win, the horses would too.

"Deal," I said, and extended my hand for a shake. "Consider yourself the official manager of Hillspring Horse Rescue."

He shook it so enthusiastically I had to brace myself.

"You won't be sorry, Boss. I promise."

"You can start by sorting out the feed and supplement order." I pulled a sheet out of my notebook where I had been scribbling some estimates. "We'll need to factor in Ruby on the alfalfa order and eventually on the feed and supplements too. I was planning to take inventory this morning."

"You got it." He beamed.

He bounced out the door about the time Andy emerged fully dressed for the office.

"Tanner is out early." He glanced out the window as he crossed the living room. "You're going to have to give that boy a raise."

"I just did."

"Really?" He paused as he packed up his laptop and files.

I showed him Tanner's proposal and gave him a quick run-down of its highlights.

"Those are really good ideas," he said as he passed the proposal back to me.

"That's what I said."

"Why don't you come to the office with me today?" He paused as he swung the handle of his laptop case over his shoulder. "You could bring Banjo and we could check on the car rental this afternoon."

I was momentarily struck speechless. Andy had never invited me to spend the day with him at work. Since everything I'm feeling is usually plastered all over my face, I'm sure he could tell I was having quite the mental debate.

"I just don't like the idea that someone followed you yesterday."

"I know. I don't like it either."

"But you're going to stay here."

"Yeah, I'm going to stay here."

"At least keep your phone with you and check in every once in a while."

I gave him the thumbs-up gesture and then made a show of grabbing my phone off the table. He kissed me, and bent to scratch Banjo's ears before he left.

I grabbed my laptop and went to work. I figured it wouldn't hurt to look into the names Patricia had given me. After all, one of them might be the one who vandalized my truck. It didn't take long to find out that Bruce Porter owned a car dealership just outside town, Auto-Nation. He smiled his thousand kilowatt, perfectly straight smile from the home page of their website. I'd driven by that lot but never really paid it much attention. I got up to find Tanner and tell him that I was going to run an errand, then realized I was stranded.

I called my insurance company and found out that they don't cover a rental on bargain rate policies like mine. I weighed my options. Renting a car gets expensive, especially when I wasn't sure how long the repairs on my truck would take. I could borrow Dad's little truck, but then would worry that he might need it and would be too stubborn to ask me to bring it back. Finally, I called the body shop and asked if they could expedite my repairs.

Randy Faraday of Randy's Towing and Randy's Repairs seemed to be a one-man show since he was also who answered the phone. He assured me he could have the tires on by this evening, but the paint would take longer. My white truck had *just* enough metal flake in the paint to make it a pain in the butt to match, so he needed to order the paint. He assured me that he could at least sand out the word so it wouldn't look as ominous if I needed to pick it up while I waited for the paint. I agreed, but that still left me without a vehicle for the rest of the day.

I refocused on my notes and Googled Ben Archer as well. There were several articles in the local paper about the basketball player who had been caught dealing drugs on school grounds and was turned in by his coach. He was sentenced to just under four years because he'd technically been an adult at the time of the crimes. I shuddered. Thinking about my Ginny or even Ashley or Tanner in that situation made my heart ache. But unless he'd been paroled or released early, he couldn't have killed Coach Griggs, because his sentence wasn't up yet. I knew that early release was a definite possibility though, and I started trying to find any information about his current whereabouts.

I'd gone down the equivalent of a warren of Internet rabbit holes when I finally gave up and closed my laptop. A quick glance at the clock on my kitchen wall told me I'd been engrossed in one search or another for over two hours. All of the scrolling had proved fruitful though. I found out that Ben Archer had been released on parole three months ago.

Chapter Fourteen

"Hey," I said as I opened the door to the stall Tanner was mucking out, "this is a weird question, but is there any way I can borrow your truck for an hour or so?"

Tanner looked like he was trying to process the question.

"I'm sorry to ask." I said, feeling very self-conscious.

"No, it's fine. I was planning to be here all day anyway." He leaned on the pitchfork handle. "Why don't I drive you?"

I hadn't considered that possibility. I stood there staring at him while the gears in my brain stripped the wheels.

"You're going to talk to those people on your list, right?" he said with a little half-grin. "It would be better than talking to a potential killer alone."

I opened my mouth to protest, but he didn't give me a chance.

"Your choice, Boss. Me and the truck are a package deal."

"Have you forgotten Heather and her shotgun?"

"Nope. And I haven't forgotten how I wished I'd been here when Braydon tried to kill you either." He glanced at his feet the way he does when he's uncomfortable.

"I'm glad you weren't," I said softly. "I know how fiercely loyal you are to me and the rescue, but I would never forgive myself if anything happened to you."

"Well, I feel the same way, so we seem to have a bit of a conundrum here." He looked up and held my gaze, but he squirmed a little as he did.

I'd watched this boy grow from a lanky, awkward teenager and was so proud of the man he was becoming. If I'd been blessed with a son, I'd want him to be just like Tanner. Though I'd like to think *my* son would be less stubborn and listen more to reason, but who am I kidding? He'd probably be worse.

He threw a couple more full pitchforks onto the wheelbarrow and then pulled it into the alley.

"I'll dump this and meet you at the truck."

I considered calling it all off and waiting until I had my own truck back, but there *was* a safe avenue of inquiry I could take. I could go back to the school and talk to Leslie Danvers, something I needed to do anyway in order to find out exactly what Coach was planning to present to the school board. Apparently it was enough to cause the parents of one of his players to have an angry confrontation with him in the school parking lot, so it might have been enough motive for murder. I remembered the article I found in Dad's attic and other news stories I'd read over the years. For example, there was the mom in Texas who tried to kill the mother of her daughter's cheerleading rival so the girl would be too grief-stricken to compete. Another case involved a father in Boston who had killed another parent over "rough play" at a youth soccer game. Recently, a father just across the state line in Missouri was charged with threatening to kill his son's coach.

I leaned against Tanner's truck and rubbed my leg. The throbbing had dulled to an annoying ache and a lot of the swelling had receded, but it still hurt when I stood for too long. I looked down the hill at the offending kicker. He looked like he could double for Black Beauty, with the sunlight gleaming off his jet-black coat. Even his thick winter hair was shiny, his *jet-black* winter hair. Dang it. That was going to stick. I might as well admit to myself I'd mentally named him Jet. I hated that his whole world had been turned upside down, the trauma of Coach likely having been killed either *while* he was riding him or at the very least in close proximity to him. And then not being returned to the home he knew. Even though he was being well fed and not abused, my heart ached because he was displaced and unwanted, even if he had kicked the thunder out of me.

"Load up, Boss," Tanner said as he closed the paddock gate.

I climbed into the passenger seat and pulled out my phone. I started to call the school, but then quickly decided that it might be better to just show up. People are less likely to tell you "no" if they're looking you in the eye.

"Where to?"

"The high school."

"I thought you already got Coach Griggs's stuff."

"I did, but I want to talk to the secretary again." I told him about Coach's confrontation with the angry parent and the planned proposal to the school board.

"Want to go all 'good cop, bad cop'?" He grinned. "I'll be the good cop."

I laughed in spite of my best efforts not to.

*   *   *

"This brings back memories," Tanner said as he pushed the buzzer beside the doors to the main entrance.

It took only a few seconds for Leslie to push the door open and look at us as though we were interrupting the Supreme Court or something. Her bird-like movements and long thin nose gave her entire persona an avian quality. She held the door open with her shoulder and wrung her hands the same way she'd done when I came to pick up Coach's things. Her mousy brown hair was pulled back in a severe bun, and not a single hair dared to escape its bonds. Her clothes, while still too big for her tiny frame, were more stylish this time. Her calf-length skirt was paired with a plain white blouse and a lovely knit cardigan.

"Did you forget something?" she asked, looking quickly from me to Tanner and back again.

"I was hoping to talk to you. I have a couple of questions."

"I'm very busy," she said as she stepped backward through the door.

I followed before she had the chance to close it, and Tanner took the cue to fall in line right behind me.

"I promise I won't take much of your time," I said, hating that I had to be the kind of pushy that I didn't like to deal with myself.

She crossed her arms and glanced back at the administration office.

"I just need to know more about the proposal Coach Griggs was going to present to the school board," I said with what I hoped was a reassuring smile. I'm not always sure, since my default facial expression seems to register on the angry/annoyed end of the spectrum.

"Oh," she said, her sharp features softening just a bit. "What do you want to know?"

She gestured for us to follow her into the office. It was a much more open design than I remembered from the old campus. The principal, vice-principal, and guidance counselor all had offices lining the back wall, only separated from the front reception area by glass walls. I'm sure the fishbowl effect was meant to convey accessibility, but I would hate never to have a minute's privacy. And I wondered how students would feel about coming to the guidance counselor if they were on full display to anyone passing by.

That thought was punctuated by the fact that Cameron Green could be seen having a rather animated discussion with the guidance counselor at that very moment. She pointed to some papers on her desk, and he gestured angrily and shook his head. The other offices were vacant.

"What exactly was his proposal?" I asked as Leslie situated herself behind the counter. "Mrs. Griggs told me that it would have affected how students qualify to play sports, but she wasn't clear on the details."

She pursed her lips and stared at me for a moment.

"Currently, our students have to meet an overall grade point average to qualify for extracurricular activities, including sports. Coach Griggs believed that they should meet the minimum grade in *every* subject in order to qualify."

"That's a bit odd, isn't it?" Tanner said, leaning on the counter in front of Leslie.

"How so?" she regarded him coolly.

"When I was playing football, I think Coach Davis would've done my homework *for* me to get me to qualify," Tanner said with a laugh. "It's just kind of weird that Coach Griggs would want a more restrictive policy."

"I don't pretend to know what his reasons were," Leslie snapped. "I just know that's what he intended to propose."

Tanner was unfazed. Although, to be fair, I've never seen much faze him.

"Do you know how many students the new policy would have affected?" I asked.

"I do not."

"Well, Bruce Porter sure thought it would affect his son," Cameron Green said as he left the counselor's office.

"Is that what they fought about in the parking lot?" I asked, watching him closely. There was something about Green that aggravated me. He could've offered me this information when I was there earlier.

"Oh, I don't know about that. I just know he'd been lobbying against it. He approached several of us teachers about opposing the proposal and asking if we'd go to the school board about it."

"Did you?"

"Did I what?"

I watched him for a beat, trying to decide if he was playing at being clueless or if he really was. He seemed to think that my attention was an invitation of some sorts. He sidled up to the counter beside me, ran his hand through his hair, and smiled broadly. I resisted the urge to back away.

"Did you go to the school board on Mr. Porter's behalf?"

"Oh. No. The school board hasn't met on the matter yet."

"*Would you* have gone to the school board?" I gritted my teeth slightly. If this schtick worked on other women, I couldn't for the life of me figure out why.

"I considered it," he said, still avoiding my questions.

I gave up on him and turned my attention back to Leslie. She was watching Cameron with the kind of adoration he seemed to expect.

"Will the proposal move forward now that Coach Griggs is . . ." my throat caught on the word, and I just let the question hang in the air.

"Not likely. At least not during *this* session."

If Bruce Porter's son would've been affected by the change, then killing Coach Griggs might have been the reprieve he needed.

"What grade is Porter Junior in?" Tanner asked from beside me, seemingly reading my mind.

"I'm not comfortable with this line of questioning anymore," Leslie said as she stood up from the desk. "I think you should both leave. Bruce Porter is an active member of our booster club and very helpful with the basketball program, and Noah Porter is a star athlete. These questions are not appropriate."

I glanced over at the guidance counselor's office. Her name plate on the door read "Johanna Vaughn." She looked stricken, and she wasn't paying any attention to the conversation taking place in the front. Her focus still seemed to be on the papers she had gestured toward while she was talking to Cameron. She shuffled through them and made notes as she did.

"No problem," I said, turning back to Leslie. "I just have one question for Johanna."

I made a beeline for Johanna's door before anyone could question or protest. I closed her door behind me, leaving Tanner at the desk with Leslie and Cameron. I gave him a little shrug. He nodded slightly in return and started talking to Leslie again.

"May I help you?" Johanna pulled a folder off a stack onto the papers she'd been studying.

"I'm so sorry to barge in here like this," I said, quickly taking the seat across from her. "I'm just trying to find out if Bruce Porter's son, Noah I believe, would have been affected by Coach Griggs's academic eligibility proposal?"

She looked from me to the front of the office. I turned slightly in my chair to follow her gaze. I locked eyes with Cameron and, just for a second, thought I caught him shaking his head.

"We don't give out any information about our students," she said firmly. "I think it would be best if you and your friend left now."

"Of course. Thank you for your time."

*   *   *

"You're going the wrong way," I said as Tanner pulled out and headed in the opposite direction from the rescue.

"We're going to talk to Bruce Porter now, right?"

"I'd rather not get you any more involved. Someone vandalized my truck, and I don't want anything like that to happen to you. Or worse."

"I *am* involved. There's safety in numbers. Besides, you don't think Mr. 'Best Deals in Northwest Arkansas' would murder us on his car lot, do you?"

"I'll bet Coach Griggs didn't think he'd get murdered either."

He didn't argue further, but he also didn't turn the truck around.

Chapter Fifteen

We pulled through the used-car side of the lot and Tanner parked in front of the office. We were met at the door by a young man about Tanner's age in a bright-blue polo shirt with the Auto Nation logo printed on the left side.

"Hey, long time no see," he said as he gave Tanner's hand a rough shake.

"Been a minute." Tanner grinned. Then, turning to me, he said, "Rory was our best wide receiver."

"That feels like a lifetime ago." Rory patted his middle. If he was heavier than he'd been in high school, it wasn't immediately obvious. "And Brynley's cooking has a way of staying with me."

"That's right. You two got married." Tanner nodded. "Guess I'm a little late on the congratulations."

Rory laughed, a good-natured, genuine laugh. "We didn't have a local ceremony. For some reason Brynley always wanted to do the Vegas thing, so that's what we did. Now, two kids later, I'm glad we saved the money."

"Wow," Tanner said, looking a bit horrified at the thought. "Two kids."

As Rory pulled out his wallet and opened it to a thick packet of photos, I ducked off to the glass office in the center of the dealership. The door was open, and I could hear Bruce Porter's booming voice halfway across the showroom, which featured a red Ford Raptor that I tried not to drool on as I passed by. I was surprised that no one headed me off before I got to his office, but no one seemed to notice me.

Bruce Porter held up a finger and nodded for me to sit down. I took the seat across from him. He seemed to be negotiating the terms of a fleet lease for what sounded like a security company. The sticking point sounded like the cost of window tint, which the person on the other end of the phone loudly proclaimed was crucial to their drivers' safety. I half-listened as I glanced around the office. It was sparsely decorated. No, scratch that; it wasn't decorated at all. There were no family photos, no knickknacks, no trophies, nothing. Just his big desk, a couple of filing cabinets, and a dry erase board that took up most of the back wall. The board featured salesmen's names, their sales numbers, and how far off they were from their weekly and monthly goals.

Bruce himself was just as sparse. He wore a nice but plain gray suit. His off-white button-down shirt was loose at the collar, and he didn't wear cufflinks. His sandy-blonde hair was cut short and neat. He wrapped up the call and then turned his blindingly white smile toward me like a weapon.

"Looking to trade that old Dodge in on something more sporty?"

"Not quite." I smiled back. "I was hoping to talk to you about Coach Griggs." I watched him closely, but there was nothing out of the ordinary. He did take on an appropriate look of concern, but there was no guilty fidgeting or aversion of gaze. Not that these absences ruled him out. He could just be innocent after all.

"What a tragedy," he said, shaking his head.

I nodded in agreement. "Did you know him well?"

"He coached my son for years," he said, squirming for the first time since I'd entered the office. "What did you want to talk about exactly? Are you here in some sort of official capacity?"

"Oh no, not official. I'm just trying to find out who might have vandalized my truck. As you can imagine, with an open investigation into Coach Griggs's death, the police aren't prioritizing a vandal. But whoever attacked my truck seems to think I know more than I do. I'm just playing catch-up."

"Well, this will be a quick visit then," he turned the smile back on again. "Because I don't know anything about the death or the vandalism."

"What did you argue about with Coach Griggs in the school parking lot?"

His smile faltered for a nanosecond. "How do you know about that?"

"He told his wife that you two had words, but he didn't get the chance to tell her what it was about. As you can imagine, in her grief she's suspicious of everything," I bluffed. I'm sure there was plenty of chance to mention it to Patricia, I just hoped he wouldn't think it through.

"It was about that stupid, short-sighted school-board proposal. But he told me he would consider revising it, so it wasn't so much an argument as it was a passionate discussion."

"Did you ask him to revise it?"

He laughed and leaned back in his chair. "No. I asked him to scrap it altogether."

"It wouldn't have made *that* much difference, would it?"

"It's not fair to these kids to switch policies in the middle of the school year. He was proposing that the new guidelines go into effect after Christmas break. That would have put some of them on immediate academic probation." The rest of his smile faded as he spoke.

"Was your son one of them?"

He narrowed his eyes, watching me as closely as I was watching him. I tried not to squirm under the scrutiny.

"Yes," he said finally. "Noah would have had to bring his history grade up. But if you're insinuating that I would fake a hunting accident to keep the proposal from going through, you're crazy. I was at a car auction all weekend anyway."

That would be an alibi Grady could easily verify. Just for a second I wondered how he knew that it looked like a hunting accident. Then I remembered that it had been front-page news, both online and in print, for days now. Just because I rarely read our local newspaper didn't mean no one else did.

"I'm not insinuating anything, Mr. Porter. I'm just trying to figure out what happened to my truck. And since a threat was carved into the door, it's pretty clear the two crimes are related." I leaned forward and took one of his business cards. "I'm sure you wouldn't mind telling the sheriff about your disagreement with Coach Griggs."

"No, of course not." He shook his head, but he didn't look as sure as he sounded.

"I appreciate your time."

I reached across the desk and shook his hand.

*   *   *

Tanner met me at his truck.

"Find out anything useful?"

"If he's telling the truth, then he has a pretty great alibi," I said as we both got in. I angled myself in the seat so I could prop up my aching leg just a little. The swelling was much better, but the ache hung on.

"Rory said Porter's been complaining about Coach Griggs since school started." He started the truck and pulled out onto the road. "He would rant about his son not getting enough court time, then turn around and rant that Coach wouldn't let him rest enough. Sounds like he was mad no matter what."

"That matches what Mrs. Griggs said too. She said Bruce Porter would call at all hours of the day and night to complain. Did Rory give you any indication if Porter has a tendency toward violence? Or if he hunts at all? I thought I might get a feel for him from his office, but that place was bare. Oddly bare, now that I think of it. There was *nothing* personal in there at all."

"Yeah, no clue if he hunts or not, but Rory did say he has a habit of throwing things in sales meetings. He likes to yell a lot too."

I was mulling that information over when my phone started ringing in my pocket. It was the auto body shop. My truck was ready, and though they'd buffed out the word "stop" that had been gouged into the driver's door, the matching paint was on back order, so it could be a few weeks before they could finish the repairs. Tanner dropped me off and cheerfully declared that he was heading back to the rescue to work on the website with Ashley.

After paying a ridiculous amount of money for new tires, I contemplated just getting a can of automotive spray paint to cover the spot and head off rust. My truck didn't have to be beautiful to serve its purpose. I also thought about looking into the cost of a decal for the rescue to cover it up, which might be cheaper too.

I had a million things at the rescue that needed attention, but decided I could spare a few minutes to stop in and see Lanie. We'd been missing each other a lot lately, and it occurred to me that I hadn't heard from her since my truck had been attacked in her parking lot. That wasn't like her at all.

Eve was on the phone when I came in, and she hooked her thumb toward the back. I nodded my understanding and walked through the doors marked "Employees Only."

Lanie was indeed at her desk, but she was packing her laptop and some files into her characteristically stylish leather tote.

"Hey," I said, thrilled to see her.

She looked up, but didn't greet me the way she usually did. In fact, she didn't greet me at all.

"Everything okay?" I asked as I watched her stuff more files into her tote.

"Wow," she said as she angrily slung the bag over her shoulder. "So you suddenly care?"

"What?"

"I've been trying for days, *days*, to have any sort of conversation with you. But you're always too wrapped up in your own orbit to notice."

Her words cut into me like a knife.

"That's why I'm here," I said slowly, quietly. "I know we've had trouble connecting lately . . ."

"*We* haven't had trouble, Mallory. Just you. The rest of the world is at your beck and call, but you can't make time for anyone else."

My first impulse was to be defensive, to tell her that I had just been busy, that life gets away from me, that I hadn't planned on Ruby being sick or getting kicked by a horse or finding a dead body. But all of it sounded hollow, like flimsy excuses that wouldn't hold back the flood of hurt she was obviously feeling. I stepped around the desk in an attempt to physically bridge the distance between us. She burst into tears.

"I know you've been dealing with a lot," she sobbed, "but so have I. And I can't handle anyone else's mess right now. I just can't." She adjusted her bag over her shoulder and put her hands up between us.

"You don't have to deal with my mess. I'm really sorry, Lanie." I tried to hold back the tears that threatened to flood down my own cheeks. "I want to be here for you. I want to hear everything you've tried to tell me for days now."

"I just need some distance," she said and angrily swiped the tears off her cheeks. "I'm going to stay with my sister for a few days."

"Oh God," I gasped. "Are you leaving Bill?"

"No, Mallory. I just need to get *away* from everyone and everything right now."

Chapter Sixteen

I felt gutted as I turned my truck toward home. The distance wasn't enough to get the sobbing out of my system, so I took the turn for Deadwood Lake instead of the one that would take me home. I knew Lanie was unhappy that we'd been missing each other, but I'd had no idea that I'd managed to ruin our friendship completely.

I pulled into the park and found a spot nestled in the pines at the back of the parking lot. I needed a secluded area where I could finish falling apart. In a spiral of self-destruction, which I told myself was self-reflection, I examined all of my recent failures: failing to tell Ginny about Andy, pushing Andy away every time he tried to get closer to me, being uncooperative and snappy with Grady.

I was still alternating between breathless sobbing and dissociative staring into the middle distance when my phone pinged with a text from Tanner.

Hey Boss. Been a while. U OK?

I sent him the thumbs-up emoji and then followed it with a *be home in a min* text. At least I didn't have to elaborate with Tanner. I fought the urge to call or text Lanie. The clingy, needy part of my personality wanted to flood her with apologies and try to make things right again, but I knew I had to let her have the space she'd asked for.

When I pulled into the drive, I angled my truck up the hill toward the unfinished quarantine pen so Tanner and Ashley could get out around it. They were huddled over Ashley's laptop on my front porch with Banjo curled up under her chair. He stretched and wagged his tail enthusiastically as I approached. Biscuit brayed his greeting from his spot on the hill behind the barn. At least I could count on not messing up with my animals. They forgave all my shortcomings.

"Wait until you see what we've come up with." Ashley waved me over as I climbed the steps.

She excitedly showed me the website they had designed for the rescue. I was instantly impressed. They'd included each horse's story with their intake and "after" photos. There was a page for lessons, complete with photos from our adorable clients. They took turns excitedly telling about their marketing ideas, which included an upcoming events page where we would outline the locations where we would be making appearances with one or more of the residents. They suggested that we bring Biscuit to the Farmers Market and let him work his charms for donations. Tanner also outlined his plan for the sponsorship program he'd included in his proposal. Sponsors would either pledge a small monthly donation or a one-time gift, and in return they would receive a Tanner original braided horsehair bracelet from the horse they chose to sponsor as well as monthly photos and updates.

"It's not live yet, we still have a little work to do, and I'd like you to get current photos of everyone," Ashley said. "I've e-mailed photo releases to all the parents, so I'll wait to publish any of those until I get them back. I just wanted you to see what it could look like."

Their enthusiasm was balm to my wounded heart.

"This is really brilliant."

Ashley beamed and Tanner looked slightly embarrassed.

"I'm glad you like it," she said.

"I've been meaning to start a website forever, but I've just never gotten it done. And this is better than anything I could've come up with." I scrolled through the pages again, and an idea started to percolate.

"I know you need to slow down a bit on the day-to-day stuff, but what do you think about running our website and social media pages? I'd love to have a social media presence, but I know I'd never keep up with it well enough to keep followers."

Ashley and Tanner exchanged knowing glances.

"We were just talking about that very thing. Tanner thought that would be a good way for me to stay involved. And I can work on it remotely from anywhere."

I smiled at Tanner. He was already making good decisions as manager.

My phone beeped its text-alert jingle and I jerked it out of my pocket hoping it was a text from Lanie. I stared at the message while my brain tried to make sense of the words.

You keep sticking your nose where it doesn't belong. That's going to get you and everyone you care about in big trouble. You can't watch them all the time.

*   *   *

"I doubt we'll be able to trace anything," Grady said, staring at the message on my phone with a fierce scowl. "But we'll try anyway."

I hugged myself. Between the creepy message and the attack on my truck I was thoroughly spooked. I'm sure that was their goal, and it frustrated me that they were succeeding.

"I don't think you should be alone."

I felt the gut punch of Lanie's absence again. I'd sent Tanner and Ashley home amid protests from both of them. Andy was stuck in a deposition but promised he would come straight to the rescue when he finished.

"They aren't really threatening me," I said, pointing to the message. "I'm mentioned, but it's more of a threat to everyone around me." *And that scared me more than anything.*

I shivered at the thought. The message was right. I couldn't watch them all the time. I couldn't make sure everyone was safe.

"It would be worth mentioning to your friends and family to stay vigilant."

I nodded.

"I'll let you know if we find out anything."

"Grady," I said as he turned to leave. I wasn't sure how to say what I wanted to say, so, true to my usual form, I just blurted out everything that popped into my brain. "I'm really sorry I've been so difficult. I know you're just doing your job, and I know I get in the way a lot."

"Where is this coming from?"

"I don't know," I lied, and shrugged. In spite of my best efforts to keep my emotions in check, a traitorous tear slid down my cheek.

"Hey," Grady took a step toward me and, much to my surprise, pulled me into his arms. "We'll get this guy. I've called in favors to try to speed up ballistics. It's going to be okay."

"It's not that," I said, hugging him back. Sometimes when he's in sheriff mode it's easy to forget our decades of shared history. "Lanie and I had a huge fight. And I feel guilty for being selfish and difficult."

"Well, I don't know anything about that. I just know that you and I are good. And if there's ever a time when that changes, I'll let you know." He patted my back, and I suddenly felt very self-conscious, gently pulling away.

"I'm sorry, I'm just an emotional mess."

"Stop being sorry. You can have emotions you know."

"Back to what you said earlier," I said, changing the subject. "You still think it was a hunting accident? That Marvin Randall shot Coach Griggs and then tried to cover it up?"

"That's what the evidence is telling me. We didn't have enough to hold him, but if the ballistics show what I think they will, then it's only a matter of time before he's behind bars."

"There are other people who have motives," I said, hoping I wasn't about to ruin another friendship. I told him about the school-board proposal and about talking to Bruce Porter. He listened patiently, but I could see his annoyance growing.

"No wonder they're warning you to keep your nose out of it. If it works, I'll start sending you creepy texts too."

"Oh *now* he grows a sense of humor," I teased, grateful to be back to our normal banter.

Grady scratched Banjo's ears before he left, warning me again on his way out the door to remain vigilant and stay out of his investigation.

I entertained the idea that he might be right, about all of it. Maybe I should stay out of the investigation, and maybe he *was* right about Marvin Randall, who had certainly been drunk enough to mistake a horse for a deer and then panic about what he'd done.

I screwed up my courage and sent a text message to Lanie warning her that those close to me had been threatened. I watched the message dots start and stop three times before they stopped completely and didn't come back. Sighing, I reached down and rubbed Banjo's head. He never got too far away from me if he could help it. He twisted and licked my hand, comforting me the best way he knew how.

I reached for the blanket I usually keep folded on the back of the sofa and remembered it was in the clothes hamper. Then I also remembered that I hadn't yet cleaned out the dryer from the morning Tanner had used it to dry Ruby's blanket. Groaning, I got to my feet and prepared to deal with what I knew was going to be an impressive mess.

*   *   *

As always in times of turmoil, I sought solace with the horses. My arms ached after scrubbing the dryer to make it suitable for human use again, and I vowed to attend to things like that in a more timely manner from then on. It was likely a hollow vow, because I know myself and my tendency to procrastinate. In my defense though, a lot had happened in the last few days, and I did have a good excuse for my forgetfulness, at least this time. On my way to the barn, I texted Andy, though he was probably still in the deposition he had scheduled that afternoon and wouldn't see it until he was finished.

Most of the little herd were grazing at the last blades of grass left on the hill above the barn. Biscuit seemed to be the only one to notice my presence. He brayed a greeting and then trotted down to meet me, his round belly jiggling with every step. I needed to cut back on his treats. He was just *so* convincing. I scratched his long ears and let him follow me down to check on Ruby.

She raised her head when I approached the fence, mouth still full of her soaked hay. She hadn't really been thrilled with the soggy mess, but I felt better knowing we were following Doc Brantley's orders to a tee. I stroked her soft nose and told her what a beautiful girl she was before she decided I had no food to offer her and went back to the hay.

Per his usual, Jet was pacing the fence in the lower paddock. I noticed that I referred to him as "Jet" every time I thought about him, and there was just no denying that's what I'd named him in my mind. He'd stopped whinnying desperately every time someone or something moved, but he was still focused on the rest of the horses. My heart ached for him all over again. I trudged down the hill, slowly and carefully on my achy leg, and tried to call him over to the gate. He tossed his head and trotted in circles, but showed no interest in being friendly. (Biscuit, on the other hand, was busily searching my pockets for any evidence of a hidden treat.) I wondered if Jet had bonded with Coach Griggs, or if he was just wary of everyone.

I gave Biscuit another vigorous scratching, then ventured into the paddock with Jet. I had no intention of adding another hoof-print bruise to my collection, but I couldn't stand him being isolated and unhappy either. I'd made a stupid mistake in getting kicked the first time, one I didn't intend to repeat. Maybe it was because I was feeling particularly isolated myself after finding out how Lanie felt, or maybe because I'd always been sensitive to feelings of loneliness: being an only child out in the middle of the country was often pretty lonely.

Jet was immediately on edge, high-headed and snorty. He tossed his head and trotted away from me, then turned back to snort at me again.

"Easy boy," I said, approaching slowly and deliberately while he continued to watch me like he thought I might eat him right there in the paddock.

He allowed me to get *almost* within reach, then just as I was about to touch his nose he threw his head back and tore off down the hill. Biscuit called after him with a scolding bray, trotting along the fence, belly and ears bouncing in time with his little legs. I considered leaving Jet to his paranoia, but I didn't want to reinforce his bad habits. I sighed and wished I hadn't started this when I was emotionally exhausted. My aching leg was just the cherry on top.

The lower paddock, which is also the smallest, lines the driveway at the top and then extends over a small limestone bluff before flattening out next to the main road. The lower half is rocky and steep and grows very little grass, so I don't use it a lot. And because it isn't used much, it doesn't have the nice, worn horse trails that crisscross the rest of the property. I could see Jet through the trees and brush at the bottom fence, pacing there like he'd done at the gate. I braced myself against the trees and picked my way slowly off the limestone ledge just in time for Jet to roll back on his haunches and launch past me like an Olympic eventing champion.

"Are you kidding me?"

I watched him charge up the hill, bucking occasionally as he went. I hesitated at the bottom of the ledge, trying to decide if it was worth aggravating my leg further to keep trying to catch him and ultimately decided it wasn't. I made my way to the bottom fence and hoped that the ancient, makeshift wire gate wouldn't disintegrate when I tried to open it. I didn't want to climb back up the hill in the paddock, opting instead to go down to the road and come back up the driveway.

After cursing myself for not clearing the lower fence row, and fighting through enough greenbriers to trap a sasquatch, I stumbled out into the paved road. I rounded the corner to grab my mail before tackling the climb back home and found a black truck parked off the road facing my driveway. A black truck with a dented front fender.

Chapter Seventeen

Grady had warned me that Marvin Randall drove an older F150 with a dented front fender. I knew instantly that I was looking at his truck, even before I could see him in the driver's seat through the open window.

"Hey!" I yelled toward the truck, and started jogging toward it as fast as I could, ignoring the increasing pain in my leg.

Marvin looked at me, threw the truck in reverse, and slung gravel in my direction as he made a U-turn into the road. I watched him swerve dangerously and then lose control, smashing into a sycamore on the bank of White Oak Creek. I stopped in my tracks for a second, but the nurse in me couldn't ignore that he might be injured, even if he had no business being there. Even if he'd been the one to kill Coach Griggs. He needed to be held accountable, and he had to be alive for that to happen.

I jogged down the middle of the road, calling 911 as I went. A plume of steam rose from his busted radiator. His air bag had deployed, and he was very still. I took a second and did a scene survey. It looked safe, so I opened the door as he started to stir. It groaned and crunched as the metal ground against twisted metal.

Marvin Randall turned to face me, his head and hands trembling.

"I'm . . . so . . . sorry," he said between gritted teeth. He attempted to get out of the truck and failed, causing us both to fall to the ground in a heap.

I quickly raised up on my knees defensively, but it was apparent that he was in no shape to attack anyone. His whole body was shaking uncontrollably.

"When was the last time you had anything to drink?" I asked.

He started crying, rolled onto his side in the dirt, and curled into the fetal position.

"When the sheriff told me . . . I killed that man . . . I don't remember nothing . . . I'm not ever going to drink again . . . Oh God! I killed someone!"

"So you quit drinking when Sheriff Sullivan took you in?" I suspected that Marvin was in the throes of delirium tremens from alcohol withdrawal.

"Yes," he sobbed.

"Okay, help is on the way." I looked him over the best I could in his current position. He had a nasty gash on his forehead, and I had nothing with me to stop the bleeding. I rocked back on my heels to stand up, and he suddenly grabbed my wrist.

"Please don't leave," he said, still sobbing and trembling. "I only came to ask . . . if you saw me . . . saw anything . . . that day in the woods. Did you? Did you . . . see me kill him?"

I looked into his pleading eyes. "I didn't see you before we met on the trail."

He looked even more anguished, curling in on himself again as he released his hold on my wrist. He started groaning and then lurched up onto his elbows, vomiting into the grass. I didn't know if it was the DTs or potential head trauma that was causing his nausea, I just knew that he needed help, and fast.

Almost as if on cue, I started to hear ambulance sirens in the distance.

"Hang on, they're almost here."

*   *   *

It didn't take the paramedics long to get him assessed and loaded up, leaving me to wait for Grady, again. Considering the number of times I'd had to call him recently, I felt like I should pay higher taxes or something. While I waited with Marvin Randall's truck, I clicked through my text messages. Andy still hadn't seen the message I sent him earlier: it still displayed Sent and not Read. I started to call Ginny, but she was far enough away that I felt she was safe. Then I suddenly realized I hadn't warned Patricia Griggs. I also wanted to know if she'd received any threatening calls or messages.

I dialed her number and listened to it ring until a message came on and told me that her voice mailbox was full. I followed it with a text asking her to call me back; this kind of information was best suited for a phone call rather than a text. I was about to dial her number again when the sheriff's SUV pulled in behind the truck, followed closely by Randy's Towing. Corporal Darrin Bailey looked through the truck while I filled Grady in on how I'd found Randall in the driveway.

When I'd finished, Grady scratched his chin and sighed.

"I hope you'll listen to me from here on out," he said. "I told you he was following you."

"I know it doesn't always look like it, but I *do* listen to you."

"I'll head to the hospital, talk to our friend Marvin."

"You'd better hurry. It wouldn't surprise me one bit if they don't ship him to a bigger facility, one with an ICU. He's in pretty bad shape."

He grunted in response, then turned to Darrin. "Finish with the truck. I'm going to run Mallory home."

Darrin nodded.

"I can walk," I offered, which Grady completely ignored. I didn't bother arguing, just followed him to the SUV and climbed in.

We didn't talk during the short drive to my house, and I didn't linger when he pulled in behind my truck.

"Thank you," I said as I pushed the door shut.

He gave me a chin lift in response, but his attention was focused on the call he was already making. I watched him disappear back down the road and then made a call of my own. Patricia Griggs's line went to her full mailbox again. I suddenly felt uneasy. I went into the house and grabbed my purse. Banjo whined after being neglected all day. I rubbed his impossibly soft ears and gave him a chew bone. Thankfully, he's easily distracted.

I sent another text to Andy. *Can't get ahold of Patricia. Worried after getting those awful texts . . . Might head over there.*

I waited to see if he would respond and talk me out of it. I gave him a full two minutes and then jumped in my truck. I tried to keep myself from speeding on the way to Patricia's house but failed miserably. My truck slid in the loose gravel in front of her house as I came to a stop. I couldn't explain the urgency I felt, but I knew it was warranted as soon as I saw her door swinging open in the breeze. I jumped out and ran for the porch. I could hear little Timmy barking with every breath inside.

I winced with every other step, but took the stairs two at a time anyway. I followed the frenzied yaps through the house toward the back porch. By the time I'd run through the house, I was thoroughly out of breath. I'd like to think it was more from pain than the fact that I'm woefully out of shape, but I doubt that was the case.

Timmy scratched at the back door with his tiny fuzzy feet, ignoring me. I opened the door, and he shot out like bullet, racing down the steps to Patricia, who lay crumpled at the bottom. I hurried down to her, afraid of the worst seeing the unnatural angles of all her limbs. I pressed my fingers into the side of her neck, feeling for the pulse in her carotid artery, and was pleasantly surprised to find it beating against my touch. From my angle beside her, I could also see her chest rising and falling reassuringly.

I pulled out my phone to dial 911 for the second time that day when I heard a motorcycle fire up in the direction of the barn. I told the dispatcher what I'd found and what services I needed while I circled the house and ran toward the barn, just in time to see someone in a black hoodie speed away on what looked like a dirt bike. I'm grossly uneducated about motorcycles, but that was my best guess.

"Hey!" I yelled as they sped through the yard and passed my truck.

Whoever it was, they never looked back.

*　　*　　*

I sat with Patricia and her bitey little dog while I waited for another ambulance, making sure that she continued to breathe and have a heartbeat and being careful not to move her until paramedics arrived with the necessary equipment to protect her spine and neck. I'd retrieved a quilt from the sofa to cover her and keep her warm. I wondered how long she'd been lying there, because whoever was on that bike had enough time to ransack most of the house. This was a fact I hadn't noticed right away, but in my quick search for something to keep Patricia warm, I saw that the cabinets had been emptied and every drawer in sight dumped on the floor. I carefully covered her up.

All the while Timmy was threatening to kill me from the ankles down. In between his snarls and yaps, I told Patricia to hang in there, that help was on the way, and that I wouldn't leave her. I held her hand in one of mine and tried to keep the tiny buzzsaw from eating me alive with the other one. When the paramedics arrived, Timmy's attention was at least divided so he was only trying to kill me part of the time.

Grady wasn't far behind the ambulance.

"What exactly possessed you to make a beeline over here?"

"Hello to you too," I said, trying to hide the fact that my hands were shaking. It was too late though. Grady doesn't miss much and he'd already noticed. And something about being *seen* gave my brain permission to dump all the feelings it had been holding at bay. Tears streamed down my cheeks, and I angrily swiped them away, furious that my default reaction to any strong emotion is to cry.

Grady softened slightly. Timmy had finally settled a bit in my arms, that is until Grady reached out to pet him, and then he turned into a little furry buzzsaw again. Grady pulled his hand back slowly.

"What caused you to race over here after I dropped you off?"

"I couldn't get ahold of her," I shrugged. "Nothing happened. I just needed to see if she was okay." My voice broke as I watched the ambulance leave, lights and sirens blaring.

"Start from the beginning. Tell me every detail."

Chapter Eighteen

Retelling yet another encounter to Grady left me utterly exhausted. It felt like all I'd done for days was tell Grady or Darrin about the latest disaster. The worst part of it all was that people kept getting hurt.

"Are you okay to drive?" Grady asked as he walked me to my truck.

"I'm fine," I lied.

He reached to open the door, and that set Timmy off again. I had almost forgotten I was carrying the little monster around. I hesitated, unsure of what to *do* with him. I couldn't leave him there. Grady's deputies would be searching through the house for hours, Patricia didn't have a yard, and I had no idea when their son was going to arrive. I put him in the front seat, and he used the opportunity to whirl around and snap at me.

"Stay!" I waggled a finger at him and shut the door.

"I need to go check on the horse," I told Grady. "Patricia told me their son is coming, but I don't know when he'll be here. I guess I'll take *that* home with me." I pointed toward the yapping fur ball in my truck.

"I'll go with you. Don't touch anything if it looks like it's been disturbed."

It turned out *disturbed* was an understatement. The barn had been *torn apart*. Even the feed bin had been dumped. The saddles and tack were strewn on the ground. The two saddle pads had been ripped apart, fleece scattered around like it had been thrown in every direction. The boards behind the feed bin had been pulled away from the supports and the tack room floor was in pieces. I wondered how one person could have possibly done all that damage.

"I can't get to the feed," I said, the shock catching up to me. I realized how stupid that sounded as soon as the words were out of my mouth, but suddenly I couldn't process everything that had happened over the last few days.

I braced myself against the fence and felt a soft nose against my forearm. Coach Griggs's big, chestnut gelding was nuzzling me with a gentleness that made my heart melt. I rubbed the big star on his forehead and leaned into his warm breath.

"We're going to have to process the whole barn," Grady said, snapping me back to reality. "You can't use that feed right now."

"I'll bring some over later then," I patted the horse again and wished I'd asked Patricia what his name was. "He still has some grass in the field. He'll be fine until I can get back with feed and hay."

"Don't worry about it. I'll make sure he's fed after we get the scene processed."

I checked the water trough and found it full. Grady alternated between talking on the phone and talking into his radio, so I didn't interrupt. I waved as I headed back to my truck, and he nodded back. I expected Timmy to attack me the minute I opened the truck door and braced myself for his tiny wrath, but he just growled halfheartedly from the passenger seat.

"It's okay," I told him. "Your mama is going to be fine."

*   *   *

Timmy bit me twice as I tried to extricate him from the truck and get him inside. The second assault drew blood, and I made a mental note to schedule my tetanus booster. Banjo met me at the door, bouncing up on his hind legs in an attempt to get a look at what I'd brought home, which started a whole new round of snarling and snapping from Timmy. I locked the doggy door, left Banjo in the house, and put Timmy in the backyard. He took a few steps, then turned around and glared at me until I went back into the house. I watched him from the back window, and as soon as I was out of sight, he started sniffing around some. I decided to leave him out there for a little while to give us both a break from one another while I washed my wound in the kitchen sink.

I'd called Tanner on the way home, filled him in on the latest developments, and tried to talk him into staying home until this all blew over, but I knew I was wasting my breath. He adamantly refused. I'd also left a voicemail for Andy when I hung up with Tanner. By the time Andy called me back, my finger was throbbing in time with my leg.

"I'm coming over right now," he said, and I could hear road noises over the line. "Lock your doors and just stay put, *please*."

I made an affirmative noise. I hadn't even told him about Patricia yet.

*   *   *

"I can't leave you alone at all, can I?" Andy grinned as he refilled my wine glass.

I managed a halfhearted smile in response. He'd listened patiently while I told him about my crazy, traumatic day.

"Sorry, bad joke."

"I'm just exhausted," I said, settling into the crook of his arm. "And I miss Lanie."

Timmy growled when I moved, growled at *any* movement. I'd brought him inside before Andy arrived and he'd promptly attacked Banjo, who didn't have a violent bone in his body and had no idea how to handle his tiny fluffy assailant. I finally got them separated without further injury to me or either dog and settled Timmy into a box where he could feel secure. I cut a door in the side so he could come and go freely, and I did *not* look forward to taking him outside later.

"I don't know Lanie as well as you do, but I'm sure this will blow over." Andy rubbed my arm as he spoke.

"I'm not so sure," I said around the lump in my throat. "I think I've really screwed things up."

"You didn't mean to ignore her. You've been dealing with a *lot*."

"She's right though. I've taken her for granted, leaning on her every time I need a friend, and I'm never there for her. Not really, not like she is for me. I've been selfish, and not just with her. I just about ruined everything with you too." My voice cracked and I turned to wrap my arms around his waist.

"You didn't. I'm not that easy to run off." He kissed the top of my head. "Even though that makes me sound like a creepy stalker."

I laughed and he squeezed me again.

I started telling him about what I'd found out about Ben Archer and Bruce and Noah Porter, but I must have dozed off, because the next thing I knew sunlight was boring into my skull through my closed eyelids. Andy had covered me with the quilt I keep on the back of the sofa, and at some point during the night Timmy had curled up next to me, all snuggled in. Asleep, he didn't look like a snappy little demon. I hated to disturb him, but I don't think I'd moved all night and my whole body was stiff and achy. As soon as I sat up, he started growling again, but he wagged his little stump of a tail. I talked softly to him as I coaxed my joints into an upright position. I felt like my jeans had nearly cut me in two while I slept. It might be fine for skinny girls to sleep in jeans that are already a bit snug, but my little roll of belly fat was *not* happy with the lack of proper pajamas.

It didn't take much encouragement to get Timmy to follow me outside. Banjo gave him a wide berth. My sweet dog was used to me bringing home random fosters of all species. But this was the first one he hadn't instantly won over, and that included the baby bobcat Tanner had found tangled in hay wrap on his parent's farm. Banjo did his business quickly and then followed me back inside. I left Timmy outside to allow him a little privacy.

I texted Grady to see if he knew how Patricia was doing. I knew that I wouldn't be able to find out anything if I called the hospital because I wasn't family. I was worried because, as a nurse, I knew that head trauma causing a loss of consciousness as long as hers is a very serious thing and her prognosis would be guarded.

I showered in the guest bathroom so I wouldn't wake Andy before his alarm went off. Thankfully, my procrastination with the laundry had paid off and I had clean clothes in the dryer. I pulled on a set of comfy sweats and settled on the sofa with my phone and notebook. Rest had invigorated me and the sense of dread and defeat I'd felt yesterday was replaced with determination and focus.

I'd previously only had the most tenuous idea of where to start with Coach Griggs's murder—hadn't even really been one hundred percent convinced he *had* been murdered. But the vandalism of my truck, the creepy text, and finding Patricia like that solidified the knowledge that his death had not been accidental. There was also no way that Marvin Randall was responsible for his death, not when I looked at the totality of the evidence. Whoever killed Coach Griggs was looking for something, first on his body and then, when they didn't find it there, in his house and barn. I had to wonder if they'd found what they were looking for.

I picked up my phone to call Lanie, knowing that she's an early riser and needing someone to bounce ideas off of, then felt a pang in my belly when I remembered I couldn't call her. I wasn't going to let years of friendship go without a fight though, so I texted her instead.

I'm so sorry, Lane. I'll figure out a way to make it up to you. I love you my friend.

I clicked out of the messaging app. I didn't want to see if she opened it or not. I opened up my Facebook app. It was unlikely that Bruce Porter had killed Coach Griggs, but I hadn't ruled him out completely; he just seemed like a lower priority until proven otherwise. Whoever had been on that dirt bike had been smaller than Bruce Porter, slender and long-limbed. I added Noah Porter to my list of possible suspects. Just because it had been Bruce who argued with Coach Griggs in the parking lot didn't mean that Noah wasn't the killer.

I searched his social media accounts and found his Facebook account locked down to just his profile photo. Instagram, however, was a treasure trove. He took a selfie nearly everywhere he went, multiple times a day. On the Saturday when Coach Griggs was killed, his selfies included another boy and a girl in a series of photos at Silver Dollar City. From the time stamps on the photos it appeared that they had spent all day there. I put a question mark by his name. He could have scheduled the photos to post on that day. There was no way to tell when the photos were really taken. Instagram deletes the metadata attached to photos when they're uploaded. I learned that from a malpractice case we'd investigated at my former law firm when the physician we were investigating tried to prove that he was home with his family the night before he botched a surgery and not out doing lines of cocaine with his former frat buddies. He'd used an Instagram photo to try to prove it, and our tech team couldn't prove that the photo wasn't taken that night because the metadata had been erased. Luckily, there was more evidence that led to his conviction.

I started a new list of things I needed to talk to Grady about, the first being whether or not Noah was actually at the theme park on that fateful Saturday. Then I turned my attention to the next name on my list. I searched for "Ben Archer" and "Benjamin Archer," but nothing came up in our area for anyone that looked like the mugshot I'd already found. Stalking people on social media was easier before Facebook updated their privacy settings, which overall was a good thing of course. But it made research and investigating a bit tougher, especially when I no longer had access to any of the databases and resources I'd had when I was a legal nurse consultant. Granted, I hadn't typically work on murder investigations, focusing instead on malpractice and insurance fraud. I hoped that what I'd learned about investigating would serve me again. I didn't find him on Instagram or Twitter either.

I stretched and decided to take a break while I made a pot of coffee. I was just finishing up when I heard a little yap at the back door. I'd completely forgotten Patricia's poor little dog in the backyard. I hurried to open the door. Timmy rushed past me and made a dash for his box.

"Hey. Little Buddy, are you hungry?"

His ears perked up. I fixed Banjo's breakfast and took him outside so he could eat it in peace, suspecting that Timmy was probably food aggressive in addition to all the other ways he was aggressive. With Banjo safely outside, I served Timmy his breakfast. Much to my surprise, he dug right in, gulping the food like he was really enjoying it. I'd half expected him to be finicky. After he finished his food, he retreated to his box and curled up. For all his bluster and aggression, he seemed to be settling in fairly well.

I turned as I heard Andy yawn behind me.

"Good morning," I said, happy to lean into his arms.

"I hope you were comfortable. I couldn't bring myself to wake you last night."

"I slept like a log. I guess I needed the rest."

"I'm going to work from here today." He tightened his hold on me just a little. "If you don't mind."

"I'll be fine if you need to go in to the office. Tanner should be here anytime."

"I thought you sent everyone home?"

"You know Tanner. He wouldn't agree to stay home. And it was enough of a battle to just get him to leave for the night."

I pulled the towel off my head and started the task of trying to tame my wet curls. I decided that I would just pull it back in my signature ponytail. After all, I'm a creature of habit, and if anyone saw me with styled hair, they'd probably think I'd been replaced with an alien clone.

"Still, I'd rather be here today, if that's okay."

"You can't work from home until this investigation is over."

"Let's just take it one day at a time."

I hesitated for a moment. I wanted to find Ben Archer and I wanted to identify the two kids in the photos with Noah Porter. If their social media posts corresponded with his, then he probably really had been at the theme park. I was afraid Andy would try to talk me out of it, but the truth was that he hadn't *ever* chastised me or second-guessed me for poking around. He'd always just been supportive and helpful.

"I'm going to try to find Ben Archer," I blurted out.

He watched me for a moment like he was waiting for me to say more.

"I figured you would," he said when I didn't. "Nothing I could say, or Grady, or anyone else, has ever stopped you, and I'm not so deluded that I think you'd start now."

"Oh," was all I could manage.

I've always been *aware* of my faults and flaws, but until the last few days, I'd always thought I was better at hiding, or at least managing them. But Lanie had confronted me with my tendency to be self-absorbed and Andy was pointing out my stubbornness. I felt raw, exposed, and vulnerable.

"That sounded far angrier than I meant for it to," Andy must've seen the look on my face. "I just meant I know what you're up to and I'm not going to try to talk you out of it."

"Because it wouldn't do any good anyway," I said, quietly. Even though I knew they were both right, I still felt the sting of being confronted with my shortcomings.

"I'm sorry. I didn't mean to hurt your feelings."

I nodded. I knew he didn't mean to, but I couldn't turn the hurt off like a switch either. I hugged him, to comfort us both.

*   *   *

Tanner pulled in behind my truck just as I opened the paddock gate. Biscuit started honking with renewed vigor at the arrival of one of his favorite people. I waved my hello and my phone dinged with a text message.

It was Lanie.

You don't have to make it up to me. I'm mad at you, and I need some time to get myself together, but we'll work it out. I just don't have any room for anything except my own stuff right now.

I nearly jumped from sheer joy. She could be mad at me. Hell, *I* was mad at me, but she wasn't *done* with me. I typed back with giddy, shaking thumbs.

I'm here when you're ready. If there's ANYTHING I can do to help, I'll drop everything, I promise.

She read it but didn't respond. But that was okay. She'd reached out and that was enough.

"Boss," Tanner said with an urgency that snapped me out of my elation. "I have news."

Chapter Nineteen

"After we saw him at the dealership, Rory insisted I come over for dinner to meet his wife and kids, and he wouldn't take no for an answer. I'm glad he didn't, because I found out Bruce Porter wasn't at the car auction like he told you he was." Tanner fidgeted as he spoke, barely able to contain his excitement.

"How does he know that?" I could barely contain myself either. Buoyed by Lanie's reassurance, I felt revitalized. "Porter is too cheap to hire an assistant, so he farms out the secretarial duties to the salesmen. Rory is in charge of processing expenses. There weren't any receipts from that weekend from the auction, not from Porter, anyway. He sent another salesman, Anthony Decker, to the auction. The only receipts from Porter that weekend were here, in Hillspring. He turned in a gas station receipt and a restaurant receipt, both labeled 'networking expenses.'"

"That's interesting," I said, the gears already spinning in my brain. "How did you get him to share all that?" I was duly impressed.

"It didn't really take any effort. Two beers in and he started ranting about what a cheap jerk Porter is but he can't afford to quit because the commission is so good. That's the kicker here, we can't let on where this information came from. I can't cause him to lose his job."

I nodded. "Did he happen to tell you whether Mr. Porter hunts or not?"

"Not exactly, but he showed me Porter's Facebook post from last Christmas. Apparently, he told the employees the dealership was barely scraping by and he couldn't afford their usual bonuses, then turned right around and posted a picture of his family's new indoor pool."

I tilted my head and blinked, trying to figure out what Christmas had to do with hunting. Tanner must've noticed, because he added, "When he was scrolling back through Porter's posts, I saw several pictures of him posing with his kills."

"Why would he lie about something like that? It would be really easy to prove he wasn't there."

"My guess? He just didn't take you seriously. He figured he could tell you anything and you wouldn't have any way to check up on him." Tanner shrugged. "That, or he just panicked and blurted out the first lie he could think of."

Biscuit seemed to have decided that he wasn't getting enough of our attention and wiggled his way in between us. We both doubled our efforts to find all his itchy spots.

"That's not all," Tanner said as he rubbed the donkey's little chest. Biscuit clearly appreciated the extra effort, turning his head and flopping his lower lip. "He told Rory to order flowers for Patricia Griggs and then insisted that he would deliver them himself."

"You think he used that as an excuse to attack her?" I shook my head. "The person I saw on the dirt bike was smaller than Bruce Porter. I know I didn't get a great look, but I'm sure of that."

"So, Noah Porter then?"

"Maybe."

We went around feeding and mucking, taking frequent breaks to give Biscuit the attention he seemed to think he needed more than food or air. All the while, I was trying to figure out how to use the information Tanner found out without betraying his promise to Rory.

I sat down on a bale of hay outside Ruby's stall and tried to pull up Bruce Porter's Facebook page. It was private. Rory must've been on his friends list. I'm not sure what I thought I would find there, but at least it made me feel like I was doing something.

"Why don't we follow him?" Tanner said as he opened Ruby's stall door.

"What?"

Ruby almost shoved her head into the halter. She didn't seem to enjoy being in the barn, and her favorite part of the day was being turned out in the little pen below it.

"We could follow Porter and see if he tries anything." Tanner shrugged. "I've been thinking about it. He has motive, right? Even if it wasn't him, he could want to protect his son."

"You don't think it's a bit of a stretch for him to *murder* someone over high school basketball?"

"I know I played football, but I'll bet basketball is pretty much the same. And what I know of high school sports, I'm surprised people aren't murdered more often. Some of those parents took it all *way* too seriously."

I knew he was right. Ruby nudged him gently with her nose, trying to urge him through the door.

"I better take her out," he laughed. "But I'll stick around today, and we can start watching Porter tonight. If he or Noah was desperate enough to kill and then hurt Patricia looking for something, they're not going to stop until they find it."

"I don't think that's a good idea," I said, using the stall door to pull myself up. "Besides, we don't really have anything solid pointing to him. I haven't found Ben Archer yet, and Patricia seemed to think he was important enough to mention."

"So, let's find him today and watch Porter tonight," he called back over his shoulder.

I spent the entire time while we finished the morning chores trying to talk Tanner out of it. We were still arguing about it when he followed me to the house to finalize the feed and supplement order. Timmy took particular exception to yet another person intruding into his general vicinity and barked ferociously from the safety of his box. When he realized that Tanner wasn't going anywhere, he turned around in a few circles and settled for grumbling occasionally.

"With all due respect, Boss, I'll just go alone if you don't want to go with me."

"It is *not* that I don't want to go with you. It's that I don't want you to go at all!"

When I turned around, Andy was leaning against the wall in the short hall, an amused smirk on his face. Tanner and I took turns pleading our cases to Andy, who listened patiently, nodding or making affirmative noises every so often. When we both ran out of steam, he held his hands up, either to keep us quiet or in surrender, I wasn't sure which.

"It seems to me that I'm best suited to find out where Ben Archer might be. I have a few connections I can call on and I'd be more comfortable talking to him myself."

I stared at him for a moment while it sank in.

"You're on board with this?"

"I feel like this is probably the least of the evils." Andy looked from me to Tanner. "I'm not thrilled about the idea of you two pulling an amateur stakeout, but talking either of you out of *anything* is an exercise in futility."

Tanner grinned. I wasn't sure whether to be flattered or insulted.

"What if we're focusing on the wrong person? I'm almost certain it wasn't Bruce Porter on that dirt bike."

"It could've been someone he hired," Tanner interjected. "Or it could've been Noah. Either way, keeping an eye on the two of them seems to be a pretty good idea right now."

"How are we going to watch both of them?"

"You can follow Noah and I'll follow Porter. When they go home, we can meet up and join our efforts." Tanner said this so matter-of-factly that you'd think he was an old pro.

"I'm not comfortable following a kid," I said, even though Noah looked more like the person I'd seen than his father. "That just doesn't feel right."

"Okay then, we'll go together. Safety in numbers and all that."

The rest of the day went faster than I thought it would. It's easy to stay busy when there are animals that need tending. Between the two of us, we managed to catch Jet and successfully integrate him into the little herd with minimal squealing and little general nonsense. He seemed more relaxed with the other horses, even though Biscuit hadn't fully warmed to him yet and kept pinning his long ears at him whenever he strayed too near. After that, we picked up where we'd left off with the quarantine pen and made good progress. It would take only a few more workdays to have it ready for use.

By the time we were supposed to leave, I was exhausted. I wanted to get cleaned up, at least a little, before I left. Not that anyone was supposed to see me if I was following a suspect, but I wasn't sure even I wanted to be cooped up in a truck with me if I didn't clean up a little. I washed quickly and found Andy and Tanner waiting for me in the living room when I came out.

"Good, I'm glad you're both here," I said when both sets of eyes turned toward me.

I grabbed my notebook off the counter and motioned for them to follow me to the table. I wanted to talk through everything again since they both seemed so eager to jump in. One thing I knew from my past as a legal nurse consultant was that collaboration and review of evidence were extremely important.

"Nothing adds up or points in any one direction," I said as I opened the notebook. "It could have been *anyone* in those woods that day."

"The initial evidence supports the theory that it was a hunting accident," Andy said. "And you said Grady told you the caliber matched Marvin Randall's rifle, right? So, the theory makes sense that he killed Mr. Griggs, panicked, then tried to hide the body and the orange vest."

"But that doesn't explain why Coach had so much weird stuff hidden on his saddle and tack and why someone would break into his house, attack his widow, and ransack the place," Tanner said, leaning forward and pointing to my notes.

"No, it doesn't," Andy conceded. "But we don't have a clear motive for anything but an accident either."

"The only motive we've been able to find so far is the feud between Coach and Bruce Porter over the policy proposal," I chimed in. "I know Ben Archer threatened Coach when he was caught, but to wait years to exact revenge?"

"Which is just one more reason we need to see what Porter and his son are up to." Tanner sat back and crossed his arms like the matter was settled.

"We'll see what he has to say. I'm meeting Mr. Archer for drinks when he gets off work." Andy glanced at his watch. "And if I'm going to be on time, I'd better get going."

I nodded, impressed that he'd already found Ben Archer.

"How did you find him?" I asked, feeling torn. I wanted so badly to sit in on that meeting.

"I'll fill you in on everything when I get back." He stood up and kissed me on the top of my head. "Be careful. Please."

"I could just go with you," I said. "I don't think we need to watch Bruce Porter. There's no way he was on that dirt bike."

"Ben Archer *is* an ex-con." Tanner said. "Maybe we should all go."

*   *   *

Our ill-conceived stakeout plan was quickly abandoned in favor of accompanying Andy to Fayetteville to meet with Ben Archer. He worked at an Agri-Dyne processing plant and was planning to meet Andy at Buffalo Wild Wings for drinks. Andy had a connection in parole who had put him in contact with Ben.

"He sounded genuinely upset that Coach Griggs was killed," Andy said as we pulled into the parking lot.

"Maybe he's a good actor," Tanner said from the back seat. "You guys go in first and I'll follow in a few minutes. I'll sit close, but not so close it's obvious."

Andy and I exchanged smiles.

"Sure thing," Andy said over his shoulder as he got out.

I scanned the bar as soon as we entered, but didn't see anyone who resembled the mugshot I'd Googled again on the way over. We sat and ordered, a light beer for Andy and a Primo Margarita for me. The smell of the wings made my stomach growl. I could eat my weight in chicken wings, and that would be—well—a lot of wings.

I was still trying to decide whether it would be weird to order some teriyaki wings when Andy elbowed me and directed my attention to a young man staring at us from the end of the bar. His gaze didn't waver when we both looked up at him. He just continued to sip his bottled beer and watch us.

He looked nothing like his mugshot, except for the piercing black-brown eyes. His hair was longer and pulled back in a low ponytail and he wore a long, full beard. His arms were fully sleeved in black tattoos; the only one I could make out at that distance was a huge cross on his right forearm. He drained the rest of the bottle, got up, and walked toward us. He held out a hand as he approached and Andy shook it.

"Andrew Hannigan. This is Mallory Martin."

"You found him?" he asked as he gestured to a table.

We took the table next to Tanner, who was doing a miserable job of being inconspicuous. He stared too long, snapped his head around like he'd been electrocuted when Ben glanced in his direction, and attempted to hide behind a menu that the server was trying to retrieve from him. It was a really lucky thing Ben didn't seem at all concerned with anyone else.

"I did."

He flagged a server over and ordered another beer.

"Everything that's happened to me is because of him." He said quietly, and clasped his hands in front of him on the table.

Chapter Twenty

I'd braced myself for anger, resentment, and a hatred that had been simmering in jail over the last few years. I was wrong.

"If he had *just* turned me in, I might have turned out vastly different. But he didn't." Tears welled in Ben's eyes as he spoke. "He came to see me regularly, even when I was still furious with him. Even when I was awful to him. He was a steadier presence than any of my family. They wrote me off after I was convicted."

I was touched by how fondly he spoke of Coach Griggs, but I also found myself wondering why Patricia didn't know any of this. Ben's name was the first one she'd given me when I asked who might want to hurt Coach. Like Tanner had suggested earlier, he could've just been a really good actor.

"You can imagine our initial skepticism after your threat in court. And then for Douglas Griggs to end up dead so soon after your release," Andy said, quietly but firmly. I'd seen him switch on Attorney Mode when he represented me, but I never got tired of watching him in action. He was normally so quiet, gentle, and understated that it was fascinating to watch his edges sharpen and the softness harden.

"No, I get it," Ben replied. He didn't seem offended at all. "I said some horrible things, only half of which were recorded. But I owe my life to that man. If there's anything I can do to help, I'll do it. I was at work the day he was killed, and I'll sign anything you need to look at the security footage."

If it was a bluff, it was an impressive one. I couldn't imagine how he could fake his employer's security footage. I still wondered, though, why Patricia had named him so quickly.

"I'm sure Sheriff Sullivan will want to take a look at that. And I'm sure he'll appreciate your cooperation," Andy said.

"Like I said, I'll do anything to help."

I decided this would be a good time to jump in. "Why did Coach Griggs's wife still think you might hurt him? If he visited you and kept in touch, why did she think you might be responsible for his death?"

"All I know is what he told me. He said she didn't believe I was sincere, that I was just playing him to get what I wanted."

"What did she think you wanted?" I asked.

"I don't really know. He gave me a little money here and there, so I could get socks and stuff. Not anything that ever amounted to much. It meant a lot to me, and still does, but it didn't break the bank or anything." Ben took another long swig of his beer.

"I think I reminded him of his boy," Ben said thoughtfully as he picked at the label on the bottle. "He overdosed, you know? And I think he wanted to sort of save me, since he couldn't save his son."

I hadn't known that Coach Griggs had lost a child. My heart ached for him. Just imagining that sort of loss took my breath away and made my rib cage feel tight.

"Patricia was his second wife." Ben was still picking at the label. "I didn't get the impression he bonded real tight with her kid."

I was beginning to realize just how little I knew about Coach Griggs. He'd treated me much the same way that he'd treated Ben, kind of taken me under his wing when I was struggling and helped me far more than he was obligated to; not that failing math is similar to getting caught dealing drugs. But we hadn't kept in touch over the years, and I couldn't even remember if he was married to Patricia when I was a student or not. I assumed he wasn't, since I'd just found out he had a *first* wife, but I didn't know that for sure.

"Can you think of anyone who might have wanted to hurt him? Did he share anything with you about being threatened or anything like that?" I asked, just throwing out a wide net to see if it caught anything.

"No, but I wouldn't know. I hadn't seen him since they released me," Ben looked at me as he spoke, but he was still working on that label. "He did say something odd though, during one of his last visits."

I waited for him to elaborate.

"What was that?" Andy finally gave up and asked.

"He asked me if any of the teachers had been doing anything illegal while I was there."

"Like what?" I asked.

"He didn't say, just asked me if I knew if anything was going on."

Andy and I looked at each other. Ben didn't seem to want to continue unprompted.

"What did you tell him?" I asked.

For the first time, Ben looked nervous. He shifted in his chair and glanced around the restaurant.

"Do you think what I told him got him killed?" He asked Andy.

"It honestly looks like hunting accident," Andy said, which wasn't entirely dishonest. It did *look* like an accident, even if only by design. "We're just following up on a few things to be thorough."

I wondered what Andy told him to get him to meet with him. Were we impersonating police officers?

Ben leaned in conspiratorially and whispered, "I told him there was a rumor that if you were failing a certain class, you could pay the teacher for a grade boost and bring your average up—you know, if you needed to play sports or something."

"Was the rumor true?" Andy asked.

Ben shrugged. "Who knows? Could've just been kids talking crap."

"Who was the teacher?" I asked.

"Look, I don't want to hurt anyone with a stupid rumor." Ben waved the server over and requested another beer.

"Did you tell Coach Griggs who was rumored to be the teacher?" I asked.

"Yes."

"Who was it?" Andy asked him again.

The server arrived with Ben's third beer. He took a long sip and looked from Andy to me.

"I understand that you don't want to spread unfounded rumors. I can promise that we'll be as discreet as possible with the information. I'm not interested in hurting anyone's reputation either," I said, and I meant it. I'd been on the receiving end of harmful rumors not that long ago.

"Coach Griggs," he said quietly as he attacked the label on the new bottle. "The rumor was about him. But it didn't make much sense because it was after he retired, and I don't know how he was supposed to change anyone's grades. I always kind of thought someone started that rumor to throw off suspicion from someone else."

"So, you think the rumor was true?"

"All I know is that it wasn't Coach Griggs. But some kids who could barely pass anything didn't have any trouble getting their average high enough to play sports. At least the kids with money, anyway."

We thanked him for his time. Andy paid our tab, gave Ben his card, and told him to contact us if he thought of anything else that might help. I looked longingly at an elderly gentleman's plate of hot wings on my way out the door, but I didn't think it was the right time to order some for myself.

The drive home seemed to take twice as long as it had on the way to meet Ben. Maybe it was anticipation of what we might find out or apprehension about his character that had made the distance seem shorter. I'd been lost in thought most of the way home, while Andy and Tanner discussed everything from football to hoof care.

"What if it *was* Coach Griggs who was selling grades?" I blurted out, my thoughts bursting out into reality.

"That might explain why someone wanted to keep him quiet," Tanner said from the backseat. "And why someone was willing to hurt Mrs. Griggs to hide the evidence."

"Maybe we can use that to force the killer into the open," I said, looking nervously from Andy to Tanner.

"What do you mean?" Andy asked.

"We could ask Bruce and Noah Porter if they'd heard that rumor. If either of them is guilty, he might panic and incriminate himself."

"Or he could panic and try to shut up the next threat," Andy said, shaking his head.

"It might be better than just trying to follow them blindly, hoping they do something out of the ordinary."

Andy opened his mouth to say something, but my phone rang before he could speak

It was Ashley.

"Hello Ash—"

"Mal, someone cut the fences and let the horses out," she said breathlessly. "We've got them all back but Jet. Biscuit won't let anyone in the barn, but we put enough of the fence back together to keep them in the front paddock."

"Is everyone okay?" More than a little panic crept into my voice.

Andy glanced at me, concerned. Tanner leaned forward to try to hear the conversation. I switched the call to speakerphone.

"They're all freaked out and Biscuit won't let anyone in the paddock but me, but everyone seems alright. I can't find Jet anywhere though. Luis, Jeff, and Lexie came over to help, and Luis has headed out on horseback to try to find him. There are hoofprints everywhere, so it's hard to tell which direction he might have gone."

The thought of Luis out in the dark, trying to find a black horse, caused my chest to feel tight.

"Philip?" Tanner asked.

Philip had been a problem for my late neighbor, Albert Cunningham, and then later for me as well. He had cut Albert's fences, trespassed, and harassed him until Albert filed for a restraining order. I'd had to do the same, and honestly, I hadn't seen any sign that he'd been back on my property since he was served with the protective order. The thought that he'd been lurking around this whole time unnerved me more than a direct threat.

"I don't know," Ashley answered Tanner. "I came out to work on some low jumps and ground poles for lessons this weekend and they were already out when I got here."

Andy hurried home as fast as he dared on the curvy roads. We pulled in just as Luis, sporting a bright LED headlamp and atop one of the Cunningham Quarter Horses that was probably worth more than my entire place, house included, emerged from the tree line. He wasn't leading a black horse.

I got out of the car before Andy had even come to a complete stop. "I'll check the dogs," he said before I shut the door.

"Thanks," I said over my shoulder.

"I didn't see any sign of him," Luis called as he approached.

"Thank you so much for looking." My voice was unsteady, and I tried to stay calm. Falling apart wasn't going to help anything.

Biscuit started frantically braying and pacing the fence. I jogged over to him. He stopped pacing, but continued to bray as I took his head in my hands and spoke softly to him. It only took a few minutes to calm him down, but when I tried to leave him to go back and talk with Luis and Ashley he let loose again and tried his best to follow me through the gate. I hesitated, but then pulled the rope halter off the fence post and slipped it over Biscuit's little nose. If he was going to be frantic when I left, I would just take him with me. Content to stay by my side, he followed me over to the quarantine pen where Luis was talking to Ashley and Tanner. Andy met me there.

"The dogs are fine," he said. I reached for his hand, but Biscuit squeezed in between us. Andy patted his back.

"I don't think he went up on the mountain," Luis said to Tanner. "I left word at the barn to call me if he tries to go to the horses up there." He did a little chin lift toward the Cunningham farm on the hill above my rescue. "I think he headed toward the creek. It's hard to tell since there are hoofprints everywhere, but that was where the others kept looking when they came up the hill."

"I'll go see if I can find him," I said, handing the lead-rope over to Tanner, but Biscuit wouldn't have it. He almost pulled the rope out of Tanner's hands trying to follow me.

"I'll take him with me." I gently took the rope back. "Luis, thank you so much for your help."

"You shouldn't go out in the dark," Luis said firmly. "We don't know who cut your fences. We can put the word out up and down the road to watch out for him, and I'm more than happy to come back at first light and help look. I know the others would help too."

"He's right, Mal." Andy circled Biscuit's little round rump to stand beside me. "It's just not safe to head off into the night."

"We can't just leave him out there," I pleaded. "What if he gets out on the road? He's black and they'd never see him until it's too late."

"There's nothing in that direction to draw him out that way." I recognized Grady's voice behind me instantly. "He's much more likely to stay close to either your horses or the Cunningham herd."

I turned around to see his familiar tall, Stetson-topped frame silhouetted in the porch light. I'm pretty sure my mouth fell open at the sight of who was with him.

Chapter
Twenty-One

Heather Rogers was clutching Grady's arm like she thought she might get lost on the way across my yard. I hadn't seen Heather since she had served me with a lawsuit alleging that my and the Cunningham horses were polluting the creek she used to irrigate her organic farm. Although we were neighbors, we definitely were not on friendly terms. I was very surprised that she was there with Grady, even though they had been dating for months now. Then I noticed that her long, patchwork, boho coat was covering a sleek slip dress, and that they had probably abandoned a date to come to my rescue.

"He's not been here long enough for this to feel like home," I said, gathering my wits about me. Biscuit made a soft whuffling sound as Grady approached. He reached out and scratched his long ears.

"That's even more reason he won't want to leave the other horses," Grady countered.

"Did Philip Atwood do this?" Ashley demanded, arms crossed.

"We don't know who's responsible," Grady said in his well-practiced way.

"Well, this would be just like him, wouldn't it? He cut the Cunningham fences multiple times," she said. "Didn't he?" she asked Luis.

"It's true, he did."

"Why don't you go check on the horses, make sure everyone is alright and get them settled down while I talk to Ashley about what she found," Grady said, while Heather glared at me.

"Thank you both for coming out," I said directly to her. "I really appreciate it."

"I'll take care of everything, Boss," Tanner said as he took the lead rope from me. This time Biscuit followed him quietly, as he seemed to assume that we had the threat handled now. I knew Tanner was trying to prove himself as rescue manager, and I was going to have to sit down and have a talk with him. I didn't expect total dedication 24/7, and I didn't want him to feel that he had to take on everything by himself to prove to me that he was capable. This wasn't the time for it though, so I let him take Biscuit back to the paddock and check on the others.

Ashley ran through what she'd already told me on the phone: that she'd come out to work on some obstacles for the weekend's lessons and found the fences cut. What she had added to Grady that she hadn't told me was that, on the way here, she'd seen a dirt bike speeding toward town, and the rider had been dressed all in black.

*   *   *

By the time everyone left, I had worked myself up into a fine state of worry about Jet. Logically, I knew that what everyone was saying was true, that it would be hard to find him at night and my leg wouldn't allow me to go blundering through the woods. But my heart wanted to grab a flashlight and search until I found him no matter how long it took.

I had to talk Tanner out of staying in the barn loft for the night. He was more furious about the vandalism than I'd realized and was determined to catch the culprit if they came back. He finally agreed to go home, but promised he would be back at first light to help with the search for Jet. By the time I crawled into bed next to Andy, even my bones were exhausted. I thought I wouldn't be able to turn my brain off and go to sleep, but I think I was out before my head even hit the pillow.

*   *   *

Morning brought another flurry of activity. I'm pretty sure Tanner showed up *before* first light since he'd already done most of the work before I even dragged my caffeine-deprived butt out of the house. And Ashley wasn't far behind him. I really hoped she wasn't missing classes to help us. Biscuit was back to his endearingly annoying self and was playfully pulling at the hem of Tanner's jacket while he tried to push a wheelbarrow of pine shavings to the stalls. Tanner's big bay gelding, Zeus, stood tied to his little two-horse trailer. He'd pulled as far up the driveway as he could to make room for any other vehicles that might show up.

Tanner adored Zeus from the minute we'd brought him to the rescue. I hadn't gotten along with him quite as well, because he'd exploded out of my trailer right on top of me. After that initial blowup, he'd proven to be a pretty laid-back horse, and Tanner adopted him as soon as he was legally available.

Luis rode over from the Cunningham farm on the same gorgeous gray Quarter Horse that he'd ridden the previous evening, and he brought Lexie and Duncan with him, both riding horses that could grace the pages of *Horse Illustrated* magazine.

Lexie Moss had come to the rescue several times to visit the horses, and her love of animals was evident from the beginning. She was one of the Cunningham full-time staff and was responsible for the breeding program, embryo transfer, and foal management. She was younger than I but older than Tanner and Ashley, and possessed the kind of effortless beauty most women only dream about. She looked as elegant in her jeans and North Face vest as most people do in a ball gown and heels. Her long auburn hair was pulled back in a fishtail braid that cascaded over her slender shoulder.

Duncan Knapp followed Lexie and Luis on a sorrel mare with four white socks. He was a short, wiry man with wild gray hair and a heavily wrinkled face that always reminded me of a gnome's. I wasn't sure what his official title or duties at the farm were, but he was one of the nicest people I'd ever met, and he had a quiet, soft way with the horses reminiscent of Tom Dorrance and Buck Brannaman, two of the natural horsemanship greats.

"I thought we would fan out over the mountain," Luis said after tipping his baseball cap in greeting. "The mares were whinnying up that way this morning. He might have doubled around last night, and we all know the country up there pretty well."

"That sounds great," I said. "I can't thank you all enough."

Duncan waved me off. "You helped me look after a sick filly all night when Mr. Cunningham, God rest his soul, was out of town. This is the least I can do."

"Seems we've all been in your debt," Lexie smiled down at me. "I seem to remember you helped me change a flat when I first started out here."

"That's not debt. It's just what neighbors do." I blushed.

"Exactly." She winked at me. "And it's not like our former employer didn't give you plenty of grief."

"It's not nice to speak ill of the dead," Duncan said, looking a bit stricken.

"Not ill, just the truth."

Duncan still looked a bit offended, but didn't argue further. We all turned toward the sound of a car engine and crunching gravel. I hoped it wasn't Grady. I was already feeling guilty for monopolizing so much of the sheriff's time. It wasn't Grady.

I closed my mouth, which had fallen open when I saw the "Heather's Happy Organics" decal on the side of the white SUV. I crossed the driveway to meet her.

She got out carrying a large basket covered with a fitted floral cloth.

"Look," she said before I had the chance to speak. "I've been trying to figure out a way to apologize, but I've never threatened anyone with a shotgun before and they don't make greeting cards for that. So, I figured this was as good a way as any."

She held the basket up between us.

"I made snacks for the volunteers and cookies for the horses." Then, looking away nervously, she added, "and I dropped the lawsuit. Albert's sister contacted me after she was served as the new owner and let me know that he had been using harsh fertilizers on the driveway and front grounds and had ordered an increase in usage after I first spoke with him. She promised me they would discontinue the use and look for more environmentally friendly ways to maintain the property."

"Wow. He could certainly be vindictive, couldn't he?" I shook my head at the thought of such pettiness. I instantly felt guilty as I thought of Duncan's earlier admonishment.

She nodded in agreement.

"There aren't any greeting cards that say, 'Sorry I thought you might've murdered my neighbor' either, so let's call it even, shall we?"

She let out a breath in a rush, like she'd been holding it in.

"Deal," she said with a broad smile.

"The house is unlocked, make yourself at home. My dog, the heeler, is friendly. The little guy is a monster, and he bites, so steer clear of him."

"Yeah, Grady said you'd taken in the little beast," she laughed. "I brought a table and some spiced cider. I'll set up out here, if you don't mind."

"That will be great," I said, marveling at her generosity. "Do you need any help?"

"No, I've got this. You go find your horse."

"Heather," I said, taking a step toward her, "thank you."

She turned around from the open hatch of her SUV and smiled warmly. Maybe it was the fact that I hadn't slept well, or the worry over Jet, but my eyes filled with unshed tears. I'd hated the dispute with Heather over the runoff, and while I'd hoped that she would eventually find out that my rescue wasn't polluting the creek, *this* was more than I'd ever expected.

"Hey, Boss," Tanner called from the paddock, drawing my attention away from the feast Heather was unloading from her SUV. I met him at the gate.

"I was going to saddle River for you, but he's thrown a shoe."

"Dang," I said leaning around him to look at River, who was lazily munching hay. "And you don't have to saddle my horse."

I swear Tanner blushed. "I know, I just want to help out."

"You *do* help, more than you realize, but you don't have to wait on me."

I looked up the hill to Tunie, who was watching the goings-on warily. Tanner followed my gaze.

"I don't think that's a good idea," he said looking from Tunie back to me.

"It'll be fine. She's the only other one that's shod." I lamented not having Goldie shod. She was fine barefoot just doing lessons in the paddock but would need shoes on trails in the woods. Stormy probably had the healthiest hooves of any horse in the rescue, but he was also the oldest, and I sure wasn't going to ask our elderly resident to pack me around. Tunie snorted and tossed her head, almost as if she'd understood our conversation.

Ashley coordinated the exchange of everyone's phone numbers so we could all stay in touch during the search. She really was amazingly efficient. She had drafted a master list and set everyone on a check-in schedule in just a few minutes.

It didn't take long for me to get Tunie tacked up, even though she danced and pinned her ears back the entire time. She looked beautiful under my trail saddle, her dappled-gray coat a nice contrast to the black leather. When we'd first started working with her after she'd gained weight and settled in, I was afraid that pain was causing her behavioral problems. But after a full battery of tests and evaluations, Doc Brantley and an equine chiropractor determined that pain wasn't her issue. I spent months trying to form any sort of bond with her, as did Tanner and Ashley, but none of us had any luck. She preferred her meals to be on time, but otherwise she just didn't have much use for us.

She turned a few circles when I climbed on from the mounting block but didn't buck me off, so I considered myself off to a good start. Tanner held the gate and managed to keep Biscuit from joining me. He climbed on Zeus quickly, then we headed down the driveway while Luis, Lexie, and Duncan headed up the hill. Andy waved at us from the porch. Tanner gave Tunie a wide berth, since she pinned her ears and snapped at Zeus every time he got within reach.

Luis was right. There were hoofprints *everywhere*. The horses had clearly enjoyed exploring the area. I am definitely not a tracker, and I wasn't sure where to start looking once we passed the mailboxes at the end of the driveway.

"Maybe he went toward the lake?" Tanner seemed as unsure as I was.

"It's really weird that he hasn't stayed close to the other horses. Makes me worry," I said. I looked in the direction of the lake. "Can you see anything that looks like a trail? Or any sign at all?"

Tanner reined Zeus across the road and searched the ditch. I did the same a little farther down, for all the good it did me. I had no idea what I was looking for. I finally gave up and turned Tunie back toward Tanner. She'd stopped protesting every new direction and was looking around like she *might* be enjoying the experience. I made a mental note to take her out more. Maybe that was the missing key to unlocking our bond. Even if it wasn't, I would gladly take her for a trail ride if she continued to seem like she enjoyed getting out. It only took a moment for her long strides to close the distance.

"Most of the land in that direction is fenced," Tanner said, pointing back toward Hillspring. "But the old Newton place is open. And except for the storage place, nothing around the lake is fenced."

"Yeah, I think you're right. If he isn't up on the mountain, that's the most logical direction. I'll take the old road, if you want to loop around and meet me?"

"Sounds good Boss." He nodded, and then paused for a moment. "You guys seem to be getting along pretty well."

"She seems to like the adventure." I reached down and patted Tunie's neck.

We parted ways and Tunie didn't even look back. I wondered why I'd mistaken her grumpiness for being uncooperative. Horses are as varied in personality as humans, and maybe Tunie was just not the warm fuzzy type. She strode confidently down the overgrown road, which was barely even a road anymore. I tried to look everywhere at once, alert for any movement that might be Jet.

The old split-rail fence that had once lined the road was broken and rotten. I'd never seen the property in its heyday, but I'd seen photos, and this whole area had once been the manicured route that used to take tourists to the Newton Family Resort. It had been popular in the fifties and sixties but fell into disrepair in the seventies when the original owners died. It closed down for good in 1985 and had sat abandoned since then. Every few years there were rumors that someone had purchased it and planned to start something new and fabulous there, but so far nothing had ever panned out.

As we navigated the overgrown winding drive, I let my mind wander. I *knew,* based on Ashley's description, that the same person who hurt Patricia cut our fences. There was no way it could be a coincidence that someone dressed all in black riding a dirt bike was at both crime scenes. I had more questions than I had answers, and that bothered me. I still wasn't sure why Coach had been murdered, and without a clear motive it was hard to nail down suspects. I urged Tunie to a gentle stop and pulled out my phone to text Darrin.

Any chance you can tell me if you've had any luck finding out what was on that USB drive? Or what that key goes to?

I squeezed my legs and Tunie picked up the pace again. She was definitely proving to be a great trail horse. I hated the fact that I had missed out on both of us enjoying rides over the year that she'd been with us.

It didn't take long for Darrin to respond.

Nothing on the key yet. USB drive just has grade records, test scores, and sports rosters.

"Why would he hide that?" I asked myself out loud. Unless he'd been the one selling grades after all.

I asked Tunie to stop again and called Andy. I told him what Darrin had just texted me.

"Would you call Darrin and tell him what we found out from Ben Archer? Maybe Coach had gotten himself in over his head and the policy proposal was a way out."

"Sure. Send me his contact information."

"I need to find out if Coach could even access grades and manipulate test scores. Can you find out if he still did any teaching at all? Maybe he subbed regularly after he retired. No, scratch that. I'll go talk to Leslie at the school this afternoon. I want to see her face when I ask."

"I'll go with you. I have a meeting this afternoon I can't reschedule, but I can go with you after I'm finished. I'll give Darrin a call now."

"You don't need to go with me. I'll be fine at the school."

"I don't really want you going anywhere alone right now. We can argue about that later. Right now, just be careful and send me Darrin's information."

I sent it right after we hung up and then urged Tunie into a walk again. The path wound through old-growth hickories and oaks that were hanging onto their brown leaves. We'd had a few frosts already, but the oaks were always the last to drop their foliage. The first snow, or God forbid ice storm, would finish stripping them for the season. Tunie's hoofbeats crunched the leaves that *had* fallen, and I strained to hear any other possible signs that Jet was nearby.

We'd just crested a gentle hill and started down the other side when I heard a whinny in the distance. Tunie's head jerked up, her ears shot forward, and she stopped in her tracks. She waited a moment and then whinnied back, shaking me as she did. The horse in the distance answered again and I urged Tunie into a trot in that direction. I hoped it wasn't Zeus.

Thankfully, Tunie kept whinnying and the horse kept answering her. The worrisome part was that he didn't seem to be moving. I prayed that he wasn't hurt. We finally came through the overgrowth and crossed into what used to be the main grounds in front of the old resort's main building.

I pulled out my phone and called Tanner, but this time I didn't ask Tunie to stop. Jet was whinnying frantically and pawing the ground. I squinted, trying to see if he was okay, as Tunie picked up the canter I'd asked for. I couldn't see anything wrong, except that he seemed to be tied to a tree.

"I found him!" I said as soon as Tanner answered. "He's tied to a tree in front of the resort."

"I'll be right there," he said, and disconnected the call.

I quickly dismounted and secured Tunie to a tree close by. Jet snorted and pawed. I spoke softly and approached slowly, careful to keep the halter and lead rope I'd brought with me contained. The last thing I wanted to do was spook him now. I wondered how anyone had caught him, given how hard he'd been for me to catch. It also didn't make any sense why someone would tie him up that far out in the woods, where he wouldn't be easily found. He lowered his head, and while he still snorted occasionally and watched me warily, he let me approach him.

Someone had rigged up a makeshift halter out of what appeared to be a drawstring and tied him with a length of electrical wire or cord of some sort. It was an unfortunate testament to how loyal and obedient horses can be. He stood there in a tether he could easily have snapped in two, but he had been trained to stay put. His training wasn't perfect though; it looked like he'd pawed all night long. But my breath caught in my chest at the thought of what might have happened if we hadn't found him.

I patted his neck gently and pulled a treat out of my pocket. He ate it greedily, then nuzzled my pocket for more.

"Chew on that, Buddy," I said as I eased the halter over his nose. He raised his head and nodded a few times, but he didn't bolt, thankfully. Once I got it buckled, I slipped the drawstring off from underneath and reached to untie the cord.

I heard shouting, and then gunshots rang out through the forest, echoing with a *crack* off the abandoned resort building. Jet jerked backward, reared, and nearly pulled me off my feet as I struggled to keep hold of the rope. He shook his head and another shot exploded in the quiet forest. I didn't have time to think about whether the shots were close or where they might be landing before Jet started pulling again, dragging the lead rope through my hands. I hissed at the rope burn but willed myself not to let go. Just because the whole area was marked with "No hunting" signs didn't mean everyone respected them.

I was still trying to calm Jet down when I heard an engine fire up on the hill behind me. A four-wheeler maybe? Thankfully, Jet settled down almost as fast as he'd spooked, and I led him back to Tunie. I was thankful that I was wearing a large hunter orange vest, and I wanted to put that vest between whoever was hunting and the horses.

The engine seemed to be getting closer. Both Tunie and Jet pricked their ears toward the approaching noise, which seemed to be approaching *very quickly*. I scanned the ridge above the resort grounds for movement, but the overgrowth was too thick to see anything. I started to move into what was left of the clearing to get a better view when the dirt bike crashed through the brush behind us and sent dirt and leaves flying toward us in its wake. Both horses pulled at their tethers, snorting and spooking at the noisy machine. The rider, wearing all black and face obscured by a black helmet, turned back to look at me briefly before speeding down the old road that I'd taken.

Just a few seconds later, Tanner and Zeus crashed through the brush behind the dirt bike. Zeus's ears were pinned back, and he dug into the ground; powerful legs gobbling up the distance between them. It all seemed as though I was watching an action movie unfolding in slow motion. Finally, the dirt-bike rider gained the upper hand and disappeared out of sight, leaving Tanner in the proverbial dust. Thankfully, he conceded defeat and didn't continue the pursuit. Tunie and Jet, both still looking toward the sound of the retreating dirt bike, snorted, and Jet started pawing again.

As Tanner urged Zeus into a trot back toward me, I realized that the gunshots had not been fired by a trespassing hunter. They were meant for *us*.

Chapter
Twenty-Two

Tanner was excitedly retelling how he'd ridden up on the shooter taking aim at me for about the hundredth time while I unsaddled Tunie. We'd waited at the old Newton Resort building for Darrin and Calvin Burns to search the area. Tanner had ambushed the shooter, causing him to leave the shell casings behind. Darrin said he was sure they were going to match the type that had killed Coach Griggs. He said they'd also found evidence that the killer had waited all night, watching the area for me to show up, which both thrilled and terrified me. On one hand, I hoped there would be fingerprints or DNA to identify the killer. But it was one thing to vandalize my truck and let my horses out; it was another entirely to set a trap for me and lie in wait to kill me.

Ashley had organized the volunteers to repair the cut fences, so everything was back to normal when we returned. Jet was settled safely in a stall, making up for lost time by gobbling his hay. Tanner had unsaddled Zeus and tucked him into the stall across the breezeway.

I pulled the saddle off and slung it over the paddock fence. Tunie turned toward me, and instead of pinning her ears like she normally did, she nudged me with her nose, just once, and when she was finished, turned back to stare at the other horses on the hill. In spite of the near-death experience I'd just had, I was thrilled by this tiny gesture. It was the closest any of us had ever gotten to receiving any affection from her. I scratched her withers, that prominent rise of the spine at the base of a horse's mane, and she bobbed her head a little. We just might become friends after all.

I turned Tunie out in the newly secured upper paddock and slumped against the gate post. Tanner didn't seem to appreciate how dangerous our situation was, how close we had both come to suffering the same fate as Coach Griggs. It was scary enough to think about being the target of someone who'd already proved they weren't afraid to kill, but the thought of something happening to Tanner or anyone else I loved was just too much.

Suddenly, Andy was at my side, quietly telling me to breathe.

"You're okay. You're safe," he whispered. He put my hand on the center of his chest. "Feel me breathing? Breathe with me. In through your nose, out through your mouth."

It hadn't registered that I was having a panic attack, that I'd started to hyperventilate and my vision had narrowed to a tunnel in front of me. As my breathing started to return to normal and my world widened back out, I realized that he was whispering and standing between me and the small crowd in the driveway. I fell into him, causing him to take a half-step backward to regain his balance, but he responded to my hug just as fiercely.

Andy led me back to the driveway, where he'd set up some makeshift tables and seating. He'd used some boards and the saw-horses from the quarantine paddock for tables and the larger logs from the wood pile for seating. I was amazed at the number of people who had gathered there. Luis, Lexie, and Duncan sat at my little bistro table on the porch, each with a cup of spiced cider and a muffin. At the sawhorse table, Ashley and Darrin sat talking with . . . my dad! I had no idea when he'd come and glanced around for his little beat-up truck. And there it was, parked in the grass behind Andy's Lincoln.

"Here, you can take my seat," Darrin said as I approached. "I've got to get back. I just couldn't resist one of Heather's turnovers."

"Thank you." I slumped down onto the log, grateful to get off my feet. I seemed to be exhausted all of a sudden.

"You've had quite a morning, Punkin," Dad said, reaching across and patting my hand. I hated that he'd gotten involved, but if I was being honest with myself, I was glad he was there. "I like your fella, Mallory. You don't have to hide him." He hooked a thumb toward Andy, who was getting spiced ciders and snacks from Heather's table.

I felt my face burn, and Ashley did her best to look preoccupied with her phone.

"I'm not hiding him, Dad. I've just been busy." I felt like a teenager who just got caught sneaking in late.

"I like what you've done out here, and the horses all look great," Dad said with a wry smile. I knew this wouldn't be the last I'd hear of it, but he was granting me a reprieve in front of Ashley.

"Thanks," I said and smiled up at Andy, who had returned with our drinks and muffins. "Now if I can just keep them all safe."

"Hopefully, those shell casings will help Sheriff Sullivan find the killer," Andy said.

Dad scoffed. "It'll take them forever to get everything they need. You need to figure out who's behind this before someone else gets hurt."

Andy choked on his cider. "Someone like Mal? I've been supportive of this up until today, but this was just too close. It's too dangerous to keep this up."

"It's too late for all that." Dad waved his hand dismissively. "The killer *laid a trap* for her. He's not going to stop now. It's even more important for her to continue after all this. Plus, she's going to have to cancel lessons and keep people away until this is over."

My stomach did a flip-flop. I hadn't considered that, but he was right. I couldn't risk my students and their families. I looked up at Ashley, and she nodded.

"On it," she said. "I'll reschedule to start with."

"Offer a refund," I said, inwardly cringing at the thought of losing money.

"I couldn't help but overhear," Luis said from behind me. "We've been talking, and we'd like to help keep an eye on things over here until this is all sorted out. Like a neighborhood watch. We can take turns."

"I can't ask any of you to endanger yourselves that way." I shook my head.

"You aren't asking," Duncan said with a finality that didn't invite argument.

"In that case, I'll return the favor. I've been looking for an excuse to ride more. I can help look after the back fences."

"Deal," Luis said.

The three of them thanked Heather for her excellent food, then mounted their horses to leave, waving as they headed down the driveway.

"It's settled then," Dad said. "I'll come out and stay and keep an eye out here. They're going to watch from over there, and you can figure this mess out."

"Dad, you can't just leave your house." I struggled to find more reasons to discourage him. I loved my dad, but he was eighty-five years old, and while most people would never guess his age by looking at him, I could see how he'd slowed down since his bout with sepsis a few years ago.

"Nonsense. I brought a bag with me. I'm here to stay until this is over."

*   *   *

I helped Ashley make sure all the volunteers were accounted for so we could feature them on our new social media pages, and several people had their photos taken with Biscuit, much to his delight. Ashley even signed up a new student for lessons, one who wasn't bothered by having to wait until we were sure the grounds were safe. She was a quiet, timid young woman I didn't recognize, and she would be our first adult beginner. Ashley was as excited as I was about expanding the lesson program to include more age groups.

Dad raised an eyebrow when he realized that Andy had stayed the previous night, but he didn't say anything. After he'd moved into the spare bedroom, fixed himself a pot of coffee, made instant friends with Timmy, and settled himself on the sofa with the remote, I went back outside to help Heather pack up when the last of the volunteers left. But not before I'd marveled at the little dog who was happily curled up beside Dad on the sofa. Timmy had never even offered to growl at him!

"Heather, this was so generous, and everything was just delicious."

"I'm glad we finally cleared the air."

"Me too. Were you able to salvage any of your mother's heirloom seeds? I felt so terrible about that."

"I was," she said quietly. "Not all of them, but I did save some."

"I'm so sorry."

"Thank you." She paused her packing and looked at me intensely. I squirmed a little under the scrutiny. "Grady really thinks a lot of you."

I felt my cheeks burning again. "I think a lot of him too. He's like the big brother I always wished I had."

She smiled broadly and resumed gathering the compostable paper cups and plates she'd provided for her amazing muffins, turnovers, and pastries.

"I would love for you and Grady to come over for dinner sometime," I said. I started to gather the leftover food and pack it in the shallow totes.

"That would be nice."

When Heather pulled down the driveway, I noticed that Tanner was carrying hay to Ruby, who'd once again been settled into the small paddock below the barn. I wondered if we should continue trying to quarantine her since she'd just been out and in close proximity to everyone else for who knows how long. But I decided to worry about that later.

Andy met me on the porch.

"I'm going to head in to the office," he said, his mouth drawn into a thin line. "I think you've got plenty of people looking out for you."

"Are you coming back tonight?" I noticed his duffle bag was slung over his shoulder.

"I'm just taking this home to do some laundry, water the plants, and check on things," he said, following my gaze to the bag. "Just promise me you'll be careful, whatever you decide to do."

He descended the steps and headed for his car.

"Are we okay?" I hated how vulnerable and pathetic that sounded, but I *felt* vulnerable and pathetic, so it stood to reason I would sound that way.

He stopped and turned around.

"I'm trying to come to terms with the fact that you're going to continue to look into this case and endanger yourself. And your own father is encouraging you to do it!" He threw his free hand up in exasperation.

I didn't know what to say and started to tell him that I wouldn't, that I would leave it all to Grady, but I stopped myself. I didn't want to make a promise I couldn't keep, so I just watched him leave.

Chapter
Twenty-Three

Forward motion kept me from giving in to worry and obsessing over whether Andy and I were over or not. If I got too still, I started thinking about the facts that I'd almost been murdered that morning, my best friend was angry with me, and my boyfriend was disappointed with me. I was the common denominator, and because I wasn't sure how to fix either relationship, I concentrated on finding a killer.

I pulled into the school parking lot and hoped that Leslie would let me in again. She hadn't been exactly welcoming on my previous visits. I took a moment to compose myself and quiet my thoughts.

"There's nothing else of Coach Griggs's here," Leslie said over the buzzer at the front doors.

"Actually, I was hoping to speak with you," I answered.

There was a pause and then the doors clicked open. She was waiting for me at the door to the administration office. The principal and vice principal's offices were vacant again, and I wondered if they ever kept office hours. Johanna looked up briefly from her computer, then got up to hang a "Meeting in Progress" sign on her door before closing it. Leslie took her position behind the front desk.

"Excuse me for just a moment," Leslie held up one finger, then picked up the phone receiver. "Send Noah Porter to the office please," she said after a brief pause.

I froze. Did she think I was there to speak to Noah Porter? I realized I'd asked a lot of questions about Noah on my previous visit, but I couldn't imagine that she thought I was there to talk to him. I waited awkwardly, and thankfully it was a short wait. In no time he came bursting through the doors with two other boys.

"Dylan! Thomas! Go back to class," Leslie scolded. "Neither of you was asked to report."

"We were coming to pick up the permission slips for Mrs. Banks. She said she left them up here, and since Noah was coming anyway . . ."

Leslie handed over a stack of papers and shooed the boys out the door. She turned back to Noah, who was the thinner version of his father, same easy smile, same sandy-blonde hair.

"Someone found this in the parking lot." She reached under the desk and pulled out a black motocross helmet.

"Who turned it in?" Noah looked at her skeptically.

"I wasn't the one who received it. I was just asked to make sure you got it back."

"Okay, thanks." He turned on his heel and left, helmet tucked under his arm.

Granted, I hadn't gotten the *best* look at the helmet the dirt bike rider had been wearing, but it sure looked like the one Noah had just taken away.

"What can I do for you?" Leslie said, snapping my attention back from the door.

"I was wondering if Coach Griggs did any subbing after he retired?"

She regarded me for a moment, lips drawn into a thin line, then crossed her arms as she sat back down behind the desk. She seemed to have decided that answering my question didn't pose a threat, because she finally nodded and said, "Yes. Why?"

I ignored the question.

"Did he have access to grades?"

"Well, it would've been very hard for him to record scores if he couldn't access the system, wouldn't it?"

"Was that the extent of it? Could he *just* record scores, or could he alter grades if he needed to?"

"Why would he need to?" Leslie unfolded her arms and leaned forward. "I don't know what you're trying to imply, but I won't be party to tarnishing his good name. Coach Griggs was a phenomenal coach, and he was a good man."

"I don't want to tarnish his name either—he was my favorite teacher when I attended high school here—but I also don't want that to keep me from finding the truth," I said quietly. "I've learned that there has been a rumor circulating for some time that he might have been exchanging money for a boost in grades."

What I could only describe as shock and horror washed over her face. She regained her composure just as quickly.

"I can assure you that if something like that were going on here, we would know about it and put a swift end to it. This will be the second time I'm going to ask you to leave. And this time, I need you to not come back."

But as I turned to leave Leslie stopped me at the door.

"Meet me at Brewed Awakening at five. I can't talk here."

*   *   *

I drove straight to Andy's office from the school. Once there I bypassed Sherry and made a beeline for Andy's open door. If he'd been with a client or on the phone, I would've had to wait, but thankfully he was alone and appeared to be going through his notes. He looked up when I came in. I couldn't tell if he was annoyed to see me or not. I shut the door behind me.

I took a deep breath and blurted it all out. "I know I keep messing things up, and I'd love to be able to tell you that I'll magically get myself together soon, but the truth is that I'm probably always going to be a disaster. I know you'd rather I stayed out of the investigation, but I can't promise that, and I really hope you'll decide I'm worth the hassle."

I'd hoped he'd be amused by my words, or, failing that, even *angry* would be something I could deal with, but he wasn't either of those things. He seemed sad, and that scared me.

"And I guess I'm not great at giving you the space you need to decide either," I said as I sank into one of the two chairs facing his desk.

"Clearly." He finally gave me the tiniest smile.

"I'm not good at this. I'm not good at relationships."

"I'm a little rusty myself."

"If you are, I haven't noticed. In *my* defense, Ethan was my high school sweetheart and we got married young, so I haven't had much practice." I tried not to give in to the emotions whirling around in my head.

"I'm sorry for the way I left things earlier. I shouldn't have left until we'd talked it out."

"Please don't apologize. It makes me feel worse than I already do. I can't imagine this is the kind of relationship you dreamed about when you moved here."

He laughed. "I didn't really give that much thought. I honestly hadn't considered getting into another relationship after losing Blair."

We had only talked briefly about Andy's late fiancée. All I really knew was that she had been diagnosed young with an aggressive form of breast cancer, and by the time it was detected it had already spread everywhere. She lost her battle less than a year after diagnosis. I'd been curious and creeped her Facebook memorial page, then wished I hadn't. It felt intrusive and unsavory to learn about how beautiful and wonderful she'd been before Andy was ready to tell me.

"I'm glad you did."

"I've really got to finish this brief before I leave today and I have a lot of information to work through," he said, gesturing to the piles in front of him.

"I'll leave you to it. I hope you'll come back this evening. I know having Dad there isn't ideal for having a private discussion, but I'd love to see you."

"Let's plan on the morning. I'm going to have dinner with Mom tonight and I'll come by tomorrow."

"That sounds great," I said with a smile that I hoped hid how terrified I was that he was deciding I wasn't worth the hassle after all.

* * *

I pulled into the driveway to find Ashley still there. I thought I'd talked her into working on the social media accounts from home until it was safer. I'd given up on trying to discourage Tanner.

She put her hands up as soon as she saw me coming. "Before you say anything, I *am* going to clear out. I was just working on getting everyone's contact information uploaded on a shared document so that we all have access wherever and whenever we need it. I rescheduled the lessons, and everyone was super nice about it. And I've made a list of the kinds of photos I need you to upload and e-mail to me to get up on the pages."

She handed over the list.

"Wow. You and Tanner could teach classes in overachieving. How did I get so lucky?"

"Fate," she grinned.

"Anything else I can do to help, besides sending the photos?"

"If I think of anything I'll let you know." She pulled her keys out of her pocket. "Tanner's in the house trading football stories with your Dad." She rolled her eyes.

"Oh no," I said in mock horror. "They'll be at it all night!"

She turned to get in her car.

"Keep track of your hours, I don't want to short you for all of this extra work you're putting in."

"Sure thing, Boss Lady." She saluted before shutting the door to her little Nissan pickup.

I could hear Dad telling the story of how he'd sacked the rival team's quarterback during the homecoming game his senior year before I even opened the door.

"What did you find out?" Dad asked before I could get into the house.

I told him about Noah and the helmet and my conversation with Leslie.

"Noah Porter a skinny little fella like what you said the motorbike rider was?" Dad asked scratching his chin.

"He's not really little, but it's hard to gauge height when someone is seated and speeding away from you."

"But it looked like him?" Dad pressed.

"I want to tread very lightly here, Dad. We're talking about a kid. He's got his whole life ahead of him."

"Technically, he's an adult," Tanner said. "He's eighteen."

"That's splitting a pretty fine hair," I said. "It still doesn't feel right to target someone that young."

"You can find out if he might be a suspect without ruining his life or acting creepy," Dad said. "Look at his Face Space thingy or his Insta-Picture or whatever you call that Internet nonsense and see if he has a dirt bike like the one you saw. Five bucks says if it *is* him, he's posted pictures of it."

"You might be onto something there, Dad." I didn't tell him that's exactly what I planned to do while I waited for the time to meet Leslie at the coffee shop. I noticed Timmy curled up beside Dad on the sofa on my way by. I couldn't believe how the little beast had taken to him. I pulled out my phone to call Grady and ask about Patricia and found that I had several missed calls and a voicemail. I punched the play button on my way to my makeshift home office to retrieve my laptop.

Um, hello. I got your number from the sheriff. You don't know me, but I'm Rhett Allen. Patricia Griggs is my mother. I understand you, um, found her. I'd like to talk to you if possible.

He repeated his number even though it showed up on my caller ID. I closed my bedroom door and called him back.

He picked up on the first ring.

"Mr. Allen?" I said. "Mallory Martin. I'm sorry I missed your call."

"Oh yeah, um, I understand you found my mother, is that right?"

"Yes, Mr. Allen, I'm so sorry."

"Rhett, please," he said. "The sheriff said that she was unconscious, that she didn't tell you anything about her attacker, but I wanted to hear that for myself."

"He was right. I'm afraid she was unconscious when I found her. Have you been able to see her yet?"

"No, I'm actually not quite there yet. I had to drive in, long story, but I should be there this evening. I'm going to the hospital first and I don't know when I'll be able to get to Hillspring." He took a deep breath. "The sheriff said you have her dog?"

"I do. But he can stay as long as you need him to. He's taken quite a liking to my dad."

"Really? I didn't think that little monster liked anyone but Mom. That really helps, though. I wasn't sure how I was going to manage. I've got a neighbor caring for Doug's horse, but I worried that awful dog was going to bite someone." He let out a nervous laugh.

"It's no problem, really. He's . . . delightful."

"Are you sure you got the right dog?"

It was my turn to laugh. "Would you mind letting me know how Patricia is doing when you get there? They can't tell me anything since I'm not family."

"Yes, yes, of course I will."

We ended the call with an agreement to keep in touch.

I'd just opened my laptop when I heard a car in the driveway. I started to ignore it and let Dad deal with whoever it might be, but I was afraid it might be someone with rescue questions, so I beat him to the door. I'd no more than opened it when Lanie burst inside and threw her arms around me.

"I heard someone tried to kill you this morning," she said into my shoulder. "My God, what if something had happened to you and the last thing I said to you was awful?"

I glanced back at Dad and Tanner, who were watching us intently.

"Let's talk in the office," I said and led her down the little hall.

"I'm really glad you're not alone," she said.

"I'm glad *you're* here," I said and gestured for her to take the seat at the desk. I took the armchair in the corner.

"I'm still thoroughly aggravated that I spent days trying to talk to you and you're so self-absorbed that I had to throw a fit to get your attention," she said, unshed tears glistening in her eyes.

"Gee, Lane, thanks for that," I chuckled.

"But," she paused for effect, "I'm prepared to admit that I've been overly dramatic lately. And it scared the crap out of me when Bill told me what happened this morning. I don't want to lose you, Mal."

"I don't want to lose you either, Lanie. You're the closest thing to a sister that I've ever had." I leaned forward and took her hand. "Now, *please* tell me what you've been trying to tell me."

She took a long, deep breath and closed her eyes for a moment.

"Bill and I decided to do one last round of in vitro," she said in a shaky voice. "That first morning I called you, I was going to tell you that we'd tried again, and my doctor felt confident that it could still work. But later, I started spotting and I knew it was going to be like all the other times, that it didn't work, and I was never going to be pregnant."

"Oh, Lanie, I'm so sorry," I closed the distance between us, knelt in front of her, and pulled her into a hug.

She hugged me back, but then sat back to look me in the eye.

"It isn't like all the other times, Mal. I'm pregnant."

Chapter
Twenty-Four

I'd *whooped* so loudly that Dad and Tanner came in to check on us. After a round of hearty congratulations, they excused themselves back to the living room.

"Lanie, this is just the best news. I am so happy for you both."

"I don't want to go through this without you." Her smile faded and she put her hands protectively over her belly. "This could all still go wrong."

"I will be here every step of the way." I hugged her again.

"It might be a bumpy ride. I've taken enough hormones to kill an elephant, and I'm blaming that, at least partially, for why I've been so dramatic and irritable."

"I'm not afraid. We can work through all of it."

"Now," she said when we'd both returned to our chairs, "who's trying to kill you?"

It took a while to fill her in on everything that had happened since we last spoke.

"Which leads me to Noah Porter's Instagram account," I opened my laptop, typed in his name in search field, and turned it toward her.

"Geez, he's just a kid," she said, frowning.

"I know. If it's him, I have to be one hundred percent certain." I turned the laptop back around. "I want to be one hundred percent certain of *anyone*. I've been on the receiving end of rumors like that, and I don't want to put anyone else through that."

"True. What's your plan?"

"I'm going to go through Noah's photos until it's time to meet Leslie, then depending on what she has to tell me I'll go from there. There's no clear motive right now, so I think I'll try to focus on identifying the dirt-bike rider. We know they likely hurt Patricia and they certainly tried to hurt me. It's a logical conclusion that they also murdered Coach Griggs."

"That sounds like a solid plan."

"We'll see, I guess. In the meantime, it might be safer for you to steer clear of me, especially now."

"Do you think the killer is going to try again?" She looked horrified, as though that hadn't occurred to her before.

"I think there's a good chance. Anyone diabolical enough to set a trap and then wait all night for me is probably not going to give up that easily."

"Mal, that's terrifying." She put her hands protectively over her belly again.

"That's why I feel such an urgency to figure out who's responsible," I said, wringing my hands. "And I think that's messed everything up with Andy."

I launched into a monologue about all of the mistakes I'd made in my new relationship, from failing to tell my own daughter that I was seeing Andy, panicking when he tried to include me in his life and decisions, to this latest failure. I barely took a breath, but she listened patiently.

"I know this sounds like a cliché, but if you're meant to be together, it'll work out."

"I'm sure you're right." I nodded to myself.

"You look through the Insta and I'll see if I can find him on TikTok," she patted my hand and pushed my laptop toward me. I took it and started scrolling.

I looked through photos of Noah and the same kids I'd seen with him at Silver Dollar City, plus a few new kids, some of them I recognized from the basketball team photos. I didn't have to search very hard to find a photo of him and three other boys posed in front of mud-covered ATVs and dirt bikes. I'd known that I would find something like that, though. No one has a motocross helmet for their bicycle. What I didn't expect to find was a smiling Cameron Green standing in the middle of the group.

"What do you think it means?" Lanie asked after I'd explained who Cameron was and how I'd met him.

"I don't know. But it's weird that he would mention Bruce Porter as a potential enemy and then I find out that he buddies around with Noah in some sort of . . ." I paused while I looked at the photo's accompanying hash-tag again, ". . . 'Mad Mudder Club.'"

"Yeah, that's odd," she agreed.

We visited for a little while longer, then she left to meet a delivery truck at Junk & Disorderly. I took my laptop to the kitchen table, listening to Dad and Tanner. They'd switched from football to local politics. Dad was incensed about a recent city council upset and new proposed taxes inside city limits.

I pulled out Ashley's list and started scrolling through my photo files. She wanted before-and-after photos for all of our current and past rescues. Those were easy to find. I kept a separate file for each horse, and each photo was dated. But she also listed "some shots that highlight the rescue" and "pretty pics of the area." Those were harder to choose from. There were so many. I loved photography and took photos of the area and wildlife every chance I got. I ended up sending far too many and had to follow up with an apology text.

Sorry, I got carried away. You don't have to use all of the photos, just use what you want.

It took only a few seconds for her to respond.

LOL, no problem. I'll get started this afternoon and send you the link when it's done.

"You guys want me to put on a fresh pot of coffee before I go?"

"Where are you going?" Tanner asked.

I forgot I hadn't told them about meeting with Leslie. I'd told Lanie all about it, but I hadn't told them. I gave them the abbreviated version.

"I can tag along and stay out of sight, like I did with Ben Archer," Tanner offered.

"I'd rather you stay here and help Dad keep an eye on things. Anyway, she wanted me to come alone, and she knows what you look like."

He argued briefly but not enthusiastically. I promised to text when I got there, at least once during the meeting and after we finished. So when I pulled into the parking lot of the adorable coffee shop that sat just off Main Street in Hillspring, I sent the first of those texts. I then pocketed some cash and my phone and headed inside.

Just about everything in Hillspring is located on a hill or in a hollow, blending in with the unique topography of the area rather than forcing it to conform to the buildings. Brewed Awakening, however, was built *into* the hill and looked like something out of Middle Earth. It even featured a round front door painted red.

Amber Camp

The sign to the left of the menu said, "Ask us about elevenses." Even though the baristas weren't in costume, it still felt like you were walking onto a movie set. It was one of my favorite places in Hillspring. I'd never met the owners, or if I had, didn't realize it. They had to be wonderful people if the atmosphere in their coffee shop was any indication.

Despite having windows only in the front due to being mostly underground, it was bright, warm, and welcoming inside. Pumpkin-spice everything hadn't yet given way to peppermint and Christmas carols, so I was reminded of pumpkin pie as I scanned the tables for Leslie. She hadn't arrived yet, so I took a table for two by the back wall. No one was sitting close by, so I hoped it would give us a bit of privacy.

I ordered a caramel cold brew and opened my phone to the Facebook app. I knew Noah Porter's profile was locked down, but I hadn't yet searched for Cameron Green. I didn't have a reason to until coming across him smiling in the photo of the Mad Mudder Club. His privacy settings were limited to a few teaching memes and his various profile pictures, which he seemed to change pretty frequently. Most of them featured a smiling Cameron posing with either his dirt bike or his latest quarry. He hunted every season from duck to deer, and I added a new suspect to my list.

"Thank you for meeting me here," Leslie said as she sat down across from me.

I'd been so engrossed in my scrolling that I hadn't noticed her approaching. So much for my powers of observation.

"No problem," I said, tucking my phone away. "What did you need to tell me that couldn't be said at the school?"

She looked at me for a moment, and I felt uncomfortable under the intensity of her gaze. She then waved the server over and ordered a half-caf soymilk latte before turning her fierce expression back to me.

"Those rumors crop up every so often, and we work really hard to quash them before they do any real damage," she said quietly. "They're like a fungus you just can't kill out."

"Do you think there's some truth to it then? If the rumors keep coming back, there must be a reason, right?"

"The reason is usually spoiled little brats who have nothing better to do than stir up trouble," she spat the words at me like I'd started the rumor myself.

"I can certainly understand how damaging that might be if the rumors ever gained traction. You've never found any evidence that Coach Griggs might have been bending the rules just a bit? Or maybe helping some students more than others, which led someone to think there was more going on?"

Leslie stared at me again with that unnerving intensity. The barista at the counter called her name, and she went to pick up her latte. She sighed as she sat back down.

"I'm not the one who investigates such matters. It was up to our principal, Travis Kramer, and our vice principal, Preston Hanson. I wouldn't be privy to their findings."

She held her head a little higher, suggesting to me that she was bitter about this fact.

"But I know that Coach Griggs was always held in high regard and there was never any indication that he did anything untoward."

"What about Cameron Green?"

Something flashed in her eyes, but I wasn't sure what it was. Fear? Disgust? It was gone as quickly as it showed up, and she sipped her latte before speaking.

"What about him? Are you just fishing now?"

"Have there ever been any rumors about him?"

"I'm sure there have been rumors about all of the teachers at one point or another. But nothing that has reached administration that I am aware of."

I tried to gather my racing thoughts. I wasn't even sure how Cameron Green might fit into all of this, so I wasn't sure what I needed to ask.

"But the rumors about Coach Griggs did?"

She nodded and took another sip of her latte.

"Would you be willing to see if you can find out anything about the investigation?"

"How could that possibly help?" She frowned and looked around like she was trying to make sure no one was listening to our conversation.

"Establishing motive would help a great deal. If Coach Griggs was . . ." I searched for a diplomatic way to say it, ". . . involved in a misunderstanding, it might explain why someone wanted to kill him."

She wrapped her hands around her mug and seemed to be considering my request. That she hadn't just refused to answer me and stormed out was a good sign.

"I'm not going to endanger my job," she said, staring into her mug.

"I wouldn't want you to," I said honestly.

"But I'll see if there's anything I can find out. I'll let you know." She got up abruptly, returned her mug to the counter, and left without looking back.

Chapter Twenty-Five

It was dark thirty before I made it back to the rescue. I hate daylight savings time. I'd called Grady on the way home and told him I'd discovered that Cameron Green had a connection to hunting and dirt bikes, but I'd omitted the part where I asked Leslie to find out anything on Coach Griggs's potential shady dealings. He was his usual unenthusiastic, noncommittal self and took the opportunity, once again, to remind me to keep my nose out of it. I felt a pang of guilt that I was betraying people I cared about every time I followed the impulse to investigate. I warred with myself the entire rest of my short drive home, alternating between deciding that I really *would* keep my nose out of it, then turning around and deciding to try to talk Andy and Grady into understanding my perspective.

I wandered out to barn before going inside and found that Tanner had yet again done everything that needed doing. Biscuit trotted down from his pile of hay, "honking" as Tanner calls it, with every step. He immediately rubbed his little head on me, then started searching my pockets for treats. I'm sure some trainers would scold me severely for spoiling him the way I have, but I honestly just can't resist his charms. He wasn't too disappointed by the lack of goodies when I chased down all his itchy spots instead.

When I finally pried myself away from Biscuit, I headed inside, cursing myself for not picking up some takeout on the way home. However, as the heavenly scent of pinto beans and cornbread greeted me as I walked through the door, I was glad I'd skipped the takeout. Any bean purist will tell you that you should slow-simmer them all day to achieve the perfect soup, but anyone who's lived around my dad for any length of time knows that he can replicate those results in a fraction of the time. Even though I've watched him do it my whole life, knowing the process involves minimal water and a hard boil, I still can't fix them the way he does.

I was surprised to see Tanner still there. He looked at me sheepishly.

"Hey, Boss. Jasper insisted I stay for supper," he said self-consciously.

"Of course, you're welcome." I clapped him on the shoulder and helped myself to a large bowl of beans and cornbread.

"Well?" Dad asked, taking the seat at my kitchen table across from me with his own bowl. Tanner followed suit and helped himself.

"I don't know any more than I did. Leslie confirmed that there have been multiple rumors about Coach Griggs. And she reacted really strangely when I asked about another teacher, Cameron Green."

I took a big bite and closed my eyes. It had been way too long since I'd let Dad cook for me. As I chewed, I opened my phone to Cameron Green's Facebook account and pulled up the photo of him with his dirt bike. I slid the phone across the table to Dad and Tanner.

"He just happens to be in an off-roading club," I said. "And while *that* bike is blue and white, he might have a black one too. Or borrowed one. I think he's about the right size to be the person on the black dirt bike."

Tanner started scrolling through the photos.

"Good. That's good. That's something you can take to Grady." Dad nodded as he spoke.

"Already did."

"What was his take on it?"

"He told me to stop my "sloppy little investigation.""

"Of course, he did!" Dad laughed. "He *has* to say that. He can't openly support you because he's the sheriff, but he never hesitates to use the information you bring to him, does he?"

I thought about that while I took another bite.

"Did you see this one?" Tanner asked, and pushed my phone back in front of me.

The photo featured Cameron Green in the foreground, astride his blue-and-white bike, black helmet under his arm. He was flanked by Noah Porter and one of the other kids I recognized from Noah's Instagram photos. Noah was holding his black helmet under his arm just as Cameron did, beside his *black* bike.

"Why does everything come back to this kid?" I asked with a heavy sigh.

"You don't want it to be him," Tanner said. He looked disappointed.

"No," I said, honestly. "He's just so young."

"Look at what's been done. A man was murdered, his widow viciously assaulted, and an attempt made on your life. It doesn't matter how old the killer is, as long as he's stopped." Tanner spoke passionately. "Whoever did this, whether it was Noah or someone else, is capable of just about anything."

"You're absolutely right and I agree with you. But I don't have to be excited about it."

Tanner unlocked his phone and started scrolling.

"Seems like he would be really easy to rule out," Dad said, and popped a chunk of cornbread in his mouth.

Tanner looked up from his scrolling, and we both stared at him.

"Well, the person who shot at you," he pointed at me with the rest of his cornbread, "waited around all night for the chance. If Noah was at home last night, then he isn't your killer."

"It's not like I can just waltz into his house and start asking about alibis," I said. "He was at school today, and he didn't look like he'd been up all night."

"You didn't blink an eye after an all-nighter at eighteen either," Dad pointed out.

I suddenly had an idea. "I could ask him about Cameron Green," I said triumphantly.

"How does that help?" Tanner asked.

"They're in that off-roading club together. I can approach Noah by asking him about Cameron's history with the club and where they ride together. And then I can lead into asking him about *his* whereabouts."

"He's not just going to tell you that he tried to kill you," Tanner said.

"No, but that's part of how we used to investigate medical fraud and malpractice claims. We would ask questions to try to establish points that we could either prove or disprove. For instance, when I was a legal nurse consultant, we had a case that involved Medicare fraud. The physician was padding his bill with visits, tests, and procedures that either weren't performed or shouldn't have been performed. But he was well-liked among his staff and patients. We finally cracked the case by establishing that he'd been somewhere else during some of the times when he was supposed to be online for telehealth visits he'd been billing for. No one wanted to tell us outright that he was doing these things because he had them all convinced that it wasn't really happening. It took interviewing people separately and establishing facts and timelines that we could compare against the billing data to catch him at it. Once we'd established that he'd been lying, the whole house of cards came crashing down."

"I guess you can catch Noah at practice tomorrow," Tanner said.

"They're practicing tomorrow? How do you know that?"

Tanner pointed at his phone. "His latest photo. The caption says, 'See everyone at practice tomorrow,' and he tagged the team."

"Huh," I said. "Does it happen to say what time?"

"Yes, actually. There's a discussion about it in the comments. They're all pretty unhappy that the stand-in Coach is making them start at seven AM on a Saturday."

"Yuck. I'd be pretty unhappy too," I said.

Then I remembered that Andy was supposed to come in the morning, but I didn't know what time. I knew I needed to tell him I wouldn't be there, but I was afraid that would be the last straw.

"Thanks for supper," Tanner said as he pushed his chair back and rose to his feet.

Timmy, who had been curled up at Dad's feet, growled at the movement but, on realizing it was Tanner and not me who had moved, settled back down quickly. Banjo got up from beside my chair, glared at the little dog, and trotted into the living room.

"Anytime," Dad said, grinning from ear to ear.

"See you in the morning, Boss."

"You should take a day off once in a while," I said.

"I will. Someday." He grinned and pulled his baseball cap on over his curly mop of hair.

"That boy is good people," Dad said when Tanner had closed the door. "Ashley is too. You're lucky as the day is long to have those two."

"Don't I know it," I agreed.

I pushed my empty bowl back and rubbed my belly. It was so good I wanted more, but I already needed to unbutton my jeans, so I decided to stop before I was absolutely miserable. Besides, the persistent thought that I needed to call Andy was making me miserable enough.

Dad started gathering up the dishes and turned the water on in the sink.

"I'll wash those," I said, jumping to my feet.

"Nonsense. I don't get to feed people very often anymore. I'll clean up."

"You're welcome out here anytime, you know that, right?"

He pulled me in for a hug, and I held on for a long time.

"Everything okay, Punkin?"

I started to lie and tell him I was fine, but when I opened my mouth, it all came flooding out. I unloaded on him, telling him about everything that had happened in the last week and ending with the conflict with Andy. By the time I was finished, tears were rolling down my cheeks and I got mad at myself all over again for crying.

Dad ushered me into the living room and guided me to the sofa, gathering up the little growling demon-beast on the way.

"I like that boy Andy. And I like that you're finally seeing someone again," Dad said as he situated Timmy on his lap. The little furball looked like he'd finally found Heaven. "But if he can't accept you for who you are, *all* that you are, it isn't going to work."

Banjo jumped up on the sofa and half-laid in my lap, glaring back at Timmy. I hugged him close and buried my face in his shoulder.

"Same with Ethan. He's a good man and he's a good father to Ginny. But you two never did mesh well."

"It isn't unreasonable for Andy to want me to stay out of danger," I said as much to myself as to my dad.

"Nope. It isn't. But say you do. Say you wipe your hands of all of it right now. What then? How long before you start to resent Andy and it all falls apart under the weight of that resentment?"

I groaned. "Stop making so much sense and just let me wallow in my misery for a little while."

Dad reached over and patted me on the knee. We sat together in silence for a while before I excused myself to make the phone call I'd been dreading to make.

The call to Andy rang several times before his voicemail picked up. The breath I didn't realize I was holding came out in a rush, and I had to struggle to find the words to leave a message.

"Hi, um, I just wanted to let you know that I might, um, be gone in the morning when you come. Or you could just call first. Whatever works for you. See you then."

I cringed as I ended the call. I would have had to work really hard to sound more like a babbling moron. I managed to talk Dad into staying put on the sofa with Timmy while I washed the dishes and put away the leftovers. I readied the spare bedroom for him, but it felt weird that he wouldn't be staying in the master bedroom. The house had been his, and I still felt like a kid when he was around.

"I'm going to turn in. I've got an early day if I'm going to catch Noah at practice in the morning."

"Goodnight, Punkin." Dad smiled as he stroked Timmy's round little head. "I'm going to stay up for a bit and read."

I grabbed a melatonin from the medicine cabinet and hoped that it would help turn my brain off and let me sleep.

Chapter
Twenty-Six

I yawned as I pulled into the school parking lot beside another white F150 a few years newer than mine. It also had an intact paint job.

"Are you sure I can't go in?" I asked Tanner as he opened the passenger door.

"Boss, don't make me stick my foot in my mouth again," he said with a grin. He was referring to his earlier statement that, based on our ages, *he* would blend in better and cause less suspicion than I would.

"Just like we went over," I reminded him, and he saluted me through the window.

I had never anticipated how hard it would be to wait for Tanner to get back. I couldn't focus on the emergency book I keep in my console, and I'd already combed through Cameron Green's and Noah Porter's social media accounts, at least the posts that I could access. I was just about to do some mindless scrolling through Pinterest when my phone rang with a number I didn't recognize.

"I apologize for not calling yesterday," the male voice said when I clicked on the call. It took me a minute to figure out that it was Patricia's son, Rhett.

"No problem. I'm sure you had plenty to deal with. How is your mom?"

"She's awake!" he said with a rush of breath, sounding so happy and relieved it made me smile. "She gave her statement to the sheriff this morning. I'm afraid she didn't get a good look at her attacker though."

"That's wonderful news! That she's awake, I mean." I wondered if it would be tacky or not to ask what she *did* remember about her ordeal.

"She's going to need some rehab and we're trying to figure out what that's going to look like, but one of the first things she asked was about that dog."

"Please assure her that he can stay as long as she needs. He and my dad are becoming great buddies."

He laughed. "That's hard to believe, but I'm glad."

"I'm so sorry to ask this, but does your mom remember anything that might help us identify the person who hurt her? I wouldn't ask, but I believe the same person tried to kill me."

"Wait, what?" his voice took on a slight squeak. "She told the sheriff everything she knows."

"Did you happen to hear what that was?"

"Not all of it. I did hear her ask him if he still thought Doug's death was an accident. But I don't think she can help you."

"I understand. I'm so glad she's doing well." I wanted to ask more questions, and I wanted to ask if I could speak directly to Patricia, but it didn't seem like the right time. He thanked me again for taking care of Timmy, promised to keep me updated, and we hung up.

I flinched as Tanner jumped into the passenger seat.

"We should go, *now.*"

I glanced back and saw Noah Porter talking to his dad and pointing toward my truck. I didn't waste any time. When we'd turned onto the main road, I slowed down and looked at Tanner.

"What happened?"

"Noah seems like a nice kid, didn't have any problem telling me all about the mudding club and where they ride. But his dad was in the bleachers, and he ended the conversation before I ever had a chance to ask anything important."

I cursed inwardly.

"Bruce Porter threatened to file harassment charges," Tanner said quietly.

I cursed outwardly.

"Sorry, Boss."

"It's okay. It was stupid to question him. I can't say that I blame Bruce, I'd have the same reaction if someone was questioning Ginny."

"So, what do we do now?"

Suddenly I felt the entire weight of the past few days pressing on my shoulders.

"Maybe I should take everyone's advice and back off," I sighed.

"Sure, that's always an option," Tanner said. "Or we could try to find out what Coach was hiding that someone was willing to kill for. That's what this is all about, right? I mean, his body was searched, his widow was attacked, and their place was ransacked.

And they must not have found it, or they wouldn't have tried to kill you."

I didn't have time to respond before my phone rang over the truck's Bluetooth. Andy's name appeared on the dash display. I hesitated to answer. I didn't want Tanner to overhear how disappointed Andy was likely to be with me, but I also didn't want to let his message go to voicemail.

So I answered in the most awkward way possible, because of course I did.

"Hey!" I said with so much forced cheer that I wished I could crawl under the seat. "I'm just here, driving, with Tanner. Tanner's here too! Say 'hi,' Tanner!" I glanced over at him, nodding.

"Um, hi?" Tanner looked skeptically from me to the display.

"Hello Tanner," Andy's voice sounded equally confused. "I got your message, but it was late last night so I didn't want to risk waking you. I have an emergency client meeting this morning anyway, so I'll touch base with you when I'm finished."

"That sounds good. Talk to you then," I said and ended the call.

Then I scrolled down to the number from Rhett's call and hit redial before I lost my nerve.

"Hello?" His voice sounded muffled.

"I'm so sorry to call now, but I was wondering if I could go to your Mom's place and get some of Timmy's things to make him feel more at home? Like his bed and any special toys," I said. I really did want to help the dog settle in better while he waited for Patricia to recover.

"Yes, of course. She keeps a spare key in that cast-iron dinner bell above the wishing-well in the front yard. Just put it back when you're finished."

"Thank you, I will."

I turned the truck back toward the Griggs farm.

* * *

The house key was right where Rhett said it would be. I opened the door and Tanner followed me in.

"Oh wow," he said as we entered the living room. "You weren't kidding when you said the place was trashed."

"This is awful," I agreed, leading Tanner down the hall to the room Patricia told me served as Coach's "man cave," even if he had hated that term. "Patricia shouldn't have to come home to this. I'll bet we could get some people together and get it straightened up before she's released."

"I'm sure we can. I know Ashley would help too. I think she could organize anything."

I laughed, but he wasn't kidding. She had a take-charge demeanor, and I was often envious of her organizational skills.

"We can clean as we go," I said as I picked up some of the papers that had been thrown from the desk. I leafed through them, but didn't see anything out of the ordinary.

In less than half an hour we had cleared most of the office area, but we didn't have any evidence to show for it. I put the last of the loose files in the desk drawer and closed it with a sigh.

"Why don't we split up for a bit? I'll holler if I find anything at all interesting," Tanner said.

"Yeah, that's a good idea. I'll start in the living room."

"I'll take the barn."

While I was thinking about it, I found Timmy's fluffy little bed, which was embroidered with his name. I threw in the most worn and loved of his toys, his food and water dishes, and the

241

opened bag of his kibble. Hopefully, those things would help him feel more at home until he could come home for good. I couldn't help but feel sorry for the bitey little beast. Like Jet, his whole world had been turned upside down. I'd put the stuff in the backseat of my truck and started back inside when Tanner rounded the corner of the house.

"Hey Boss, I think I found something."

I followed him to the barn and expected him to go inside, but instead he passed the door and led me to Coach Griggs's horse trailer. He pulled open the tack compartment at the front of the two-horse trailer and stood back. I didn't see anything out of the ordinary. The saddle stand took up most of the space, and save for a stray lead rope it was empty.

"I got to thinking about that key. The one you found on the saddle. It made me wonder if it might go to something that wasn't as obvious as a file cabinet since he hid stuff in weird places, so I checked the trailer. Sure enough, it was locked. But these old trailers aren't very secure, and you can just pop it open with a pocketknife."

"You broke in?"

"Not really," he blushed and ran a hand through his curly hair. "It's hardly breaking in if it doesn't require any effort."

I frowned at him. "I don't see anything."

"No, look up there," he said, pointing to the top of the compartment.

I had to get down on my knees to see the top of the small compartment. Sure enough, Coach had used four magnetic clips to secure a manilla envelope to the metal roof of the compartment. I started to remove it, but hesitated. There was no guarantee it had anything to do with his murder, but if it did, I wouldn't want to ruin the chances they could use it in court. But I wanted to know what was in that envelope so bad!

Ultimately, I decided to leave it alone. I texted Darrin instead of Grady because I felt guilty about the amount of time he'd already spent addressing my concerns, issues, and attempts on my life. Darrin showed up in plain clothes, and I felt guilty about disturbing his weekend too.

Tanner showed him the envelope and ran through how he'd found it. Darrin gave him the same frown I had.

"You two have got to stop," he said as he bent over to remove the envelope. "I think this was the *one* thing we didn't try that damned key on."

He held the envelope in his gloved hands and turned it over to see the other side. I leaned forward to get a look myself. Nothing was written on it. I watched intently to see if he was going to open it.

"I'll just take this back to the office," he said. "And you two need to go home."

"Come on, Darrin," I pleaded. "I left it there for you. At least let us see what's in there."

"No one will have to solve my murder if Grady finds out I let you see what's in here," Darrin protested even as he opened the metal clips.

I leaned farther forward, throwing myself off balance, and had to catch myself against the trailer.

"Easy, don't make me drop it for goodness sake," Darrin scolded.

By the time he'd pulled the papers out of the envelope, Tanner and I had both crowded in to read the print.

"It's transcripts," I said. "For Lucas Porter?"

"That's Noah's older brother, right?" Tanner asked.

"I believe so. But he graduated, what? Two years ago?" I tried to remember what I'd seen on Noah's Instagram.

"Why would he have Lucas Porter's transcripts?" Tanner asked.

"None of this makes any sense," I agreed. "And why hide it? Unless he was blackmailing the Porters. Maybe he's been helping them with their grades for years."

"There's no evidence of that," Darrin said. "Not yet anyway."

"Is there anything else in there?" I bent down to try to see between the pages.

Darrin frowned at me but leafed through the pages anyway.

"Doesn't look like it," he said.

"Look, I know you can't tell us much, but can you tell me anything? I'm a target too, and I don't even know why."

"You're a target because you got in the middle of a murder investigation!" Darrin stuffed the pages back into the envelope.

"Fair enough. But I'm still in danger, even if it's my own fault."

Darrin sighed.

"You know it looked like a hunting accident to begin with. It didn't help that Marvin Randall apparently either saw Coach getting killed or stumbled through shortly after it happened, but was too drunk to make heads or tails out of what he saw. He just kept repeating enough to put him at the scene, and it really looked like he could've been our guy. But then, he went cold turkey and showed up at your place at the same time Mrs. Griggs was getting assaulted at her house," Darrin sighed again.

I nodded, hoping that would prompt him to continue.

"You don't have anything, do you?" Tanner asked.

Darrin didn't answer, but the look on his face told us everything we needed to know.

Chapter
Twenty-Seven

Tanner ran through theories all the way back to the rescue. I caught most of it, even though I felt numb. It was terrifying to think that Grady and his team weren't any closer to figuring out who killed Coach Griggs than I was. Grady had been very close to arresting Braydon Cunningham when he tried to kill me. So even if I hadn't realized he was guilty, he wouldn't have gotten away with it.

Maybe that was the biggest difference. Braydon Cunningham hadn't come home that night intending to murder his father. It had been a crime of passion, a murder in the heat of the moment. Coach Griggs's killer was calculating, patient, and cunning. They had demonstrated as much by setting a trap for me and then waiting all night for me to fall into it. Which I did, without any hesitation or the slightest clue that I was in danger. I cold chill ran through me as that thought crept in again, how close I'd come to meeting the same fate as Coach Griggs. I wondered how long his killer had waited for him in those woods.

"How did the killer know he was going to be there?" I blurted out loud as we got out of the truck. "Did they follow him out there or lie in wait like they did for me?"

"I don't have a clue, Boss."

"Patricia said Coach posted his rides and plans in a Facebook group. We should cross-reference members of that group with our suspect list and see if there's any overlap."

We checked on the horses before heading inside. Ruby raised her head and looked at us for a moment, then went back to her hay. I was so thankful that her colic hadn't recurred and knocked on the barn wood for luck. Jet poked his head out of the stall window, but snorted and jerked it away when I tried to pet his nose. There was *another* insistent nose, however, that was more than happy to be on the receiving end of any and all affection.

Biscuit leaned into me as I rubbed his little shoulders. I've loved horses my entire life. I loved everything about them, from their unique, earthy scent to the feeling of freedom you get when you ride them. So it was a bit of a surprise to me that a small, somewhat obnoxious donkey had stolen my entire heart.

"There's a job that never ends," Tanner said. "You're going to have to just walk away."

"You know I can't resist him."

"Who can?" Tanner laughed, and produced a treat from his pocket.

We finally bid Biscuit goodbye and went to the house. Dad was busy in the kitchen and the entire house smelled like cinnamon and sugar.

"What is that heavenly smell?" Tanner asked as he joined Dad in the kitchen.

"I found all the stuff to bake an apple pie, so I thought why not?"

"Well, you can count me in," Tanner said, rubbing his belly.

I worried that Dad was lonely. He'd settled in and seemed so eager to cook and entertain, which wasn't out of character for him, but I worried that I wasn't spending enough time with him. I was already carrying a lot of guilt that I hadn't gotten to see Mom enough before she died. I still lived in St. Louis at the time and was working sixty hours or more a week.

I retrieved my laptop and notepad and settled in at the kitchen table. I pulled up Facebook, then drew a blank on the name of Coach's riding group. I stared at the screen, hoping I could pull it out of the fog in my brain.

"Everything okay?" Tanner took the seat next to me.

"I can't remember the name of the group."

"Can you look at Coach's page and see if it's listed under his check-ins or likes?"

"Good idea."

Sure enough, it took only a few seconds of digging and the Hillspring Hill Riders group was displayed on the screen. There was a nice tribute to Coach Griggs, and someone had made a collage of his photos. I pulled up the members list and was surprised at how long it was. There were members from all over northwest Arkansas. None of the Porters were members.

"Can you pull up a list of the faculty and staff at the school?" I pointed to Tanner's phone.

He nodded and went to work. But that didn't pan out either. I sighed and leaned back in my chair. I propped my aching leg up in the chair opposite Tanner. It was getting better every day, but still ached some when I failed to keep it elevated enough. The horseshoe imprint had faded to ugly shades of purple and yellow.

"That was a dead end," Tanner said.

Timmy rounded the corner, took one look at me and Tanner, and growled softly. He took a few slurps of water and then trotted back to the sofa with Dad.

"I forgot to bring in Timmy's stuff," I said as I started to get to my feet.

"I'll go get it." Tanner beat me getting up.

My phone rang beside me, and I snatched it up, hoping to see Andy's name displayed there. But it was Grady. Enough time had passed for Darrin to fill him in on what we found at the Griggs's residence. I braced myself for the scolding I knew was coming.

"What did you *do*?" he hissed as soon as I picked up.

"Technically, I didn't do anything. Tanner found the . . ."

"Not that," he cut me off. "What did you do to cause Bruce Porter to come in and file an official report?"

"Oh. That." I physically cringed even though he couldn't see me.

"Yeah, *that*," he said with a heavy sigh.

"I had the idea that we might be able to find out where Noah Porter was the night my fences were cut, or at least get him to tell us something we could verify or not," I said as Tanner came back in with Timmy's stuff.

Dad started cooing over the dog again, taking the toys and bed and getting him settled into the guest bedroom where Dad was staying.

Tanner pointed at the phone and mouthed "Who's that?"

I mouthed "Grady" back.

"Well, now you have an official complaint, and I'm going to need to talk to you in an official capacity."

"I understand." I felt like a teenager being chastised by a parent. But I also knew his anger was justified. "Tomorrow?"

"No. I'm not coming in on a Sunday because you can't follow simple directions to stay out of my investigation. You can come on Monday. Bring Tanner and pray you haven't ruined his future too."

"I'll be there Monday."

He grunted something that I couldn't quite make out and ended the call. I put the phone down and hugged myself.

"I'm guessing he wasn't happy," Tanner sat heavily in the chair opposite me.

"Bruce Porter filed a complaint. We both have to go in Monday and talk to Grady. I'm so sorry, Tanner. Your mom is going to kill me." I suddenly felt tired to my very bones.

"He's got to talk to you both if that Porter fella complained," Dad said as he came in to check the pie. "It won't amount to much."

"I think you're more optimistic than I am," I said.

"Jasper's right. We didn't do anything illegal," Tanner said.

Their kind words didn't comfort me much. I was continually aware that I was acting in conflict with one of my oldest friends plus the man I was . . . what? Falling in love with? It wasn't ideal to have yet another existential crisis in front of my dad and Tanner, so I excused myself to go to the barn.

I grabbed the couple of brushes we were using for Ruby and let myself into her paddock. I tried, although sometimes unsuccessfully what with students coming and going now, to keep each horse's grooming equipment separate. Especially the new arrivals, because skin conditions can be highly contagious. Ruby watched me warily as I approached her. I allowed her to sniff the brushes and she settled quickly. I used the soft bristle brush on her face and bony body and the stiffer one for her muddy legs. She seemed to enjoy the grooming and paused munching her hay a couple of times to bob her head and flop her lower lip when I hit a particularly itchy spot. Her coat was dull and coarse. She needed deworming, but that would have to wait until she'd gained a little weight first.

After I finished with Ruby, I switched out my grooming equipment, grabbed a halter, and cautiously opened the door to Jet's stall. He tossed his head and snorted at the intrusion. He was hard to catch even in the stall, and it took several minutes to get the halter on him. It probably took longer than it should have, but I was extra careful about staying out of kicking range. When I finally got him caught, I led him into the breezeway and cross-tied him. He started pawing immediately. I was really glad we had a rubber mat on the dirt barn floor in the grooming area, or he would've dug a hole in no time at all.

I started by just brushing his shiny black coat. The differences between him and Ruby were striking. He was at near perfect weight, sleek, and well-muscled. Coach and Mrs. Griggs clearly took excellent care of their horses. I picked out his hooves and considered it a breakthrough that he only tried to kick me once during the process. He was going to be the most challenging project for us so far. Funny how that works. Ruby came to us from deplorable conditions, starved and mistreated, and she had been nothing but sweet and well-mannered.

Grooming the horses gave me a reprieve from the constant loop of worry and regret that was swirling around in my head. And even in the face of further angering Grady, potentially ruining my relationship with Andy, and putting myself in even more danger, I couldn't suppress the feeling of urgency and the need to find out what had happened.

"What's *wrong* with me?" I asked Jet as I dodged a pawing hoof. He snorted and looked at me, wide-eyed and wary.

I put him back in the stall and promised him we would try turning him out with the others in the morning. I wondered if he didn't need some time to just be a horse for a while before we started his retraining. He'd suffered multiple traumas, and this was the second big move for him in less than a year. I couldn't think of any reason that he wouldn't benefit from some downtime.

I jumped when the FaceTime ring sounded in my pocket, and then I remembered it was Saturday. I happily tapped "join" and smiled at my daughter's beautiful face that filled up my phone screen. She was the best parts of me and Ethan. She had my blond hair and blue eyes, and his high cheekbones and full lips.

"Are you at the barn?"

"Yeah, just doing some grooming. We have a couple of new additions."

"Oh!" she said excitedly. "Show me!"

I took her on a little FaceTime tour and told her about Jet and Ruby. We chatted for a long time about the sweet sorrel mare and what she would need along her road to recovery. I kept steering the conversation away from Andy because I wasn't sure if she was going to get to meet him over Christmas break or not. And every time we almost touched on that subject, the lump returned to my throat.

"Oh yeah, Grandpa is staying out here for a while. He wanted to make sure to keep an eye on me until the killer is caught." I instantly regretted saying this, since I hadn't intended to tell her that someone had taken shots at me. "You know, since we have Coach's horse and I'm the one who found the body."

"Uh huh," she said, and looked at me skeptically. "You sure that's all?"

Omitting something is different from an outright lie. And I wasn't going to lie to my daughter. So I told her. All of it.

"I don't know what to say." She looked away from her phone into the distance.

"You don't have to say anything."

"I am so mad at you. You never tell me anything until I pin you down."

"I want you to focus on your classes. Worrying about whatever mess I've gotten myself into down here isn't going to help you study."

"That is *not* the point Mom, and you know it!" She leaned into the camera. "How would you feel if I did this to you?"

"I really hope you never experience anything like this."

"I need to go," she said, shaking her head.

"Ginny, please."

"Bye Mom," she said and ended the call.

I sank down onto the steps to the loft. I'd now succeeded in making nearly everyone I loved mad at me. I was no closer to finding out who killed Coach Griggs, and now that person was trying to kill me too. I was really tired of dissolving into tears, but I could feel them stinging my eyes as I took a deep, steadying breath.

My text tone alarmed in my pocket, and I hesitated to look. I had the irrational idea that it was someone else unhappy with me. It didn't help that all of my current conflicts were completely of my own doing, completely my fault. Since my phone was set to alarm every two minutes until I addressed the text message, I pulled it out of my pocket.

Your luck will run out eventually. I almost took you out yesterday. There will be another chance. Or should I try for that curly-headed cretin instead?

I gasped as I read and reread the message. I knew they weren't going to come right out and tell me, but I couldn't resist responding: *Who is this?*

The message was green, which told me they weren't using an iPhone. And if they were as smart as they seemed to be, they wouldn't be using their own number to threaten me.

Hahahaha! I'm right in front of you and you've never suspected a thing.

Even though I knew I was alone, I sat bolt upright and looked around. My heart still pounding, I sent a screen shot to Grady. It didn't take long for him to respond.

Same number as last time?

I told him it was.

Don't have any confidence we can find out anything. Likely prepaid, but I'll try. They're trying to scare you. BE CAREFUL.

I shuddered involuntarily.

It's working. I'm scared.

I got up, closed the barn doors, and looked around the hill, *my* hill. Anger rose in my chest, replacing the fear. How *dare* some coward hide and threaten me! Emboldened by the ember of rage that started to burn in my chest, I pulled the anonymous texts back up on my phone and read them again. Then I pulled Grady's number up and called him.

"The threat against Tanner scares me more than anything else," I said as soon as the call connected.

"Is there any chance you can convince him to lay low until we catch this maniac?" he sounded tired. I could sympathize.

"I can try. But I don't think so."

He sighed. "Try *really hard.*"

We ended the call. I went to the house, dreading what I knew I had to do.

Chapter Twenty-Eight

As I'd thought, it was almost impossible to get Tanner to agree to stay away from the rescue, and from me, until the killer was arrested. Almost. Much as I hated to, I had to threaten to rescind his recent promotion to rescue manager, and the coup de grace was my threat to talk to his mother. He might be an adult, but he still lived at home, and Rachel could be very persuasive when it came to her only son.

The look on Tanner's face when he left nearly broke my heart. I couldn't help but feel an overwhelming sense of dread and defeat as I watched his taillights fade down the driveway. Dad joined me on the porch and wrapped his arm around my shoulder. Tanner had proven himself as a manager long before I gave him the title. I'd come to lean on him for everything from the day-to-day minutia to moral support.

"You shouldn't run that boy off," Dad said, echoing my thoughts. "You can tell he puts his heart and soul into your rescue."

"Even Grady thinks he should lay low until the killer is caught. Those were his exact words, to 'lay low.'" I defended my decision, maybe even to myself.

"When did you start listening to Grady?" Dad grinned as he said this, but the words cut anyway.

"Maybe I should've listened to him all along. Then I wouldn't be in this mess."

"Maybe." Dad squeezed my shoulders. "But if you had, they might not have found that vest, and the whole thing might've gotten pinned on that drunk guy."

"I don't think so. The killer would've still been looking for whatever it is that Coach was hiding."

"Well, the problem is that we can't go back in time and change it. You're here *now* and you need to get mad. Stop moping around and wishing you weren't in the middle of this and just keep going. Keep following your instincts." Dad clapped me on the back. "Now, come inside and have some pie."

* * *

The pie was heavenly. Dad had always been an amazing cook. I polished off two pieces while he continued to list all the reasons I should turn into a raging vigilante. By the end of the second piece, he was starting to make sense.

I went over everything again in my head while he talked. Why did Coach Griggs have Lucas Porter's transcripts? Honestly, I'd expected there to be something about Noah. He was the only common thread in the whole thing. And much as I didn't want to believe a kid could be responsible for murder, he was the right size and build to be the person on the dirt bike. He had connections to an off-roading club, and the helmet I'd seen in the office that day was a dead ringer for the one I'd seen at Patricia Griggs's house and in the woods. I needed to look more into the Porters before they slapped me with a restraining order.

I pulled out my phone to check Bruce Porter's dealership hours, and it dinged with a text. Again it was a number I didn't recognize. *It's Leslie. Can you call me? I need to speak with you urgently, but privately.*

I excused myself, went to my bedroom, and called the number. She picked up on the first ring.

"I hope you can understand that I'm in a very difficult position," Leslie said immediately.

"Of course." I hoped my sympathetic tone would encourage her to continue.

"I came in today under the pretense that I needed to catch up on some work. But I used this time to look into the matter we discussed, and I've found something very concerning. I cannot be attached to this information in any way." Her voice was quiet and shaky.

"What did you find?"

"I've spent the last hour trying to figure out a way to get this information to you without becoming involved. I will *not* be involved," she said those last words with such conviction that I found myself nodding along even though she couldn't see me.

"I don't know how to guarantee . . ."

"I do," she cut me off. "I've found a few additional items that belong to Coach Griggs, and I am calling you to come get them," she spoke slowly and deliberately. "Since you retrieved his other belongings, this is not likely to raise suspicion. While you are here, you will *discover* the information."

"Understood. Should I come now?"

"Yes. And come alone. I don't want to have to worry about anyone else."

I agreed and ended the call.

"Dad," I called as I gathered up my purse and keys.

"In the kitchen," he answered.

Banjo watched me hopefully, and I bent down to scratch his ears on the way to the kitchen. "Next time," I told him.

"They've found some more of Coach Griggs's stuff at the school, and I'm going to run over and grab it," I said, keeping up Leslie's story. And since she'd told me she really had found some things, I wasn't lying to him.

"Want me to go with you?"

"No, I'd rather you kept an eye on things here. I feel better knowing someone is watching over the horses."

"You bet. Be careful." He pulled me over and gave me a kiss on the forehead.

I was mostly on autopilot during the drive in to the school, alternating between hoping that Leslie had found something useful and hoping that it turned out to be nothing. Part of me hated to think that Coach could be involved in anything shady or illegal. But he had definitely been hiding something, there was no denying that.

I pressed the buzzer at the front door and heard the lock click. I pushed the door open and looked around for Leslie. The empty school was eerily quiet. Most of the interior lights were turned off, and even in the middle of the day it seemed dark and foreboding. My boots echoed on the tile as I walked past the dark administration office.

"Leslie?" I called out, my word bouncing back at me from the empty halls.

"Follow me." She'd appeared from out of nowhere at my side. I gasped and jumped, causing Leslie to frown at me disapprovingly.

"Where are we going?"

"Coach Griggs's office," she said without turning around. She pulled the mustard-yellow sweater tighter around her as she walked, her long, pleated skirt billowing out behind her. Once again, she seemed lost in the oversized clothes.

I followed her through the dark halls, then out into the blinding daylight again as we took the covered concrete path to the gym. The last time I'd been there the gym had rung out with the sounds of squeaking sneakers and shouting kids. This time, the gym was as tomb-quiet as the school. The narrow hall past the locker room was pitch black, but Leslie didn't turn on any lights as we went. Even after my eyes started to adjust, I had the claustrophobic sensation of descending into a cave. Thankfully, the light was on in Coach Griggs's office, and my irrational unease dissipated in the bright fluorescent lights.

"Did you bring a box?" Leslie frowned again, wringing her hands nervously. "Or a bag, or anything?"

"I'm sorry, no."

"It's going to look very suspicious if you're supposed to pick up items and you don't leave with them, isn't it?" I suspected she spoke with the tone she used with unruly teenagers.

"I didn't realize there were that many items," I said truthfully. "I'll make it look believable. What is the *other* information?"

She started wringing her hands again.

"It's on the computer," she pointed to the ancient desktop on the desk. "I'll walk you through it."

I sat down at the desk, and the computer came to life as soon as I moved the mouse.

"What you're looking at are the grades for the basketball team over time," Leslie pointed to the spreadsheet. "Coach Griggs was keeping tabs on every player, but only in certain classes—classes that he had subbed for—and each of those classes had students with unexplained jumps in grades. Those jumps made the difference in being allowed to participate in extracurricular activities or not."

Leslie stood back with a somber expression. I looked over the information, trying to think of all the possible explanations for it. Unfortunately, most of the explanations ended with Coach Griggs manipulating grades so that his players could stay on the team. My heart sank, and it must've shown on my face, because Leslie moved away from the desk and looked away.

"You can go through the rest of the documents," she said, her back still turned to me. "I'll go get a box for his things and you can ask any questions you might have when I get back."

She left without looking back. I suspected she was giving me a moment to digest the whole mess. Instead of ruminating on what I did and didn't want to find there, I just dove into the information. Every time there was a dip in a student's overall grades, there would be a corresponding jump in one of the other classes to compensate for it, bringing the overall GPA over the threshold for participation.

It was obvious that Coach had been manipulating grades, and here was the proof. I still didn't know how it fit into his murder, but it was something I could take to Grady. I looked around for a printer and finally found an ancient, dusty model tucked under the desk. I powered it on and printed the documents, checking to make sure the spreadsheet didn't print weirdly. As I waited for the printer to finish, I had a sudden niggling feeling that I couldn't shake.

I remembered a malpractice case tried by my former law firm that had centered around a nurse's failure to recognize a patient's deteriorating symptoms in the intensive care unit. The case had come down to the metadata attached to the nurse's documentation in the electronic health record. She'd tried to say that she *had* recognized the early symptoms of sepsis and acted on them, only to get nowhere with the attending physician, despite the testimony that she hadn't called the attending or followed the chain of command and notified her charge nurse. Her argument was that she had been targeted by administration and had documented her concerns in the patient's chart. The problem was that she'd documented those concerns a full two days after the shift in question, which was revealed by the metadata in the record. She'd accessed the chart *after* finding out that the patient's condition had declined, and she'd been named in the incident report for not recognizing the signs.

I clicked "file," then "info," and finally "version history." I stared at the screen, trying to make sense of what I was seeing. There was only one name displayed in the version history and it wasn't Douglas Griggs. Coach had been set up. He wouldn't have left something this important and incriminating to be so easily found; he would've hidden it someplace stupid and weird—like the fringe of a breastcollar.

Chapter Twenty-Nine

I quickly printed the version history too, shoved the entire wad of printed papers in my back pocket, and sat back down at the desk to wait for Leslie. When she didn't return immediately, I started poking around the other files on Coach Griggs's computer. There wasn't much there. I scrolled through rosters, practice schedules, and fund-raiser lists. I didn't expect to find anything, it was just taking a lot longer than it should have for Leslie to return with the box.

I shut the computer down and started searching around the office. I looked in all the out-of-the-way places that I'd failed to check during my first visit, like under the desk, behind the posters on the wall, and under all the drawers. Nothing. I sat back down at the desk and tried to imagine where Coach might have hidden something in the small, sparse office. But there weren't any places I hadn't already looked. As the minutes ticked by, I grew more and more worried.

I finally gave up and opened the door just in time to nearly get run over by Cameron Green. For the second time, we had ended up in Coach Griggs's office at the same time.

"What are you doing here?" he asked, as startled as I was, but he quickly recovered. "Not that I'm not glad to see you."

"I'm picking up the rest of Coach's things. I missed some stuff the first time." I didn't return his smile. "What are *you* doing here?"

"I've taken over helping with scheduling the practices. I found out this morning that I don't have the updated roster. I was hoping it was in here somewhere," he nodded past me toward the office.

"Did you see Leslie on your way down here?" I asked, looking past him in the dark hallway.

"No," he turned and followed my gaze down the hallway. "I didn't even know she was here. I didn't see her car in the parking lot."

I moved to pass him into the hall, but he cut me off.

"Where's the stuff?" he asked, blocking my path.

"In the office," I said, looking him in the eye.

"Are you going to leave without it? I thought that's why you were here."

I wanted to wipe the smirk off his face. He had rubbed me the wrong way every time I'd come in contact with him, and this time was no exception.

"Leslie went to get a box, but she hasn't come back yet." I kept my voice measured and calm, even though I was getting more annoyed and anxious by the minute. I couldn't explain why; his questions weren't unreasonable. Of the two of us, I was the one who didn't belong there.

He nodded, but the expression on his face told me he didn't believe me. I moved forward, prepared to push past him if I needed to, but he moved out of the way. As I passed him, I felt him snatch the papers out of my back pocket. I whirled around and grabbed for them, but he was too quick.

"Give that back!" I said, hating that I sounded like a petulant teenager.

He unfolded the wad and strained to look at the pages in the dark hallway.

"Seems you managed to grab a few things without that box," he said menacingly.

I lunged forward to snatch them back, but he ducked around me and hurried down the hall into the light of the gym.

The gunshot filled the gym with a crack so loud my ears started ringing instantly. It took several seconds for me to realize that the deafening sound was connected to Cameron's sudden spin and crash to the floor. He looked as confused as I was for a split second before his face contorted with pain and fear.

My brain finally caught up, and I inched forward. I guessed, hoped, that the shooter was concealed to the right of the hallway, just judging by the way Cameron had reacted when he was hit. I stayed hidden as best I could and grabbed his foot and dragged him back into the hallway with me. I peeled off my flannel overshirt and wadded it up to put pressure on Cameron's shoulder. He had started to scream, and I tried to quiet him. The shooter obviously knew where we were, but I needed Cameron to hear my instructions.

I grabbed his hand and placed it on my shirt.

"Push, *hard*," I said.

"It hurts!" he screamed back.

"I know it does, but you're going to bleed to death if we don't put pressure on that wound." I tried not to even think about the damage we couldn't see.

I reached back for my phone and found my pocket was empty. Cameron must've pulled my phone out along with the papers. I tried to find it in the dimly lit hallway, but I couldn't see my black phone in its gray case against the dark floor.

"Where's the light switch?"

"Out there." Cameron pointed to the gym, then screamed again when he pushed his hand back down on the wound.

I cursed under my breath. "Do you have a phone?"

"No," he moaned. "I left it in the car."

I cursed again and tried to remember exactly where I'd been when Cameron took the papers. I stood and retraced my steps.

"Don't leave me." Cameron started sobbing in earnest.

"I have to find my phone," I whispered.

"Use the one in the office," he said in between hitching sobs.

"Of course!" I said and shoved the door open.

I pulled the receiver off the hook and . . . drew a complete blank. I hadn't memorized a phone number in at least a decade since they're all right there in my phone, which was God-only-knows where. Then I realized I could call 911 and groaned to myself. I pushed the numbers on the keypad and waited for the call to connect. It felt like it took forever.

"This is Mallory Martin, I'm in the high school gym and someone has shot a teacher. He's alive, conscious, but needs EMS immediately. I don't know who shot him, but they're still here somewhere," I spoke as fast and deliberately as I could. "I need to get back to Cameron Green, he's the teacher who was shot. I don't have a cell phone. Just send help."

I waited for the dispatcher to confirm, then left her talking on the line. I rushed back out to Cameron.

"Help is coming," I said as I knelt beside him.

Leslie appeared at his other side.

"No, no, no," she repeated as she, too, kneeled beside him.

"Get down," I said. "He's still out there somewhere."

"You ruined everything," she hissed at me.

Thankfully, my brain wasn't lagging behind this time, and I realized immediately what she meant. She'd been the one who shot Cameron Green. And the bullet had been meant for me.

Chapter Thirty

Leslie hadn't counted on Cameron being there. She'd taken so long to come back with the box because she'd been waiting for me to give up and come find her, where she'd been lying in wait for me. Just like she had in the woods. My realization was confirmed by the bruise pattern now visible on her uncovered calf. I had a matching bruise on my leg, made by the horseshoe with the wonky nail. She'd gotten kicked by Jet too. Most likely when she killed Coach Griggs and had tried to search his horse the way she'd searched Coach's body.

"Paramedics are on the way," I said, trying not to let on that I'd figured out she'd shot Coach. "Did you see who did this?"

She looked up at me, her eyes so cold and furious that I felt a chill run down my spine.

"Don't play games with me," she spat the words at me as she rose to her feet.

I did the same, leaving Cameron sobbing on the floor between us. He needed attention as soon as possible, but I couldn't help him if I was dead, so I decided to try not to end up that way.

"What do you mean?" I tried to play innocent, but I'm sure my knowledge was written all over my face. I have zero poker face.

Leslie reached around the corner and pulled out a rifle. She slowly brought it up to her shoulder. I glanced behind me, looking for any means of escape.

"Don't bother trying to run. There isn't an exit that way," she said quietly. Somehow, her soft voice was even more threatening than if she'd yelled at me. She was just so *cold*.

"Leslie!" Cameron screeched from the floor. "What are you doing?"

"It's okay," she cooed at him. Her whole demeanor changed. "Just a few more loose ends and we'll be free."

He scooted the few inches to the wall and pulled himself up to a half-sitting position. Thankfully, it didn't look like he was losing a lot of blood. I hoped that she hadn't hit anything crucial.

"What are you talking about?" His voice was high-pitched and shaky.

"I'll explain everything later," she said, and leveled the rifle at me.

"Stop!" he screamed, and grabbed her ankle, causing her to stumble sideways.

"Cameron, my love, you have to let me finish this." She recovered and bent down to him.

I used the distraction to inch toward the locker-room door.

"You're crazy." He went wide-eyed, and his breathing quickened.

"Don't say that." The dreamy look on her face faded and was replaced by the icy stare she'd given me. "Don't *ever* say that."

She stood back up and reached into her sweater pocket. She pulled out a handful of ammunition and threw it at Cameron, who squealed when the brass shells hit him and clattered onto the floor.

"*All* of this has been for you." She was wild-eyed now, breathing heavily, and waving the end of the rifle erratically. "Coach Griggs was going to expose you along with his proposal. He had been collecting evidence for months. We just have to get rid of *her* and you're free and clear. I've made sure that when they find whatever evidence he had, they'll think it was him. I've been circulating that rumor for years anyway."

She laughed, completely unhinged now, her thin frame rocking from side to side as she spoke. I'd almost closed the distance to the locker-room door. Just a few more inches.

"Oh my God, Leslie. What have you done?" Cameron went pale, and I hoped it was from shock and not blood loss I couldn't see.

"I've made sure that you aren't in any danger." The lovesick look returned to her eyes. "And after all of this settles down, we can finally be together."

Slowly, he started to nod. That was all the reassurance Leslie needed. She smiled and bent down to caress his face, and I took the opportunity to dive through the locker-room door, gambling that it wasn't locked. And thankfully it wasn't. Once through the door, I leaned heavily against it, feeling behind me for a lock, but there wasn't one. I scanned the room quickly for anything I might use to secure the door. Leslie was screaming outside like a feral animal, sending cold shivers down my spine.

I braced myself against the door and said a little prayer of thanks that it opened inward and not out into the hall. Leslie shoved from the other side; she was surprisingly strong for her size. I remembered a video I'd watched on TikTok showing how to secure a classroom door during an active shooting incident by using a belt around the automatic closure arm. I wasn't wearing a belt, and my extra shirt was out in the hall with Cameron, so I scanned around for anything within reach that I might be able to wrap around the arm, but there was nothing even remotely close. For a high school locker room, it was amazingly tidy.

The shoving on the other side of the door abruptly stopped, and I got a wild idea. I shimmied out of my bra and tied it around the automatic arm as securely as I could, careful to stretch out the elastic in the hope that it wouldn't give when Leslie resumed her assault. I also hoped she didn't know another way into the locker room, but I didn't have time to dwell on it. I ran to the back wall where the bank of narrow windows lined the top of the wall.

I climbed up on the bench and reached for the window just as another deafening shot filled the room. The concrete-block wall to my left exploded with the impact of the bullet that missed me by inches, spraying me with sharp shards of concrete. I couldn't help it, I screamed and whirled around back toward the door. Leslie had only been able to open the door wide enough to slide the rifle through. She was struggling with the bolt as she could only reach one arm inside. I could finally hear sirens in the distance, and though logically I knew it had only been a few minutes, it felt like I'd been under siege for hours.

I jumped off the bench and searched for anything I could use as a weapon, but the athletic equipment was apparently stored elsewhere. Why couldn't there have been a stray baseball bat lying around somewhere? My ears rang as she shot into the room again. This time the bullet hit nowhere near me, but the blast was so loud in the confined space that my hearing was starting to dull.

Trotting Into Trouble

I ran to the showers, hoping to find a mop or bucket, or just anything that I could swing, and found it in the form of a loose towel bar. Two good yanks and I pulled the surprisingly sturdy steel pipe off the wall. Not wasting any time, I ran back into the main room and positioned myself just out of sight from the door. Leslie had gone quiet again, and the door was closed.

I was just beginning to wonder if she'd made a run for it when I saw the door open again. She reached inside and cut my bra loose from the closure arm. I didn't give myself time to second-guess my actions: the moment the door was flung open, I screamed and lunged forward. I swung the steel pipe with everything I had, bringing it down on the rifle and Leslie's forearm.

It was her turn to scream as she recoiled in pain, dropping the rifle as she stumbled backward. We both recovered about the same time and lunged for the rifle together, but she was quicker than me. Seeing that I wasn't going to be able to wrestle the gun away from her, I pulled the trigger, discharging the cartridge she had chambered. I hoped I could keep her busy long enough to keep her from chambering another one until Grady and his team breached the gym.

But I didn't count on how cat-quick and nimble she was, and she managed to elbow me so hard in the left temple that I saw stars and little bursts of light in my periphery. I lost my balance and fell backward, landing hard on my backside. When I could focus again, I realized I'd knocked the rifle hard enough to destroy the bolt handle, and she couldn't open the chamber to load another round.

I pulled myself to my feet as I heard Grady's voice in the hall.

"Get him out of here," his deep baritone voice echoed against the concrete walls. "Sheriff's department, make yourself known! Surrender your weapon!"

"In here!" I yelled back. "She has a rifle, but it's broken!"

Defeat washed over Leslie's face for a split second before it was replaced by pure, hot rage. She raised the rifle like a club and charged me, screaming like the feral thing she'd become. I ducked just in time and reacted on instinct, bringing my fist up fast and hard into her chin. The *thwack* when my knuckles met her jaw popped like a champagne cork and she fell, unconscious, to the ground.

Grady rounded the corner, sidearm first, took one look at my bra in pieces on the floor, and then at Leslie, before shaking his head at me.

"Clear! Shooter down!" He yelled over his shoulder. He bent down on one knee to cuff Leslie before saying into his shoulder radio that they needed EMS for her too. I cradled my throbbing hand and wished I were close enough to the benches to sit down.

Darrin, Calvin Burns, and a deputy I didn't recognize right away burst through the doorway and took in the scene much as Grady had. Once they'd taken over with Leslie, who was starting to stir, Grady stepped over her and put an arm around me.

"Are you hit?" he asked.

"What?"

"Did she shoot you?"

"Oh," I shook my head. "No."

"You're bleeding." He led me around Leslie, who was now trying to sit up. Darrin told her to be still until the paramedics could check her out in between reading her her Miranda rights. He looked up at me, concern clear on his face.

"I think I got hit by some concrete chunks, and maybe some bullet shards. I don't know," I said, and let him steer me through the hallway. "At one point she was just shooting blindly into the room."

Paramedics were tending to Cameron, who was still conscious and wailing, which I counted as a good sign. We met another team pulling a stretcher heading toward Leslie. They paused to look me over.

"In there," I said, pointing back toward the locker room with the hand that wasn't throbbing in time with my heartbeat.

Grady nearly carried me out into the parking lot. It seemed the farther we went, the weaker I got as the adrenaline started to wear off. He steered me toward an ambulance that was just pulling into the lot. The sheriff deputies who weren't inside had already set up a staging area where emergency medical services, volunteer fire, and search and rescue were checking in. I realized that when I'd called I hadn't been clear about the number of casualties, and they were expecting the worst-case scenario. I was so glad that they wouldn't be needed.

One of the paramedics jumped out of the truck as soon as it stopped and jogged over to me and Grady where I'd slumped against him.

"No GSW," Grady said, speaking in shorthand for "gunshot wound." "She may have some shell fragments, and I suspect a boxer's fracture on that swollen right hand."

He handed me over to the paramedic, whom I recognized as one of Tanner's friends.

"Levi?" I tried to focus on his face.

"Yes ma'am," he said with his South Arkansas drawl. He'd moved to Hillspring during his senior year and become fast friends with Tanner and his group. Tanner had brought him to the rescue a few times, usually on rodeo weekends when they were both competing. I hadn't realized Levi had gone into healthcare. I honestly thought he'd go pro in bronc riding.

"Let's get you checked out." He took over steering me where I needed to go.

I was sitting in the back of the ambulance when they brought Cameron out on a stretcher. He was calmer, and I suspected they'd administered pain medication. He had IV fluids hanging on a short pole attached to the stretcher, and they'd replaced my flannel shirt with a bulky gauze bandage.

Just behind him, the other team brought Leslie out on a stretcher too. She was handcuffed and strapped in. I was a bit satisfied to see that her jaw had started to swell as much as my hand and was taking on an angry purple color. She raised up as far as she could to look at Cameron. Even in her delusional, unhinged state she couldn't mistake the look of pure revulsion that washed over his face, and she started to cry.

Chapter Thirty-One

My forehead was still stinging from the antiseptic wash when I left the ambulance to go find Grady. Levi hadn't found any metal fragments or bits of concrete in my wounds, and based on his physical assessment he didn't think any bones in my hand were broken either, but still recommended an X-ray to confirm. I promised I'd get one if I had any concerning or worsening symptoms.

Familiarity afforded me the ability to wander around an active crime scene, and I was careful not to get in the way or abuse the privilege as I searched for Grady. I found him in the now well-lit hall studying the printout that Cameron had dropped when he was shot. There were deputies everywhere, collecting evidence and taking photos.

"I printed that. I think I know what happened," I said as I approached.

"Is she involved?" He pointed to the page of metadata I printed last.

"I don't think so." I adjusted the ice pack on my hand. "Can we sit?" I gestured toward the bleachers.

He nodded and followed me to a spot that wasn't under intense scrutiny by investigators. I explained why I'd been there, that I'd asked Leslie to look into the rumors about Coach Griggs before I realized that she was the one who'd killed him. I ignored Grady's increasing frown and head shaking as I spoke.

"I figured out something was up as soon as I saw the metadata on that spreadsheet. The only name in the version history was Johanna Vaughn. And the document had been created *after* Coach Griggs died. I don't think Johanna is involved, but I'll leave that up to you."

"Gee, thanks for that for a change," Grady said without looking up from his notes.

I smiled and continued. "Leslie is smart, too smart to use that spreadsheet to try to frame anyone, because she would've known that a trained investigator would look at the document properties. I think she just used it to lure me here and set another trap."

I grimaced when I adjusted the ice pack again. I was beginning to think an X-ray might be a good idea after all. My knuckles were swelling more by the minute in spite of ice and elevation.

"It was Cameron who was altering grades. I don't know the extent of the scheme, but she said Coach had been gathering evidence for months. She's in love with Cameron and thought she was doing all of this to protect him and make sure he didn't get caught."

"Just when you think you've heard everything," Grady grumbled as he continued to take notes.

"She has a bruise on her calf, the left one. It matches mine." I inched up my jeans leg with my good hand while I tried to remember if I'd shaved my legs recently. I tried not to think about it and showed him my perfect horseshoe bruise, complete with bent-nail impression. "I'm guessing she got kicked when she killed Coach Griggs. I can attest to Jet's deadly aim."

He snapped a photo with his phone.

"And she didn't find the thumb drive or the key because he kicked the thunder out of her and got away," Grady said.

"Yeah, I'm betting that's exactly what happened. And then she attacked Mrs. Griggs when she went to the house to try to find the evidence he'd been collecting."

"We found the dirt bike here in the parking lot," Grady said.

"That explains why Cameron said he didn't see her car. She didn't expect him to be here today. I think she was planning all of this to set someone up, maybe Noah Porter. She made sure I saw her return a black helmet to him when I was here earlier in the week." I shrugged.

"Well, she's not framing anyone now," Grady looked up from his notes and grinned, "thanks to your mean right hook."

"I thought you'd be furious with me."

"Oh, I am. And you'll get an earful eventually. Right now, I'm just thankful you're alive." He scooched down from the bleacher above me to sit beside me and put his arm around my shoulders. I leaned into him and closed my eyes. It was nice to feel safe after the afternoon's ordeal.

"Um, Mallory?" My eyes snapped open at the sound of Darrin's voice. "We found a phone, but it's toast. Is it yours?"

"Crap," I said as I took the shattered phone. "Yes, that's mine."

I turned it over in my hand. The light came on, but the screen was so broken I could only make out the carrier name in the top left-hand corner and what looked like multiple texts or maybe missed calls, but I couldn't tell who from or what the alerts said. It also wasn't responsive when I tried to swipe it open.

"Oh no! I need to call Andy!" I said as I realized some of those alerts were probably from him.

"Here, use mine." Grady stood and handed me his phone with Andy's contact pulled up.

"Thank you." I took it and punched the call button.

Grady stood, and he and Darrin walked back toward the hallway to give me some privacy. Andy answered on the second ring.

"Sheriff," Andy said.

"No, it's me. My phone is broken."

"Why are you calling from the sheriff's phone? Are you okay?"

I gave him a condensed version of what happened and braced myself for his reaction, fully expecting him to call it quits.

"Are you still at the school or at the Sheriff Department?" he finally asked after a pause.

"I'm still at the school."

"I'll be there as soon as possible."

"Andy," I said, not really sure how to put words to what I was feeling. "You don't owe me anything. You've been more wonderful through all of this than anyone could ask for. If this isn't working for you, I understand."

"That sounds a lot like a goodbye," he said quietly.

I sank back against the uncomfortable bleachers, thankful that Grady and Darrin were out of earshot. The air was still thick with the smell of spent gunpowder. Grady kept glancing back at me every so often, I assumed to keep track of when he could retrieve his phone.

"I just want to give you an out if you're done. I don't want to be, but I also don't want you to feel like you need to stick around

278

because I just almost got killed." I sighed and cradled the phone against my shoulder so I could put the ice pack back on my throbbing hand.

"I love . . ." I started to say "spending time with you," but Andy cut me off before I could finish.

"I love you too," he said.

I was suddenly breathless.

"I don't want to lose you, and I can't promise I'm okay with all of the choices you make, but I love you," he said again. "I'll be there in just a few minutes."

Tears had started to well up in my eyes when I handed Grady back his phone.

"Everything alright?" he asked, looming over me on the bleachers.

"Yeah," I said, stupid giddy elation all over my face. "Andy will be here in a minute."

Grady nodded, then leaned down and squeezed my shoulder.

"When you feel up to it, we need a formal statement," he said.

"Of course," I said, then remembered my right hand was a swollen mess. "Any chance I can record a statement?" I held up my hand.

"We'll work something out. That looks rough. You should really get that looked at." He winced as he said it.

* * *

Andy had the forethought to take the only taxi service in Hillspring to meet me at the school so he could drive my truck. He knew that his car would be safe overnight at his office. I followed Grady's advice, so Andy drove me straight to the emergency room, where my fractured fifth metacarpal, otherwise known as a boxer's fracture, was diagnosed and splinted. Unfortunately, our little rural hospital doesn't have an orthopedic doctor on staff, so I received a referral to make an appointment after the weekend.

The stabilization of the splint helped tremendously, as did the dose of pain medication I'd received in the ER. I think I fell asleep before Andy even pulled out of the parking lot. He drove me straight home, where Dad met me in the driveway.

"You knock her into next week?" he asked as soon as he'd opened my door, grinning from ear to ear.

"You're way too excited about this," I said, my voice slightly slurring as I struggled to wake up through the fog.

"It's over!" he said as he clapped me on the shoulder. I winced at the sudden impact. "Oh, sorry. But it's over! Now you need to let that boy come back."

"My phone got destroyed," I said, but only after instinctively reaching for it in my pocket. "But I think I have a phone list somewhere, in the barn maybe."

I turned toward the paddock and Andy intercepted me.

"You need to go inside and rest," he said. "I'm pretty sure I have either Tanner or Ashley's number and I'll get the message out."

I let him take me inside and get me settled on the sofa. Timmy growled at me from the safety of his bed, but Dad scooped him up and calmed him down. Banjo inspected every inch of me, with special attention to the splint he didn't think belonged on my hand. After propping my hand up on pillows and making sure I was as comfortable as possible, Andy started making phone calls and I dozed off again.

Ashley and Tanner were the first to arrive. I recounted the day's events to them and Dad, who'd taken his spot at the other end of the sofa. When I finished, Tanner and Ashley looked at each other and then back at me.

"I didn't suspect her *at all*," Tanner said, shaking his head.

"Me neither, until it was too late," I agreed, thoroughly disgusted with myself.

By dark, my house was Grand Central Station. Lanie came thundering through the door, Bill trailing behind her completely loaded down with groceries and takeout.

"With the ordeal you've been through, you shouldn't have to worry about food. And I doubt you can cook anyway with that hand." Lanie sat beside me and fluffed my pillows.

I hadn't had time to think about all the things that would be more difficult to do with a broken dominant hand, but cooking was definitely among them.

"I can stay a while and make sure she eats," Dad said, clutching Timmy, who watched everyone warily with his evil beady little eyes.

"If you need anything, help with shopping or anything, you just let us know," Bill told him. I smiled at Lanie's wonderful, giant, scruffy husband. Bill might look like wild mountain man, but his heart was made of pure gold.

I laid my head on Lanie's shoulder, taking immense comfort from her presence.

"Let's never fight again," I whispered.

She reached up and patted my cheek. "Deal," she said.

"Honey," she said in a tone that made me apprehensive. "Have you talked to Ginny yet?"

"Oh God, no," I said. "I don't know how to tell her what happened. She's already so mad at me."

"Do you want me to call her?" Andy asked as he took a seat in the accent chair closest to the door. "I can FaceTime her from your iPad if you have your contacts synced."

I opened my mouth to say no, but then closed it again as I considered avoiding my daughter's wrath for as long as possible.

"As much as I'd like to take you up on that, I should be the one to tell her."

He reached across the end table and patted my arm, careful to avoid my hand.

"I'll go get your iPad and we can FaceTime her together. She won't yell at me. She loves me." Lanie jumped up and headed to my bedroom.

As predicted, Ginny was absolutely furious with me. Lanie did as promised and ran interference, and by the end of the call they were making plans for the Christmas break visit. Ginny ended the call just as Grady arrived and made me vow to check in with her the next day.

Grady asked to speak to me privately since the house was nearly full. We made our way to my home office, which was currently the room Dad was staying in. Grady had a typed statement from our earlier interview and asked me to read it for accuracy. I was so thankful that I didn't have to go through the whole story again. I attested that he'd included everything I'd told him and signed it the best I could with my left hand.

"She hasn't asked for a lawyer, but she hasn't admitted anything yet either," Grady said, and pushed his Stetson back to rub his forehead. "We haven't had much of a chance to question her yet because it took all afternoon to medically clear her. You clocked her a good one." He grinned that crooked grin he has when he's really amused.

"I'm betting the evidence Coach was collecting is on that thumb drive," I said, lost in my thoughts. "And now that I know he wasn't involved, I'll bet Lucas Porter's records are further proof that Cameron was altering grades."

"Not just altering them," Grady said. "He was selling them. He copped to everything. He's made thousands off desperate players and parents over the last several years. He's named names, and we have a list as long as your arm. Most of them are just kids who paid a few bucks here and there for an occasional grade boost or for test answers. The real money came from parents like Bruce Porter. Darrin has gone out to bring him in for questioning as we speak. Oh, and you were right about Johanna. At least it doesn't look like she was involved with the evidence we have right now. Cameron admitted that she had suspicions and had confronted him about it, but apparently Leslie didn't know, or she would've been on the hit list too."

"Wow," I said as I tried to process all this. "Coach was trying to propose a policy change that would keep that from happening again. He wanted to make sure that kids had to pass each class instead of just keeping their overall GPA above the threshold. I thought he might have been guilty of the very thing he was trying to expose."

"Don't beat yourself up. You did punch the living daylights out of his killer."

"You keep mentioning that." I laughed, enjoying another emotion besides terror and dread.

"I'm impressed. I don't remember you being quite so . . . lethal."

"I'm full of surprises."

"That you are," he said, tipped his ever-present Stetson, and excused himself to get back to Leslie's interrogation.

Chapter
Thirty-Two

The next two days felt much like it had after Braydon Cunningham was caught—a blur of activity, interviews, and endless questions. The rescue was inundated with reporters, law enforcement, and people who were just curious. Donations to the rescue started to boom again, and since Ashley published our Facebook page to coincide with the first news reports that dropped on Sunday morning, we had donations coming in from all over. She was a whiz at running our social media accounts and ruthless when it came to weeding out the trolls.

By Tuesday, things had started to settle back down a bit, and I wanted to make the trip to see Patricia Griggs. She'd been moved to a rehab facility that would allow her to see her little dog in the courtyard, so Dad was coming with me to manage the little beast. Andy begged off, since he'd taken the previous day off to help manage the chaos at the rescue. Tanner wanted to check in on Patricia too, and after giving me a tremendous amount of grief for making him leave the rescue for his own safety, he'd settled back into his good-natured ways. I didn't protest when he offered to drive, since my right hand was out of commission and would be for a few weeks.

The staff was expecting us when we arrived, and they showed us to the little enclosed courtyard where Patricia could see Timmy. He'd come to tolerate my presence, only growling if I dared to touch him or crowd his bed. He genuinely liked Dad though. He would wag his tail at him and seek out his company every chance he got. Dad insisted on staying with me until my hand healed so he could cook and do the things I found difficult. Truth be told, I liked having him there and was dreading the day when he would go back to his little cabin in town. I'd started dropping hints that I'd like him to stay, but so far he hadn't let on that he was getting them.

A man I assumed to be Rhett Allen pushed Patricia's wheelchair through the automatic doors onto the smooth concrete path. The paths fanned out to various tables and benches punctuated with raised garden beds that had been mulched for the winter. The entire courtyard was enclosed by a native-stone wall that had birdbaths built into its corners. We'd positioned ourselves toward the front, under a bare-limbed tree. I was glad that the sun was shining brightly and the temperature only required a light jacket.

Patricia's face lit up the minute she saw her little dog, and the feeling appeared to be mutual. Timmy went berserk in Dad's arms, whining and straining against his harness. Dad let him down, and he took two bounding leaps and landed in Patricia's lap, where he started licking her chin, arms, and everything else he could reach.

It took several minutes for Patricia to settle him down enough to talk with us, and I dreaded taking him away from her. When he finally curled up in her lap, she reached over and took my good hand.

"Thank you," she said with tears in her eyes.

"You don't need to thank me." I could feel my cheeks burning. "I didn't really do much."

"Sheriff Sullivan told me what you did. *All* that you did. Doug would be so proud of you. He hated injustice," she said with a broad smile.

"I hear you're doing really well here." I changed the subject.

"I am. They think I might get to go home by the weekend. Rhett is going to stay with me for a few days after I get released and make sure I'm doing okay."

"We can check in on you after he leaves, if you want," Tanner said. "And I can run over and help with the horse any time."

"That's very generous of you," Rhett said. "Her neighbors have really been a godsend though. They took Doug's horse in and will continue to care for him until Mom feels up to it."

"It was Leslie all along," Patricia said, a faraway look taking over her eyes. "The smashed truck window, the stolen laptop, the prank calls. All of it. She was trying to scare him off."

"It looks that way," I said. "She did much the same to me. She vandalized my truck and sent me threatening messages." I didn't add that she'd set two traps for me as well, one of which was nearly successful.

"Why?" Patricia asked, tears welling in her eyes. "For what? So, she could impress that simpering little blowhard?"

I suppressed a chuckle at her assessment of Cameron Green. I felt that we had barely scratched the surface of Leslie's infatuation with him and suspected there would be a lot more revealed as the prosecution built their case against her. Since the incident in the gym, it had come to light that Leslie bought the dirt bike and learned to ride it in hopes of joining the Mad Mudder Club and getting closer to Cameron. It looked like she'd been stalking him for years. She had created sock-puppet accounts to follow him on social media and fake dating profiles she used to try to keep tabs on him online. She had been impersonating a home-health aide and had been visiting his parents once a week for nearly eight months.

I kept all of this to myself. Patricia would learn it all soon enough since the media had grabbed onto the case like a vice. I guess it *was* plenty sensational—small-town murder, stalking, bullet-ridden showdown—it had all the makings of a primetime documentary. I cringed at the thought. I really hoped it didn't come to that. I didn't want our wonderful little town highlighted nationally that way.

"I'm happy to keep looking after your little dog until you feel well enough," Dad said, snapping me back to reality. "We've become good friends."

"That means the world to me." Patricia beamed at him, wiping away the last of the tears with the back of her hand. "I'm so happy to know he's in good hands."

We stayed for several hours, until it was time for her to go to her physical therapy appointment. After a quick exchange of contact information and a tearful goodbye to her little dog, we were back on the road for home.

*   *   *

Back at the rescue, Dad took Timmy inside while I started toward the barn.

"You'll just get in my way," Tanner said, heading me off at the paddock gate. "I've got this."

"I get in your way?" I did my best impression of being deeply offended.

He grinned mischievously and started to answer, but we were interrupted by Biscuit's sudden alarm. He trotted down from the upper paddock on his short little legs, braying with every step. I turned to see an unfamiliar car pulling up the drive, which had been a regular occurrence in the last few days. I fully expected it to be another reporter, blogger, or curious local, but as it rounded the last curve at the top of the drive, I realized it was Marvin Randall in the passenger seat. The car pulled in behind my truck and a young woman got out of the driver's seat. Marvin got out too.

"I'm sorry to show up unannounced," he said, reluctant to look me in the eyes. "But I needed to say thank you in person."

"You don't need to thank me," I protested.

The young woman joined him, looking even more uncomfortable than he did.

"This is my daughter Lacy," he said proudly. "I wanted her to meet you too."

"Very nice to meet you. Why don't you come inside? I'll put some coffee on," I said, and gestured for them to follow me.

"We couldn't impose," Lacy said quietly.

"Not at all. Come on in."

Dad ushered Timmy outside before he had a chance to eat our guests from the ankles down and then took over putting the coffee on, since I struggled a bit with my one functional hand. Banjo greeted them both like they were long-lost relatives. Lacy cooed over him and seemed to relax a bit.

"I don't think I'd still be here if it wasn't for your kindness, Ms. Martin," Marvin said, wringing his hands in his lap.

"I didn't do anything extraordinary, I assure you."

"I'm not too proud to admit that I'm an alcoholic. I don't remember squat about that day in the woods. I know now that I didn't kill that man, but I *could* have, I was so drunk. And then when I showed up here I was in rough shape. You were kind to me. You didn't have to be, but you were."

My heart broke for him. I didn't feel that I'd been particularly kind, but was glad he felt that way.

"You're looking well today." I smiled.

"I'm sober," he laughed. Lacy didn't look like she appreciated the joke very much. He noticed and took on a more serious tone. "I'm in a program now. After I detoxed at the hospital, I got set up with a social worker and everything, and I'm not touching alcohol again."

"I'm so glad," I said.

"That's something to be proud of," Dad piped up as he poured the coffee for all of us.

"I wish it'd happened sooner." Marvin glanced at Lacy, who didn't look up from her cup.

"Well, can't change the past," Dad said as he plopped the cream and sugar on the table and took the last available seat beside me. "Just have to look forward now."

They didn't stay long enough to finish their coffee, but Marvin thanked me several more times before I watched their taillights descend the driveway. I still didn't feel like I'd done anything that deserved his thanks, but I was genuinely glad he was taking the first steps to sobriety.

The last tendrils of light filtered through the mostly bare tree limbs and gave the hillside a warm glow in contrast to the chill in the air. The scents of horses and hay wafted in on the gentle breeze, and even though it had a bite to it, I welcomed the smell of home and happiness.

Tanner waved up to me from the barn as he brought Ruby in for the night, her breath billowing out in plumes. She looked up the hill, following his gaze. I was glad she was showing signs of curiosity, and I couldn't wait to watch her personality bloom. All of our horses were special, and I loved them all, but I was going to have a very hard time giving her up. I hadn't gotten attached to a rescue that quickly or thoroughly since Biscuit.

"Come have some coffee," I called down to him, and realized I'd just thought of the horses as "ours." Sometime soon, we might have that talk about a partnership.

"Be right up."

Lanie arrived minutes before Andy and Dad put another pot of coffee on. She'd brought an ultrasound photo of a squiggly little bean and I couldn't stop staring at the blessed little critter. Lanie and Bill had tried so hard, for so long, to be parents, and I couldn't wait for them to finally have their dreams come true.

"We need to start planning your baby shower," I gushed, even though I don't have the foggiest notion how to plan anything like that. I was sure there were entire Pinterest boards dedicated to such occasions, and I could muddle through.

"I'm not due until July," she said, and then, realizing what she'd just said, "Mal! I'm due in July!" Her hands fell to her belly, not yet showing a bump.

"I know! And that gives us only seven months to work with. It's got to be epic."

I grabbed my iPad, and we started looking through inspiration posts and making notes. Tanner made a break for it about twenty minutes in with a promise to be back early in the morning so I wouldn't have to feed with my hand still in a splint. Andy and Dad kept busy discussing who-knows-what until Lanie finally ran out of steam at about nine PM. We made plans for lunch later in the week and she headed home to Bill.

Dad excused himself to turn in early, gathered up Timmy, and left me and Andy alone for the first time in days.

"Hey there, local celebrity," he grinned as he pushed his glasses back up on his nose.

"Stop it," I laughed.

"We haven't had much time together since the . . ." he paused like he was searching for a suitable word, ". . . incident."

"It's been crazy, that's for sure."

"I meant it, Mallory. I love you." He crossed the distance between us and sat beside me on the sofa. "I didn't think I would ever love anyone the way I loved Blair, but here you are."

"Bad decisions and all?" I smiled, inhaling his earthy cologne. It smelled like a combination of impending rain, fresh-cut timber, and evergreens, and suited him perfectly.

"Can't say that I love those, exactly." He cupped my face in his hand, and I melted against it.

"I love you too." My heart pounded as I said it, but it felt so good to finally admit it to myself, out loud. And as he pulled me in for a kiss, everything felt right in my world.

Acknowledgments

As always, I want to thank my amazing agent, Jill Marsal. I'm still afraid I'm going to wake up from this wonderful dream. Thank you to Jennifer Hooks for the kind words and encouragement she gave me when I needed it the most. Every author should be blessed with an editor that makes revisions feel like a celebration of growth.

Thank you to the team at Crooked Lane Books. Terri, Rebecca, Dulce, and I'm sure I'm missing countless others behind the scenes. Seriously, you are all just amazing to work with.

I'm grateful for our menagerie of rescue animals that serve as inspiration for some of the equine characters in this series, even though they're the reason I sometimes (frequently) panic about deadlines. I adore our motley crew of misfits.

Thank you to my wonderful family and friends, who are patient with my absence and never make me guilty when I isolate myself for weeks to write. I'm so lucky to have you all in my life.

Continued thanks to the members of my writing groups: Writers Win, Pitch to Published, Pitch Perfect, and A Writer's Journey. I am so glad to be able to connect with you all.